Dear Reader,

If you are a fan of my Elemental Witches or Dark Magick paranormal romance series, or have found this book via any of my erotic romances, like *The Chosen Sin*, *Jeweled*, or *Jaded*, you will find *Raven's Quest* to be a much different kind of story. *Raven's Quest* was one of the first books I ever wrote, and it's a pure fantasy romance, weaving an endearing tale of love through a world rich with magic.

If you're in need of a hero in your life, you might escape for a while with Lucan. The fourth son of a great king, he never expected—or wanted—to rule, but when his uncle kills Lucan's family and takes the throne for himself, Lucan has no choice but to form a rebellion and force his unjust uncle from the throne.

Branna is a woman of magic and mystery who comes from a country far away. When she meets Lucan she knows he's special in more ways than one. Strong and compassionate, Branna is willing to sacrifice her life for the good of her people, but the longer she knows Lucan, the harder leaving him will be . . .

I had so much fun writing Branna and Lucan, building their magical world and guiding them both toward love. I hope you will enjoy reading their story as much as I enjoyed writing it.

RAVEN'S QUEST

A N Y A   B A S T

Previously published under the name Joanna King

B
BERKLEY SENSATION, NEW YORK

THE BERKLEY PUBLISHING GROUP
Published by the Penguin Group
Penguin Group (USA) Inc.
375 Hudson Street, New York, New York 10014, USA
Penguin Group (Canada), 90 Eglinton Avenue East, Suite 700, Toronto, Ontario M4P 2Y3, Canada
(a division of Pearson Penguin Canada Inc.)
Penguin Books Ltd., 80 Strand, London WC2R 0RL, England
Penguin Group Ireland, 25 St. Stephen's Green, Dublin 2, Ireland (a division of Penguin Books Ltd.)
Penguin Group (Australia), 250 Camberwell Road, Camberwell, Victoria 3124, Australia
(a division of Pearson Australia Group Pty. Ltd.)
Penguin Books India Pvt. Ltd., 11 Community Centre, Panchsheel Park, New Delhi—110 017, India
Penguin Group (NZ), 67 Apollo Drive, Rosedale, North Shore 0632, New Zealand
(a division of Pearson New Zealand Ltd.)
Penguin Books (South Africa) (Pty.) Ltd., 24 Sturdee Avenue, Rosebank, Johannesburg 2196,
South Africa

Penguin Books Ltd., Registered Offices: 80 Strand, London WC2R 0RL, England

This book is an original publication of The Berkley Publishing Group.

PRINTING HISTORY
Imajnn mass-market edition/September 2004
Berkley Sensation trade paperback edition / February 2011

Library of Congress Cataloging-in-Publication Data

Bast, Anya.
  Raven's quest/Anya Bast.—Berkley Sensation trade paperback ed.
    p. cm.
  "Previously published under the name Joanna King."
  ISBN 978-0-425-23880-6
  I. Title.
  PS3602.A8493R38   2011
  813'.6—dc22   2010042915

PRINTED IN THE UNITED STATES OF AMERICA

10 9 8 7 6 5 4 3 2 1

This book is dedicated to Barbara Karmazin,
who taught me about passive voice while I wrote this book.
Barbara, may you and your chainsaw rest in peace.

CHAPTER ONE

Numia 1106

A COLD WIND BIT AT LUCAN'S FACE, PROMISING WIN-
ter. He dipped his head and followed the path. Fronds of
woodland ferns brushed against his thighs, and low-growing
blooms of late autumn amberdine crushed under his step, releasing
their spicy-sweet fragrance into the air. Thick with undergrowth,
the path wound its way through the forest. It led to the abandoned
temples of Akal, and to the informant who awaited him there.

His skin prickled. Something about this meeting did not feel
right, but it had to be merely his imagination. He knew this informant, had worked with him for years. He would never betray Opposition plans. They paid him too much for that. Greed was one of
the few things that kept a man loyal.

He stepped onto the temple grounds and looked around at the
crumbling rock of the abandoned structures. When the priests and
priestesses of Akal had left, it was as if they'd taken the blood of the

buildings with them, leaving only dried-out husks. Every time he came here he was struck anew at how desolate they looked.

They said this ancient place was haunted. Only the most intrepid would venture into this sacred area now. That made it the perfect place to conduct business.

Outside the vine-choked and decaying structure he sought, a crumbling statue of Akal, the God of Air, bowed its head. He knelt and kissed the statue's foot, then rose and entered the open-sided temple. He surveyed the crumbling pillars at the edge of the building and the low-hanging rafters, which ran the length of the ceiling, searching in the waning light for his informant.

A tall, thin man stepped from the shadows. "Lucan," he said.

Goten was a politician at Ta'Ror, occupying a high place in what passed for Numian government these days. Like many, he served Emperor Magnus out of a sense of self-preservation. Luckily enough, this politician had aspirations other than serving in Magnus's puppet government. Goten was gold-hungry and would betray his master to the Opposition for enough of it.

Lucan had not trusted Goten from the beginning and had never revealed his true identity. To Goten, Lucan was simply Lucan . . . a common enough name for a common enough rebel.

"Do you have it?" Lucan asked.

"Yes, but it cost me much more than I thought it would. It must be something of great value. It was heavily guarded. It took me a long time and many bribes to organize a way for a metalworker to recreate it."

Goten opened his palm, and Lucan stepped forward to look at the object. It was iron and in the shape of an eight-pointed star. The top showed a circle and within the center was another smaller, raised star. Goten flipped it over. The bottom of the object bore rows of ridges. "If only we knew what it was for."

Yes, if only.

"We'll find out," Lucan replied. Anything of great value to Magnus was of great value to the Opposition. He loosened a bag of falcon-head crowns on his belt, ready to make the exchange.

Goten's palm closed. "I took great risks to obtain a copy of this . . . this . . . whatever this is. I will want more for it."

Lucan had suspected as much. "I put extra crowns in the bag in anticipation of your needs." He handed the bag to him and took the object from Goten's palm.

The politician opened the bag and began to count the coin.

Lucan looked at the object in his hand. It was very important in some way. He just had to find the right information to tell him why.

The sound of coins hitting the cracked marble floor made Lucan look up. Valorian soldiers stood at all sides of the temple. They were surrounded. Lucan slipped the object into the pocket of his trews. "You were followed," he said sharply under his breath. "Or you betrayed me."

Goten's eyes grew wide. "I . . . I did not," he stammered in alarm.

Lucan pulled his sword from the scabbard strapped crosswise against his back. "Get behind me," he ordered.

Goten was a policy maker, not a warrior. He stepped behind him before Lucan had finished his sentence, shielding himself from the soldiers.

With his sword in hand, Lucan turned in a wary circle, surveying the soldiers. Some of the Valorian held swords, others long knives, and a handful had arrows notched in their bows. An officer stepped out from behind the soldiers. Lucan recognized the tall, blond man as Armillon, commander of the Northern Valorian Guard.

"Rebel," Commander Armillon said. "You are surrounded and outnumbered. You will drop your sword at once and come with us."

Lucan thought not. They had not rushed him. That likely meant they had instructions to take him alive. He was valuable to them because he had important information. He didn't want to think about how they'd try to get it out of him.

Information . . . He was so weary of it.

He made no move, deciding how to get himself and Goten out of the temple.

Armillon raised an eyebrow. "You delay?" His gaze shifted and he flicked his wrist. "Let fly," he ordered.

The sound of an arrow released from its bow sliced the air and behind him Goten grunted. Lucan turned and saw him kneeling on the floor, an arrow lodged in his throat. Blood pooled in Goten's hands as he clutched his throat in shock. He made a gurgling sound and slumped to the floor.

Briefly, Lucan closed his eyes. Goten had been greedy, but not a bad man.

"Dirty traitor to the throne," Armillon said in a low voice full of loathing. "Now, if you don't want to end up like him, put your sword down."

Lucan turned back around. Armillon seemed so confident of himself, so sure there was no escape. Maybe he had a right to be confident. Lucan could not go through the Valorian, or around them. He could not go under them. Glancing skyward, he remembered the wooden rafters that ran the length of the ceiling. But he might be able to go over them. The rafters were probably unstable, but they were his only option.

Slowly, Lucan lowered his sword to the floor, watching as the Valorian loosened their holds on their weapons in anticipation of his surrender. Instead of releasing his blade, he dove toward the floor, sword in hand, and rolled to the left.

"Archers, aim low," commanded Armillon.

That did not sound good. The last thing he needed now was an arrow in his leg. If they knew who he really was, they wouldn't be aiming to merely injure, they'd be trying to kill, valuable information or not.

He went for a crumbling pillar to his left and used it to catapult himself onto one of the thick, rotting rafters above. The length of wood creaked under his weight. He hesitated. It could easily break and tumble him down into the Valorian below. An arrow shot past him, and the displaced air brushed his shin. He didn't consider it any longer and moved quickly across the rafter.

Below him, the Valorian banged on the wooden beam with their swords and tried to stab him in the leg. The archers took careful aim. Lucan hurried across, offering a silent prayer to Akal that there would be good news for him at the end.

However, the end of the rafter offered little to reinforce his faith in the Gods. His heart pounding, he looked around for some way of escape. Then he saw it. Light glinted in from a crumbled section of the ceiling to his right. He would have to cross over to the next rafter to reach it. The wood groaned beneath him under the added weight of pursuing soldiers. It wouldn't hold much longer.

Lucan judged the distance to the next rafter and then leapt onto it. He balanced precariously for a moment, almost falling into the Valorian below. A loud cracking sound split the air as the rafter he'd just been on finally gave way under the weight of the pursuing soldiers, toppling them to the ground. Taking advantage of the diversion, Lucan scrambled for the hole in the ceiling. He threw his sword up first and then followed it. Rock crumbled under his hands like dried bread as he pulled himself up and out.

Grabbing his sword, Lucan ran to the edge of the roof. The Valorian were beginning to spill out of the temple, searching for him. He caught a glimpse of Armillon.

"Capture him," the commander bellowed, pointing to the roof.

But it was too late for that and Lucan knew it even if Armillon didn't. Lucan jumped to the roof of the next building. On the other side was the forest, deepening into darkness now. It meant escape. Using a large statue as a makeshift ladder, he leapt down to the ground. He headed for the secretive forests and disappeared into the thick evening air like one of the supposed phantoms of the Temple of Akal.

B RANNA STOOD LOOKING DOWN INTO THE VALLEY BE-low her. The smell of snow hung in the air. She let the harsh wind rip back the hood of her traveling cloak. The wind whipped her hair around her face, but she did not restrain the tendrils that lashed her cheeks and eyes. What lay in front of her held her unwavering attention.

In the valley below stood the gateway to Numia and behind her the wastes of Bah'ra. Their journey to Numia was almost over, but their quest was just beginning.

Behind her, a twig snapped under someone's tread. She turned to see her protector, Fiall, coming to stand next to her. He looked toward Numia. His face was blank, but his eyes were not. She placed a comforting hand on his arm. "Almost, Fiall."

"The years of waiting have come to an end. Perhaps, with the will of the Goddess, we'll finally have balance," he said.

They had been traveling for the last three weeks through the mountains and wastes of Bah'ra. It had been punishing and untamed terrain. They were both exhausted and more than ready to be back in the comforts of a civilized society.

Civilized.

But Numia could not really be called that now. Perhaps at one time it had been civilized. But when good King Gallus had been usurped by his brother, Magnus, all that had changed. With the might of the Valorian Guard behind him, Magnus had styled himself an emperor and conquered all the lands around Numia, except for magical Ileria. Still Numia tried for that free place, like locusts devouring crops.

Tir na Ban, their own homeland, had been the first to fall.

From childhood she'd had recurring dreams of coming to this place, the land of her country's oppressors. She'd dreamt of a circle of sorceresses. Herself and a priest of Solan stood in the center, powerful magic binding them as they unleashed magic over the land. It would stop Magnus's tyranny. It was the only thing that could.

Somewhere, beyond that valley below them, within the borders of Numia, the priest awaited her. She trusted the Goddess to lead her to him. In the land of their enemy lived the man who would be her consort . . . and the salvation of Tir na Ban. It was an unlikely place to find such a man, but her dreams did not lie. They had to find the priest and the Book of *Draiochta Cothrom*.

She sighed and placed her fingertips to her temple. Fatigue caused her head to ache. "Tomorrow we'll go into the valley and past the border. We'll stop and rest, gather supplies, and then travel on to the capital, Ta'Ror."

"You should try to sleep now," answered Fiall.

She'd always had horrible insomnia, but since she'd left Tir na Ban it had grown insufferable. It had started when she was eight, when the Terror had begun. The closer they drew to Numia the worse it became. "Yes, I'll try."

A lock of chestnut-colored hair fell into Fiall's eye. She reached up and tucked it behind his ear. Raised together by the priestesses of Tir na Ban, they were like brother and sister. Branna would never forget those years of living in fear of the occupying Numian force. The Valorian had been a hated and feared thing. They still were.

Fiall had never been a submissive Tirian, though. He never cast his eyes downward in the presence of a soldier, never submitted to their wishes. Branna still wondered how he'd survived the years of the Terror, when Magnus had first come with his Valorian Guard. Fiall had suffered many beatings during that time. A thin white scar ran from his forehead to his chin—a remnant of one encounter. It marred an otherwise handsome face. His quick temper was the cause of his woes. Fiall would not back down from any man. But that was the very quality that made him an excellent protector.

She turned and offered her hand to him. "Come, we'll have all day tomorrow to look at the dreaded Numia. Now we need to rest and prepare ourselves."

*L*UCAN DOVE OFF THE CLIFF AS ARROWS CREATED A DEADLY *rain around him. He hit the winter water with enough force to break two of his ribs. The water closed over his head, and every part of his body throbbed with pain.*

Despair sucked all his will away. He stayed under, watching arrows shoot into the water around him. The water would kill him and deny his uncle the satisfaction of doing it. He stayed below until his lungs were near bursting. Faces of his family, washed in a flood of blood and tears, swirled in his memories.

Valentina ran into his arms, squealing with delight that her older brother had come home for a visit. His father asked him why he persisted on such a foolish life's vocation, requested that he stay home and follow in the footsteps of his older brothers. His uncle Magnus . . . the one who'd betrayed them . . . taught him how to use a sword, a long knife, a bow, his bare hands in combat.

Then he remembered the looks on their faces before they'd died under

Magnus's blade . . . tiny, happy Valentina. Sweet Solan! He had to live to make his uncle pay for what he'd done.

Lucan pushed up from the bottom of the river, desperately fighting the current that wanted so much to claim him. He pushed up using his numb muscles and beaten body until he burst through the surface.

Lucan awoke washed in sweat and sucked air into his lungs like a drowning man. Panting, he reoriented himself. He had rejoined his men and they were encamped near Ebru. They were traveling back to Kern. Still a fugitive, still betrayed by his own blood, but no longer was he the young, confused boy he'd been.

His eyes came into focus and he saw his second-in-command, Morgan, staring at him from across the fire. "The nightmare again?" he asked in his Angelese-accented Numian. Morgan had come from neighboring Angelyn to aid the Opposition.

Lucan pushed the blankets away. "It is always the nightmare."

Morgan brought Lucan his cup. "Here, it will calm the monsters within."

Lucan hesitated.

"Come, you are no longer an initiate of Solan. You can drink now if you choose."

Morgan did not have to remind him. A day did not go by when he did not think of his past and yearn for a time when he might have chosen his own path.

Lucan reached out and took the cup. He sniffed at the liquid it contained, Pirian fire-juice. He lifted a brow and then shrugged his shoulders. "Mal'ha," he said, tipping the cup to Morgan. Then he downed the fiery liquid in one swallow. It burned its way down his throat and into his gullet, leaving a curiously sweet trail behind. The spirits reached out and warmed every part of his body. He leaned back on his blankets, giving in to his weariness and strained muscles, and relaxed. It was an escape for the time being.

Ren, one of the youngest members of the rebel force, came running into camp. He stopped short at the edge of Lucan's blanket, barely catching himself before he tripped and sprawled on the ground.

"What is it?" Lucan asked. Ren was coming off the night watch.

"The Valorian have moved north. I think we're safe now, and I've good news to relay," said Ren breathlessly. "I've just been told that our friend Armillon will be in Strobia on the morrow. The village has been instructed to honor him with a festival."

"Really . . ." said Lucan. "Have we the men available to go and honor him ourselves?"

The firelight played across Morgan's features. He smiled. "Oh yes, we do indeed."

CHAPTER TWO

B RANNA'S TRAVELING BOOTS CLICKED ON THE UNEVEN cobblestones as she ran. She risked a glance behind her and saw two Valorian soldiers close behind. Dodging a silk vendor, she ducked into an alley, the folds of her open cloak billowing behind her. She didn't know why they were chasing her. She just knew she didn't want to be caught.

In the apothecary, she'd cast a small spell of discernment in order to discover the best remedy for her insomnia. The two Valorian in the shop had not paid any attention to her until then. When the soldiers had questioned her, she'd bolted.

She and Fiall had arrived in Numia only that morning and already she was in trouble. Numia was a strict country, of course she knew that, but this strict? They arrested one for simply seeking an insomnia remedy?

Now her only chance was to get to the marketplace where the

villagers were amassing for the festivities planned for the late afternoon. There Fiall waited for her, and she could lose herself in the crowd. She placed a hand on the belt of her skirt where her athame was sheathed. She would not hesitate to use the ritual blade against the Valorian if the need arose.

Her boots pounding hard against the cobblestones, Branna turned a corner and slammed straight into a broad chest. The man grabbed her shoulders with two powerful hands, steadying her and himself. She looked up, peering from under the hood of her traveling cloak. She noted a well-shaped face with a strong jaw, and eyes the color of blue-gray star-stones from the province Pira, all framed with a shoulder-length fall of glossy hair as black as her own. Next to him was a lanky and light-haired young man. She murmured an apology and sidestepped them both.

One strong arm reached out quick as a striking snake and grabbed the trailing edge of her cloak before she could flee. "Do you run from the Valorian, woman?" the dark man asked.

She nodded. Fear ripped through her. What if this man meant to hold her for the soldiers?

White teeth flashed in a brief and feral grin. "Why flee? It's much better to fight them." He flipped aside the edge of his black cloak to reveal a long blade sheathed at his side. He released her and she ran on.

As she fled she could hear sounds of battle behind her. The two must have drawn steel against the Valorian soldiers. A wave of gratefulness and relief washed through her. Maybe not all Numians were bad.

She reached the marketplace and plunged headlong into the crowd, nearly knocking a fruit vendor to the ground. Only when she was safely enveloped in the human swarm did she slow her pace.

In the apothecary Branna had learned that one of Numia's high Valorian commanders was visiting here today. The village was required to throw a festival in his honor. It was important that she get back and share that information with Fiall.

The crowd parted and she saw him. He also wore a hooded cloak covering his hair and hiding his face. At the open collar, his necklace of three silver miniature shields glinted in the afternoon sunlight. It was his medallion of protection given to him by the priestesses of Tir na Ban. Branna touched her own moonstone raven pendant that nestled in the hollow of her throat.

She walked to him and touched his shoulder. "Fiall."

"Where have you been?" he demanded. "I was beginning to become concerned." He flipped his hood back to reveal his thick mass of shoulder-length brown hair.

She decided not to tell him about what had happened in the apothecary. It would only worry him. It would worry her too, if she thought too much about it. "I have discovered that one of the Valorian's top commanders is in this very village today. A festival to honor him is ready to commence."

Fiall smiled weakly. "Yes, it's the talk of the town. We should be going. I'll not allow you to stay here while Commander Armillon is present. It's far too dangerous."

She sighed, suddenly feeling weariness through every inch of her body. "Truly, the last thing I want to do is travel."

"Neither do I, and you need your rest. Still, I am afraid we have to move on. I'll get the horses from the stable." Fiall began to walk away.

Branna took his arm before he could leave. She spoke under her breath so no one around them could hear. "Don't you think it's curious that we should end up in this village when one of the high commanders of the Valorian is here? Armillon was one of the instigators of the Terror. Don't you see? Our quest has begun. The Goddess has led us here. This is an opportunity."

"I can see you're getting that look in your eye. I won't allow you to be endangered on the very first day that we are in this goddess-forsaken country."

"Imagine what I could learn if I was able to get into the head of a military commander, and he is not just any military commander. This is Armillon." She sighed. "You must realize that we are going to be confronted with danger on this journey. If it is not today, it will be tomorrow."

Fiall took her by her shoulders and whispered fiercely, "I won't let harm come to you today, Branna."

She smiled. Fiall said that every day. But she couldn't allow him to sway her.

"I understand that we'll be facing danger," he continued. "But I ask that we plan these things out more thoroughly, rather than jumping into opportunities as they present themselves."

"Fiall, I have a plan. It will put into use something I bought while we traveled through Bah'ra. I knew I felt compelled to buy it for some reason."

Realization dawned on Fiall's face as he remembered the item of clothing she'd purchased while at market one morning in Bah'ra's capital city. "No—"

She made a motion with her hand to cut off his words and spoke with the authority she had over him by rights of her position within the priessshood of Tir na Ban. The last word was hers and hers alone. "You must understand. I cannot dishonor the Goddess by ignoring the opportunities she puts in our path. I cannot ignore *cinnunt*. I promise I won't unnecessarily endanger myself. You must let me go now and trust me."

Fiall's grip loosened. She stepped back, looking into his eyes.

She took another step back still holding his gaze and let the crowd swallow her.

L UCAN SLID HIS LONG KNIFE INTO THE SHEATH ON HIS belt. They had not killed the Valorian that had been chasing the woman, but the soldiers would fight no more today. Now there were two less men for the rebels to have to contend with.

Quickly and silently, a handful of villagers came out and took the two Valorian away. Over the past fourteen years, as Magnus had twisted and transformed Numia into a shadow of its former self, Lucan had noticed that many of the common citizens were firmly on the side of Numia's Opposition.

Unfortunately, the Numian noble and merchant classes were in support of Magnus because of the gold crowns with which he continually lined their pockets. Magnus had made a practice of stealing as much as he could from the common classes and giving it to his Valorian forces and the upper classes to ensure his power. That was one of the things the Opposition endeavored to stop.

Lucan thanked the villagers for their help, and then he and Ren walked toward the stables. "Come Ren, we must find our mounts. It is almost time for this travesty in honor of Commander Armillon to begin. It would be better for us to be astride."

Ren fell into step beside him. His limbs were lanky, and he was as lean as a Bah'rian mountain wolf. A year ago it had seemed no matter how much food the boy consumed, which was a lot, he never seemed to put on weight. Now he was starting to reach adulthood and was beginning to fill out.

Ren had come to the Opposition almost two years ago when his parents had been killed by the Valorian for publicly criticizing the emperor. He'd been only sixteen then, but he'd had the fire of the

Gods behind him. In the beginning Lucan had tried to restrict the youth to their stronghold in the Kernian Mountains until he had a few more years on him. However, Ren would not be denied. He'd followed Lucan into every battle. The young man had proved himself as being exceptionally able with a long knife and as capable as Lucan at getting out of difficult situations.

Lucan reached out and ruffled Ren's hair in affection. When Ren came into full manhood he would be a formidable force to be reckoned with. But no matter how able a fighter the young man was, Lucan still liked to have him near when they were in battle.

The sun hung in the west, and the two moons, the Sisters, were coming up in the east. The sun and the moons were suspended at equal heights in the sky, seemingly catching the village of Strobia in the middle of a war. Late afternoon sunlight tugged at the corners of buildings as the silver light of the Sisters sought to vanquish the sun's hold.

Lucan thought the image fitting. Even now the rebel forces were in place. Soon they'd give Commander Armillon and his Northern Valorian a nasty surprise.

The Valorian . . . they'd lost their namesake the moment they'd helped Magnus overthrow King Gallus. The Valorian had no valor now. Some were simply bought-and-paid-for mercenaries, bribed into service by the promise of power and gold crowns. Some of them fought loyally for Magnus and the glory of the Numian Empire. Still many more of the Valorian had been conscripted. For a conscripted soldier to defect was to ensure the death of themselves and their families. Because of that, many served out of fear.

Lucan and Ren retrieved their horses and made their way toward the center of the village. They selected a place at the edge of the crowd. The celebration was just beginning. A piper walked into the performance area and the first strains of the "Ode to Numia" began to fill the air.

"*Sweet Solan*," Ren swore under his breath. "Could they have found a musician with less talent?"

He shifted uncomfortably in his saddle. "Not in the whole of Numia and all its provinces," replied Lucan, wincing. He glanced into the crowd and spotted Morgan, who looked up and rolled his eyes, gesturing toward the performer.

Soon there was a blast of a horn. Slaves carrying an enclosed platform parted the crowd on Lucan's left. They brought the platform to the dais and pulled back the curtains with ceremony. Armillon stepped from it. Unenthusiastic applause smattered the air. Armillon stepped onto the dais and fell into a long and self-important speech about the necessity of having loyalty to the Great Empire and its rulers.

Lucan gazed up at the clouds scudding through the sky and thought about the horse he'd reshoed that morning.

After the speech had blessedly ended and Armillon had taken his place on the dais, a hauntingly beautiful melody from the conquered territory of Bah'ra to the west filled the air. A flutist strolled into the performance area, followed by a woman. She wore a long cloak covering her body and walked with confidence and a sensual, graceful sway to her hips.

Lucan sighed. Here was another misguided woman who sought power while disregarding truth and justice. He could not think of any other reason why a woman would choose to perform for Armillon.

The woman stood in front of the commander, swaying back and forth to the music while slipping off her cloak. Her hair was so black it looked like midnight pulled into strands. She tossed that waist-length mane as she threw the cloak to the ground beside her.

That caught the crowd's—and Lucan's—attention. She wore a green gown of an almost see-through, gauzelike fabric, cut to reveal her lithe body to best advantage.

Lucan's mouth went dry as he watched her. She danced in a slow, methodical way, swaying and rotating her slender hips. How she moved made him think of long, dark nights of lovemaking and made him wonder what she'd feel like pressed beneath him on his bed. Desire coiled low in his groin at the thought.

He leaned forward in his saddle and studied her. Her pale, smooth skin would probably taste like vanilla silk under his lips and against his tongue. A thin veil partially covered a face that promised beauty. Above the veil glowed two almond-shaped eyes. They held Armillon's unwavering gaze. She was too far for him to see what color they were, but Lucan realized with a start that he already knew. They were pale green—the same color of the eyes that had peered at him from under the hood of a black traveling cloak. She was the woman who'd almost knocked him over near the marketplace. He'd never forget those eyes.

"That's the woman we just defended, my lord," Ren exclaimed. "Why ever would she . . . oh . . ." Ren colored, realizing why she probably wanted to attract Armillon's attention.

Confused and intrigued, Lucan watched her. She danced in front of the commander, her hips snapping and swaying to the music, but her eyes never left his for more than a heartbeat—as though she was enchanting a snake. Indeed, she was doing just that. Commander Armillon sat transfixed, seemingly unable to move. Yes, this one would get what she sought. She'd have power, at least for one night.

But what was that glow? A barely noticeable shimmering hung in the air around the woman. The moment Lucan noticed it, it seemed the crowd had as well. A collective gasp rippled through the spectators as they realized what it was.

"High magic," said Ren in an amazed tone.

Lucan stared. He knew of high magic, but he'd never seen it practiced. When Magnus had invaded the magical and matriarchal country of Tir na Ban, he'd taken many sorceresses hostage. He'd commanded them to cast a spell over Numia that caused a shimmering of the air whenever magic was used.

Like Tir na Ban, the Ilerians to the far northwest possessed magic. It was the only country that Magnus had yet to defeat.

"Is she Ilerian? Or is she from Tir na Ban?" asked Ren in awe.

"See the shape of her eyes?"

"They remind me of a cat's."

"Aye. She's Tirian," said Lucan. As unlikely as it seemed, the woman had escaped her occupied country to travel here. He'd lay coin on it.

Lucan's father, King Gallus, had kept a Tirian mage named Arturo who'd taught Lucan about magic. It was either a tapping into of the Universal Fabric for the purposes of obtaining information, or an outright alteration of it. High, powerful magic produced change, be it large or small, in the fabric of reality itself. It was high magic that produced the telltale shimmering.

The mage Arturo now stood with Lucan against Numia's oppressor, but Arturo rarely engaged in high magic, only passive clairvoyance.

But that woman . . . she was definitely using high magic. She was a powerful sorceress. Didn't she realize she wrote her own death warrant by being so obvious? To flaunt magic in front of a high military commander was suicide. Or worse, it meant she'd become a magical slave to Emperor Magnus. That had to be worse than death.

"Someone who had high magic might be an asset," said Ren under his breath.

"Boy, you read my mind," replied Lucan. Out of the corner of his eye, he saw the soldiers starting to move. He had to decide quickly what to do. He could stay with their plan and let the woman be taken, or he could launch their plan earlier and save her. The soldiers reached the outer edges of the crowd and began to push through it. He had to decide now.

The woman stopped dancing and looked around in confusion, breaking her gaze with the commander. Armillon shook his head and blinked his eyes, as though waking from a dream. His personal guards began to move toward the steps of the dais, preparing to go into the performance area and take her into custody.

She looked bewildered.

Lucan made his decision. He looked for Morgan. Over the heads of the onlookers, they locked gazes for a moment in silent understanding. Morgan nodded once.

"Ren, you follow me. But stay back and clear of the Valorian," he ordered. Ren nodded, and Lucan plunged through the crowd and into the performance area. He spurred his mount to a gallop, heading straight for the woman. Absurdly, she looked angry and stepped away from his horse. Angling his mount toward her, Lucan leaned down and reached out. He wrapped his arm around her waist and hauled her light weight up onto his saddle in front of him. On the opposite side, the crowd parted for his horse, and he headed for the border of the village and the safety of the forests beyond.

He desperately tried to retain a hold on the struggling woman and manage his horse at the same time. Behind them, Armillon bellowed orders amid the sounds of a newly born battle.

CHAPTER THREE

Branna struggled against her abductor. She sat precariously on the horse's withers, both her legs trailing down over one side. With a steel grip, he held her firmly around her midsection.

He'd ruined all her plans. Armillon had been right where she'd wanted him. Yes, she was grateful to this man for the help he'd given her when the soldiers had chased her, but she didn't need to be saved twice. She twisted in his grasp, trying to free herself, but the more she struggled, the tighter his hold.

"I can't outride those Valorian and battle you at the same time," he yelled. "Be still."

She twisted around and saw he told the truth. Four Valorian soldiers followed close behind. Why were they chasing them?

The man reined the beast around an oak tree, only to find a fence directly in front of them. The horse reared, almost causing them to slide off. She clawed desperately in front of her for something to hang on to and found purchase in the horse's mane.

He swore, pulled the horse to the left, and dug his heels in. The horse jolted forward. They raced along parallel to the fence until it ended, then they turned to the right. A clearing spread before them. The man slowed the horse somewhat. She guessed in an effort to determine which way to go.

She groped for her athame where she'd sheathed it in the folds of material at her waist. She freed it and raised it high. Before she could sink the blade into the man, he caught her wrist. She struggled with him for a moment, but it was a hopeless cause. Seeing no other way to free herself, she sank her teeth deep into the back of his hand. He cursed in surprise and pain and released her.

In one deft movement, she twisted her wrist free of his grasp and slid from the horse. She rolled on the grass, got up, and ran for the tree line. When she was hidden in the shadows and foliage, she risked a look behind her.

He stopped in the middle of the clearing and reined the horse around in a circle, searching for her. By now the Valorian soldiers had also reached the clearing. The man spotted them. He drew his sword and spurred his mount forward, riding toward the Valorian at a flat run. His battle cry rent the air.

She found a large tree to hide behind, ripped off her veil, and threw it to the ground. She should run, but something stayed her. The Goddess spoke to her now in the leaves of the trees and the earth beneath her feet. In the mesh of reality, the voice of the Goddess thrummed, telling Branna to remain.

Her heart pounding and her mouth dry, she peered around the tree trunk at the man who'd abducted her. He felled two of the Valorian almost at once with powerful sword slashes to the upper body. Then he rounded on the remaining two. One of the soldiers attacked him from the front, and the man swung his sword in a deadly arc, deflecting the Valorian's blow. The sound of metal on metal rang through the air as they battled. Finally her abductor landed a well-placed blow, felling the soldier. Then his sword came around and speared the last Valorian, who attacked from behind, using the soldier's own momentum to drive the blade home.

The man sheathed his sword, then rode his horse to the tree line in an apparent effort to locate her. The sound of leaves crackling and twigs breaking met her ears. She shrank down beside the tree. Aye, the Goddess might bid her stay, but good sense told her to hide.

The sound of his horse's hooves on the forest floor grew louder and louder until it finally stopped. She braved peering around the side of the tree. The kneecap of a horse met her view. She looked up and saw him staring down at her from atop his mount, a look of exasperation on his face.

"Sal'vi," he said, still a little out of breath. A fine sweat sheened his face and arms. "My name is Lucan. I suspect you are not from around here. Come out from behind that tree and I'll give you a lesson in surviving in Numia."

It sounded like a threat to her. Gripping her athame in her hand, she stood and stepped out from behind the tree.

She brandished the blade out in front of her, the tip pointed up at him. "I have spent years studying this country," she said. "I hardly think I need any more instruction. I thank you for aiding me earlier when I was being chased. However, I did not need your help just now. In fact, you completely ruined my plans—" She bit off the end of the sentence, realizing she was saying way too much to a man she did not know.

"I won't harm you. You can sheathe that blade."

She glanced down at the silvered edge of her athame and back to his face. He looked hard, this man. He looked dangerous. Maybe he was trying to trick her. No, she felt much better with her blade in her hand. "Why should I trust you?"

The leather of his saddle creaked as he leaned forward. Glossy strands of his onyx-in-shadow hair fell around his face. The dark beginnings of a beard shadowed his cheeks and chin. He narrowed intense blue-gray eyes. "I saved you. That's why you should trust me. If it wasn't for me, you'd be entertaining Magnus's Valorian on the way to Ta'Ror right now."

She relaxed her grip on the athame. He was right. The Valorian had approached her menacingly long before this man, Lucan, had scooped her up from the performance area.

"Ah, that's better," he said, leaning back. "So, you had plans, did you? I'd lay coin they involved bedding Commander Armillon. You are every bit as touched as I first thought you were."

Branna grimaced at the thought. "I wasn't planning to bed Commander Armillon. I'd sooner sleep with a Pirian socabeast. I was trying to . . ." Branna trailed off, frustrated. She couldn't say anything to this man. She turned and began to walk back toward the village. "And I am not touched," she threw over her shoulder.

"Where do you think you're going?" he called after her. "There are Valorian everywhere. You won't get fifty steps from here before they find you and either execute you on the spot or bring you back to Ta'Ror for Magnus. He'll put you in with the other captured Tirian sorceresses to forevermore serve his every little whim. That's what happens to people who practice magic in Numia. Or were those your plans all along? If they were, I'm sorry I ruined them."

She stopped in her tracks, stunned. She turned and stared at him. The athame hung from her suddenly limp fingers. "Captured Tirian sorceresses?" She shook her head as if that would clear it. "How could anyone know I practiced magic?"

"For all your many years of study you seem to have missed some very important events in Numian history."

Branna closed her eyes and sighed. "Explain, please."

"Almost the first thing Magnus did when he took power was build a gilded cage for the sorceresses he took from Tir na Ban. He used them to cast a spell on this country, which allows high magic, be it the tiniest of spells, to glitter and to glow and be recognizable to anyone that may be present. Anyone who sees magic being used is able to collect a very sizable reward for turning in the one who practices it."

A sizable reward. Branna's eyes widened, and she took several steps backward, ready to run for the trees if he made any move in her direction. She tripped over a fallen branch and sat straight down on the grass.

"Are you all right?" he asked.

She nodded.

"I mean you no harm," he continued. "I wouldn't help Magnus for any amount of money. In fact, I take great pleasure in thwarting any of his plans I possibly can." He gave her a flash of his white teeth.

Now she knew why the Valorian had chased her when she'd been in the apothecary. And . . . Morrenna's stars! A pool of Tirian sorceresses kept for Magnus's own use. Many sorceresses and priestesses alike had been taken during the Terror. The people of Tir na Ban had never known what had become of them. It was their worst nightmare come true—too much for Branna to wrap her mind around at the moment.

Instead, she sat looking up at the man called Lucan. Under his open cloak, he wore a white shirt with a soft doeskin jerkin over it. Underneath the shirt and jerkin were broad shoulders and the hard, smooth muscle of a powerful build. He wore no vest of hardened leather to protect himself. It amazed her that a man would engage in swordplay with trained Valorian while wearing no protective clothing.

His face was very well formed, almost handsome in a rough-edged sort of way. He had those eyes she'd noticed right away when she'd run into him near the village marketplace. They were the blue-gray of the deepest ocean or of the sky before a storm. His lips were full and sensual. Branna sensed those lips did not curve to a full ... true ... smile very often. Branna knew then she was picking up on the man in a deeper, psychic way.

She brought herself back to the outer. There were several things about his physical appearance that struck her right away as very non-Numian. He had longer hair than was the fashion for Numian men. A narrow section was twisted into one thin, long braid on the right side of his temple, like a traditional Numian tribesman.

The average Numian man kept his hair cut very short and was usually adamant about not having any facial hair. She thought perhaps it was because this man was simply lazy, but when she felt a little past the outer, that is not what she found. He was rebelling in every way he could, with every fiber of his being.

Also, physically, he was dark of hair. That was very uncharacteristic of Numians who were, for the most part, light of hair, eye, and skin. He was dark in a sea of light with the exception of those blue eyes, but unlike any of the Numians she'd ever met, his eyes held honesty.

"*Sweet Solan.* I can't think with you sitting there in that dress. Here," he said roughly, removing his cloak and tossing it to her. "Anyway, it's cold out here and you're obviously fatigued. You'll catch a fever."

She put the cloak over her shoulders gratefully and looked at him ... really looked at him. Here, in the middle of the clearing, she couldn't do a complete extrasensory examination of him. However, she could get a general sense of the man and whether or not he meant her harm.

She felt herself being absorbed into him. His very cells became permeated with her consciousness. It was not high magic that she did now but simply a magnification of the psychic skills everyone possessed. She tuned in to all that was Lucan, going past the outer. His memories slid past her like the driving rain, too fast for her to see in detail, only enough for her to feel.

He was strong, not only of body but also of mind and spirit. He possessed sharp intellect as well. Also, surprisingly, Branna found a touch of the mage buried there. That bit of feyness glimmered like a gem buried deep in a mountainside. It must be brought forth and polished for its true value to be realized.

Suddenly, there was a flash of pain that made her wince. She withdrew immediately. She would not probe further, having no wish to violate the sacredness of his past. Even so, she came away knowing Lucan was special. The Goddess was telling her to trust him, and so she would.

A sharp cawing came from above. She tipped her head up and saw a raven, black, sleek, and soaring. Yes, the Goddess definitely approved.

She dropped her gaze back to Lucan. "My name is Branna," she said, standing up.

But Lucan was distracted by the sound of horses—many horses—in the distance. They all seemed to be headed straight for the clearing.

"I can fight off three or four Valorian on a good day, but not thirty. So I suggest if you value your pretty neck and don't wish to feel the kiss of Valorian steel against it, you mount . . . now."

Branna didn't want to leave Fiall behind, but it looked as

though she had no choice. Fiall could track her magically. She took the hand Lucan offered and pulled herself up behind him. She wrapped her arms around his waist, and they took off into the forest.

F ROM THE TIME THE WOMAN WOUND HER ARMS AROUND him, Lucan began having trouble thinking straight. First, there was the bewitching scent of skyflower that surrounded her and enveloped him as well. Skyflower was found only very high up in the mountains and smelled fresh and light as a meadow wind, with just the slightest bit of spice. She must have bathed in soap made from it every day for all her life, because, *Solan*, the smell seemed to be a part of her very skin.

Second, he could feel her slender thighs pressed up against the backs of his legs and her breasts and stomach brushing his back. He found himself attuned to her every breath, movement, and sigh.

Aye, it was damned distracting.

And there was no time for distractions. He needed to concentrate on getting free of the pursuing Valorian. They were far behind now, slowed down by having to find the tracks his horse had made in the grass of the clearing. He pushed his horse hard, but even at the fast pace Lucan was setting the Valorian would eventually catch up to them. They needed to hide their tracks soon. Losing the Valorian meant he'd also lose Ren, but that could not be helped. Ren knew to return to Kern, the Opposition stronghold in the east.

"Ai'yah!" Lucan spurred his mount into a new burst of speed and altered their course to the north, toward the Marcai River. The water would erase any tracks they made.

They hit the water at a flat-out run. Chilly river water, displaced by his horse, sprayed up, drenching their legs and misting them to the tops of their heads. Lucan guided his horse along the shallows, up the length of the river.

The Marcai was broad and swift. In late fall, it was especially dangerous because it was swollen with autumn rain and its currents could be deadly, but he knew of spots where it was shallow enough to cross.

They passed up two such spots, and he opted to take the third. They waded in and let the horse swim across. The cold autumn water soaked them to their waists. On the opposite bank, he guided the horse upstream in the shallows for a distance, then found a rocky place, where their tracks would not show, to ease the horse away from the river and back into the forest.

Once again in the woods, with their tracks successfully covered, Lucan breathed easier. In fact, he breathed in a whole two nostrils full of skyflower. Even wet with river water the woman smelled of it.

"We'll go to Kastum. There I know one who will take us in for the night and we can trade our wet clothing for dry," he called back to her.

Lucan could hear her teeth chatter as she answered. "How long of a ride is it to Kastum?"

"Not far, Branna." He tested her name out on his tongue for the first time and found he liked the taste of it. "Hold on."

CHAPTER FOUR

THE OLD WOMAN SAT ON A COBBLESTONE STREET IN Kastum, reaching out a timeworn hand toward Branna, her fingers gnarled and grasping. Unnameable tragedy and hunger had etched deep lines of sorrow on her face. "Succor, my lady, please."

Since they'd stabled the horse, Branna had seen many such people. The Numian commoners walked with bowed heads and sagging shoulders. She'd grown up knowing the face of desperate hunger, but seeing it here, in the very homeland of Tir na Ban's oppressor, jarred her.

Branna reached for her small pouch of crowns, but Lucan stilled her hand. She shot him a look of irritation before she realized he had some of his own coins in hand.

He knelt and pressed them into the woman's palm. "There, take this."

The old woman's face lit up. "Oh, thank you, sir." Her brow furrowed and her eyes squinted. "You look so very like King Gallus," she said, wonderingly. A tentative smile softened her mouth and showed two rotten teeth. "I saw him once, long ago, he and his fine lady queen. Aye, you look very like him."

"It's not the first time I've heard that," said Lucan.

"Gallus was a proper and just ruler." Her face darkened. "Unlike his brother."

"I'm sure King Gallus looks on from Vallon in horror at his brother's actions," answered Lucan. "Unfortunately, Gallus can do nothing from the Overworld except look on. It falls to us to change things."

Lucan stood up and backed away, taking Branna by the arm. "You should not speak so openly," he said. "It will bring you nothing but pain."

Pride overcame her wrinkled and filthy features. "I'll say what I wish."

"Try to take care then," Lucan said. Then he pulled Branna down the street after him. The old woman again called out her thanks.

They reached the house they sought and knocked on the door. A woman just a few years older than Branna answered. She had hair the color of the sky in the morning, deep golden red, and pale blue eyes. A black bodice pressed and pushed her ample breasts to near overflowing her white chemise.

"Lucan!" The woman planted a kiss on his cheek, looked over his shoulder, and spotted Branna standing behind him. Her mouth tightened as she pulled away from him. "Who is this?" she asked Lucan. A subtle moue pulled at her lips.

"Sandria, this is Branna, a friend of mine from Bah'ra."

Branna noted the lie and assumed he had his reasons for telling it.

With one encompassing flicker of her pale eyes, Sandria took in Branna's wet, torn dress, muddied slippers, and tangled hair. In sudden self-consciousness, Branna pulled Lucan's cloak, which had come open, around her tightly. A gust of wind blew and she shivered.

Sandria flashed a gracious smile that did nothing to conceal the undercurrent of dislike Branna felt from the woman. "Come in. You must be chilled to the bone." Sandria backed away from the door, allowing them to pass her and enter the narrow residence.

A stairway leading to the second floor dominated the entryway. A sitting room lay to the right, and a cooking area could be seen in the back, behind the stairs. Dresses, wigs, and costumes covered almost every inch of available space. They were thrown over the stairway banister and tossed over all the chairs and the settee in the sitting room. There was also a table strewn with swatches of fabric, needles, and spools of different colored thread.

"I need your help, Sandria," said Lucan.

"Of course." The woman sidled up to him and brushed herself against him like a house cat. "You know I'll do anything for you."

Lucan cleared his throat uncomfortably and glanced at Branna.

Branna looked away and pretended to be very interested in a girdle encrusted with false pearls draped over the chair to her right.

"We need a place to stay tonight, and she"—Lucan nodded toward Branna—"needs something else to wear."

Sandria's gaze rested on Branna once again. "Yes, I'd already guessed that." She pushed past Branna and rummaged through a pile of clothing that was jumbled on a footstool. From it she pulled a white gown made of a heavy type of muslin. Then she walked around the table and plucked a pair of boots from the floor. She handed it all to Branna.

"Thank you," said Branna.

Sandria turned on her heel and crooked a finger. "Follow me." She led them up the stairs and into a room. It had a low, sloping ceiling and was filled near to bursting with bolts of fabric in every imaginable color and texture. Sandria went to a closet in the corner, pulled out a bedroll, and laid it on the floor.

"I have only this one other room besides my bedroom." Sandria cast her pale gaze on Branna. "You can stay in here." She said no more, but by the heated look she gave Lucan, it was only too clear where she wanted him to stay.

Branna looked away. She shouldn't care where this man, Lucan, stayed the night. Obviously, he'd enjoyed this woman's physical attentions before, so why not again?

Sexual magic was a freely given and beautiful thing. It was not an area for feelings of possessiveness and personal claim. Sexual magic was used for ritual or to strengthen a bond with one you appreciated or loved. In order to make their bond stronger, their combined magic more powerful, she'd been saving her own sexual magic her whole life for the man who would be her consort in this quest. It was for the priest and no one else.

She endeavored to make her tone light, though she could not quite coax her mouth into a smile. "I thank you very much for your hospitality. I'll be very comfortable here."

Lucan went to the closet, pulled out another bedroll, and tucked it under his arm. "I will take the sitting room floor. We must part Kastum at the first dawn light. I'd like to pay our bill for the clothing and our lodging now, Sandria."

Sandria looked somewhat dismayed. She said good night to Branna, followed Lucan out of the room, and closed the door.

Several minutes later, Branna heard masculine footfalls outside in the hallway and then on the stairs. All fell silent after that. Branna changed her clothes and laid down on the bedroll. She sent a mental message to Fiall, letting him know she'd found a safe place for the night. She knew she'd reached him, because she caught a flash of him within her mind's eye. He stood in the woods near the Marcai River.

She tried to sleep, but, as usual, she couldn't. Thoughts of the strange twist her journey had taken crowded her mind. She'd come here to find a priest and she'd found a rebel instead. For surely, that was what Lucan had to be. He had not been forthcoming with information, but psychically, rebel was written all over the man.

A rebel . . . but no priest. Had the Goddess led her astray? Branna squeezed her eyes shut. That was not possible. She'd just have to be patient and wait to see what *cinnunt* brought her.

T HE SMELL OF SKYFLOWER TEASED HIM FROM HIS SLEEP. Lucan awoke and saw a flash of ethereal white out of half-closed eyes. He opened his eyes fully and saw Branna. She stood with her back to him, in front of the sitting room window, looking out. He was happy to smell skyflower again. After they'd parted last night, he'd missed that scent.

The muslin gown she wore fell all the way to the floor, hugging her narrow waist and hips. Its sleeves were voluminous and too long for her. They hung past her hands. The neckline was also somewhat too wide, and one side had slipped down over a smooth shoulder, baring vanilla-silk skin.

He stretched and tossed the blanket back.

Hearing him move, Branna turned toward him. "Oh, I didn't mean to awaken you," she said.

"It's all right." He stood and went to stand beside her. The light seeping in from the early morning sky swathed her in starshine. It limned the fair curve of her cheek in a silver hue as magical as the woman herself. Her long-lidded eyes looked deep and dark.

He yawned and then rubbed at his chin. Her hand shot out to

catch his. She turned it to the moonlight outside and exposed the half circle mark of her bite, coated with crusted blood, on the back of his hand.

Lucan smiled thinly. "You've marked me for life, it seems."

Her long, cool fingers grasped his wrist. "I'd forgotten about that or I would've treated you sooner."

"We have no herbs nor simples. What would you have treated me with?"

She looked up at him in surprise. "With myself," she replied.

"Ah . . . with magic," he said in amazed comprehension.

"Yes. Come over here and sit down." She led him to the settee and lit the candles, which stood on a table beside it, amid a clutter of spools and needles. She motioned toward the mess. "Sandria is a seamstress?"

"Costume maker, actually," Lucan answered. The primary costume maker for the Opposition, in fact. But there was no need to reveal that much information.

They sat together on the settee. He'd never had a magical healing before. He couldn't say he wasn't a little concerned about the prospect. But all misgivings vanished when she placed his hand on her thigh.

She must have sensed his sudden arousal because she hesitated for a moment, her shadowed eyes rising to meet his gaze slowly.

"Healing in this way is not always practical. Magical healing doesn't work with very grievous or mortal wounds. These types of injuries are the ones that take people to the Goddess . . . or Solan of the Overworld, depending on your religion. They are the domain of the Deities of the One alone. And the person being healed must be sensible, wanting to take part in the healing. The person must be willing to be healed on every level. It is two-way endeavor. I help you to heal yourself. So . . . do you wished to be healed of this wound, Lucan?"

"Aye."

"Do you wish to be healed on every level, and will you assist me in my assistance of you?"

"I'll do as I'm able, my lady."

"Very well then." Branna's eyes went out of focus, and the magical shimmering began. It started around her head, then extended outward, like heat rising in the distance on a very hot day.

"Ummm . . ."

Branna's eyes came back into focus, and the shimmering evaporated.

"What exactly am I supposed to do?" he asked.

"Simply allow." The shimmering resumed. She placed one of her hands under his and the other over it. Heat radiated from her palms.

After a few moments her hands grew cool. The shimmering stopped, and Branna examined his hand. The wound and the blood were gone, but a faint scar still marked it—an impression of teeth marks. Her brow furrowed, as did his. It was strange. She'd only bled him a little. The wound was not so grievous as to leave a scar.

She caught his gaze. "Seems on some level you truly did want me to mark you for life."

He smiled faintly. "Aye, perhaps."

She seemed suddenly uneasy and released him. She stood and went to the window, wrapping her arms around herself as though she was cold. The action caused the neckline of the dress to fall even farther down her shoulder.

She turned suddenly. "I have many questions for you, Lucan."

"I'm sure you do, as I have for you, but it is not the time nor place for them. Today we'll go somewhere safe where we can speak freely."

She turned back toward the window. Every line of her body bespoke the frustration she clearly felt. "Am I crazy for trusting you . . . rebel?"

Lucan didn't blink an eye. "I don't know. Am I crazy for trusting you . . . Tirian?"

She whirled and came toward him. "How do you know I'm Tirian? I could be Ilerian, couldn't I?" Anger made the slight accent she had even more pronounced. Lucan tried not to smile.

He shook his head. "No, you're Tirian. Of that I have no doubt."

"How could you know? There are not so many Tirians in the world." Her eyes flashed with pain at her own comment.

"How I know is a topic for a conversation we'll have later."

"So you think I'll aid you in your efforts to bring down Magnus, do you? That's why you helped me to escape yesterday," she accused.

Lucan did not refute her words. "I would make a guess we have similar goals," he said carefully.

She stood with her arms crossed and saying nothing for several long moments. "Fine," she said finally. "We'll have our conversation later . . . in your . . . your safe place. As though there could be somewhere safe in all of this goddess-forsaken country. But we leave now, this very moment. It's almost first morning light anyway."

Lucan rose from the settee and regarded her calmly. "That's agreeable."

They caught and held gazes for a moment. It seemed she was almost challenging him for some reason. He didn't know what inner conflict she was trying to resolve.

In any case, he suddenly had his own war to wage. For one terrible moment, he thought he would reach out and cup her cheek in his hand, just so he could feel the soft curve of it. Abruptly, she turned and went toward the door, taking away the option.

Lucan followed her.

CHAPTER FIVE

BRANNA KNELT BY THE ALHORN PLANT SHE'D FOUND. The cool, verdant strength of Terrestra's energy spiraled up from the ground. She held out her hand, palm down, and savored the gift of power. A breeze stirred the fine hairs around her face. She sank back on her heels and closed her eyes.

She stayed that way, eyes closed, head bowed, for several long moments and allowed the power to wash over her and calm her. Fiall grew near. The distinctive pattern he made in the Universal Fabric pulsed through her as he came closer.

She and Lucan had traveled slowly and cautiously all morning because of the Valorian in the area. Now they'd stopped in a clearing to let the horse drink from a stream and give themselves a rest. They'd both been quiet, each lost to their own thoughts.

She opened her eyes, unsheathed her athame, and cut a bit of the plant. Alhorn was a good healing plant to use when magic was not an option.

When she stood, she found Lucan's star-stone gaze on her. His blue-gray eyes were filled with a heat that had little to do with the warm midday sun that shone down on them. Every muscle in his body seemed to be attuned to her in that moment. She returned his gaze steadily, not wanting him to see how much he disturbed her.

Her examination of his memories had shown he was of no threat to her, and he seemed pleasant enough, and unquestionably in control. But beyond all that, deep within him, there was a kind of ferity. Branna wondered if it was related to the pain she'd felt within him yesterday. She could glean nothing from him emotionally. This man had learned long ago to control his feelings.

All she knew was that, Goddess, the man made her uncomfortable.

He walked toward her, and her hand tightened on the grip of her athame. He reached out. She looked at his upturned hand, not understanding what he wanted.

"Give me the herb," he said.

She opened her hand to him. He placed his hand over hers, and she felt his heat, his essential body's energy radiate from him and warm her skin. He placed his fingertips at her wrist and ran them down the length of her palm, catching the small bits of herb as he went. Tingles rippled through her hand and up her arm at his touch. A current of reaction passed from him to her and sent a jolt straight up her spine.

She tore her hand away. The rest of the alhorn fell to the ground. Lucan grasped the remaining herb and regarded her without a word. It was as if he tried to make her uncomfortable. Anger flared within her.

He turned and went to the horse's saddlebags. "I'll keep the herb in here until we arrive at Kern."

That he'd given up that bit of information piqued her interest enough that she forgot her anger. She sheathed her athame. "Kern? Is that the safe place you talked of earlier?"

"It is." He deposited the herb and drew up the lacings of the saddlebag, then turned to her. "Is it true the high priestess of Tir na Ban is called Raven and is chosen by a bird of the same name when she is but a babe?" Raw curiosity showed in his eyes.

"Yes, it's true. The raven is the messenger of the Goddess. When the old high priestess has lived her life fully and reaches a certain age, or if a young high priestess is to be called to Vallon unexpectedly, a raven will alight upon the cradle of a newborn girl."

He shook his head. "*Solan*, the far-bloods have always amazed me."

The people of Tir na Ban and Ileria were often referred to as the "far-bloods." It was believed a race that originally came from the stars had seeded the two magical peoples.

"It is in that way that the Goddess makes it known which one will follow in the footsteps of the older." Branna sighed wearily. "It has always been so and shall always be so, even if Magnus kills us down to our last two women," she finished. She knew sadness had crept into her voice, but she couldn't help it.

"You look tired. It is all right if you wish to rest. Lay you down and sleep a bit."

"I cannot. I'm plagued with insomnia, and even when I can sleep soundly, I am prone to nightmares . . . and other dreams," she replied.

"I'm plagued with nightmares myself. Your other dreams, are they prophetic ones?"

"Aye, prophetic." Branna didn't mention how disturbing they

were. She knelt by the stream and cupped her hands in the water, bringing the cool liquid up to her mouth for a drink.

"Are the dreams why you're here?"

She rocked back on her heels, gazing up at him speculatively. Truly, this man had more than just a touch of feyness within him. "I came to Numia to find a man," she said carefully.

He grinned briefly, showing straight white teeth. "Just any man?" he asked.

Her mouth threatened to smile. She looked down at the ground. "No, just one very special one."

Before Lucan had a chance to inquire further, the sound of hoofbeats filled the air. He went for the mount and pulled his sword from its scabbard attached to the saddle.

Two horses with riders stepped from the tree line at the far end of the clearing.

Branna scrambled to her feet. "Fiall."

Behind her protector trailed a gelding ridden by the young man she'd seen yesterday with Lucan. His hands were tied and his mouth gagged. Shame lay heavily upon his hunched shoulders. Fiall had the reins of the boy's horse tied to his saddle's pommel.

Fiall spotted Lucan and dismounted in a smooth movement. He drew his broadsword and began advancing toward the other man. "Get back, Branna," he commanded.

"Fiall, this man is a friend. He means me no harm," Branna said. But her words did not stop the Tirian warrior's stalk.

Lucan stood his ground. He indicated Fiall's prisoner with the tip of his sword. "You cut him free . . . now," he said, threat clear in his voice.

"No, wait! Lucan, this man travels with me!" exclaimed Branna.

Lucan appeared not to hear her, intent only on freeing the boy. He walked toward Fiall, and the two met in the center of the clearing. They looked like wolves with their hackles raised. A low chord of violence sung through the air between them.

"Despite what it looks like, he means the boy no harm," she said.

"This man travels with you, Branna?" asked Lucan.

"Yes."

Lucan raised his sword, ready to engage Fiall. "Then tell him to release Ren, or I'll allow my blade to quench its thirst on his blood."

"Fiall, let the boy free. He aided me yesterday and does not deserve such treatment," said Branna.

Fiall made no move. "I found the boy tracking you out of Strobia." He made a frustrated sound. "They're Numians. They are not worthy of our trust."

"Fiall, let him free," she ordered again.

With clear reluctance, Fiall walked back to the boy's horse and used his sword to cut the rope that bound Ren's wrists. The boy reached up and undid his gag. He rubbed at his chafed wrists and glared at Fiall.

Lucan turned and walked back to the horse, placed the tip of his sword in its scabbard, and slid the blade home. He placed his hands on the horse's flanks and, in a gesture of weariness, bowed his head for a moment. Then he detached the sword and scabbard and secured it crosswise to his back as though he expected additional trouble.

He half turned toward Branna as he did this. "If he travels with you, then he travels with us, I guess?" He didn't sound pleased at the prospect.

"I did not wish to be parted from him yesterday, and I won't be parted from him today," she replied.

"What makes you think we're going anywhere with you?" asked Fiall from afar.

Lucan turned toward him. "Stay here if you wish. I'll travel faster without you. But I'm telling you that you'll be sorry once you feel the kiss of Valorian steel against your throat. We planned a surprise for the Valorian in Strobia yesterday, and that means today this region is swarming with soldiers."

"We've seen them, Lucan," said Ren.

"Where?"

"Just past the Marcai and again outside Kastum."

"Well, that settles it. We ride."

Lucan helped Branna to mount and then swung up behind her. She was once again enveloped in Lucan's strength. His chest was hard and soft all at the same time against her back. His masculinity was an intoxicating thing, and it stole her breath for a moment. She closed her eyes and calmed herself, then opened them to watch her protector.

Fiall mounted and dug his heels in, coming close to Lucan's mount, but not too close. Branna could tell by the set of his jaw that he was headed straight for a good brood.

She closed her eyes and grimaced slightly. It had not been a good first meeting between Lucan and Fiall. Drawing steel against each other on first sight did not bode well. They would have to get along if they were to accomplish their shared goals. And Branna realized already that they did have shared goals. As piqued as her anger was by the rebel's desire not to give up any information until they reached the place, Kern, she knew she'd be willing to offer her aid to him.

She tried to ignore Lucan's arms around her and his strong hands on the reins in front of her. She'd noticed them that morning when she'd performed the healing on him. She remembered his fingers running the length of her palm and shivered. An image rose of those strong fingers tangling in her hair, drawing her toward him for a kiss. She tried to put it from her mind.

"You said something about how you'd planned a surprise for the Valorian back in Strobia. What did you mean by that?" she asked him.

"That's one of the things I don't want to talk about in detail right now."

"Really. It's a secret, is it?"

Lucan ignored her question. "You and your man escaped your occupied country and traveled a great distance to arrive in Numia. You two must have some reason for that. Do you care to tell me?"

Branna sighed and then was silent. He'd made his point. She didn't want to reveal anything more than she had to, and neither did he. "Fiall is not my man. He is not my servant nor is he my consort. He is like a brother to me, and he is my protector," she snapped.

"I could name a couple of other things he is," Lucan murmured.

Ren came riding up on their left side. "Are you all right?" Lucan asked him.

Branna saw the youth color. "Aye, I'm fine," he replied. Humiliation was obviously his most grievous injury.

"Branna, this is Ren . . . Ren, Branna," Lucan said.

"Sal'vi, my lady. I recognize you from Strobia," said Ren.

"As I do you. I thank you for your aid. I'm sorry you were repaid in such a way. Fiall thought only to protect me."

"I would've done the same in his place, although I'm chagrined he captured me. He came upon me like a shadow, my lady," Ren said wonderingly. "I'm merely satisfied he didn't use steel on me."

She felt Lucan shudder as he said, "As am I, Ren . . . as am I."

She knew then it was fear that had caused Lucan to react so harshly toward Fiall. Lucan felt an acute responsibility for the youth for some reason. What she didn't know was why her protector had acted that way toward Lucan.

For the duration of the ride, Fiall followed behind, dead set on not entertaining conversation. Although Lucan did try to coax him into a better humor once the rebel himself was in one. But Fiall simply growled at his attempts and then became silent.

Eventually Branna noticed that Lucan gave up trying to make idle talk and began whistling instead. That seemed to annoy Fiall, thus making Lucan's whistling all that more robust and cheerful.

Branna sighed.

After a while, fatigue overtook her. She let herself fall back on Lucan's chest. She found it strange she would be able to drowse in the arms of a near stranger. This man was the remedy for her insomnia that she'd been looking for. It was her final thought before sleep took her truly well and deeply for the first time in four days.

When she awoke, the Sisters shone full and bright in the night sky, providing enough light to travel by. In the early morning, they finally stopped to rest.

The bit of sleep Branna had gotten seemed to do her worse than none at all. She sat down on the ground and leaned against a fallen tree limb. Fiall went into the woods in search of a stream they could hear gurgling in the distance. Branna was thirsty also, but she was far too tired to move. Ren busied himself with the horses.

She watched Lucan walk to the easternmost part of the small clearing. He detached his scabbard and placed it to his side. He did the same with the long knife sheathed on his belt. Then he knelt and turned his face skyward, letting his arms dangle at his sides. His glossy black hair brushed his shoulders. He closed his eyes and his lips moved in prayer.

She watched with intense curiosity. It was a pious scene. At first look she would not have guessed such a man to be so devoted to his Gods.

When Lucan finally returned, Branna tried not to stare at him.

She looked down at her lap and pretended to brush something from it. Fiall returned with his drinking horn full and offered it to her. She put it to her lips eagerly and let the cool, sweet water slide down her throat.

Lucan extracted two pieces of cloth from his saddlebag. "Unfortunately, I'm going have to ask you to put these on for the rest of the trip," he said.

"What do you mean? As blindfolds?" asked Branna.

"If you're to travel on with me, you must wear blindfolds. It's important you don't see where I'm taking you. Branna, you may have gotten a good look at who I really am yesterday in Strobia, when you did that thing I felt you do." Branna's eyes widened in surprise at that. Most did not feel such mental examinations. "But I don't have such magical skills," he continued. "I don't know what manner of people you truly are."

She stood up and went to stand by Fiall. To blindfold a far-blood was to take away their abilities. The far-blooded needed their eyes to perform almost any type of magic. They needed to be able to isolate an area of reality in order to look beyond it, to the Universal Fabric under and behind it. She knew Lucan probably didn't realize the level of trust he was demanding from them.

"But you know that Branna and I might help in your plans," Fiall said icily. "You have an agenda, but you are not willing to share it with us, even though we're a part of it. Yet, you are willing to ask such a boon."

Branna was impressed. She had not realized Fiall had gleaned that much information. It was buried deep within Lucan.

Ren broke in, casting a look of keen impatience toward Fiall. "He's not that way. You don't even know him," he spat with vehement defensiveness.

"It's all right, Ren," Lucan said. "Yes, that's true, Fiall. I didn't save Branna from the Valorian purely from the goodness of my heart. I think I know what you are, or least where you come from. And I think you and I might be able to help each other."

"There's no way you could know where we come from," scoffed Fiall.

"You are Tirians."

Fiall went silent. Branna understood his shock. They had done everything they could . . . from their clothing, hairstyles, even their very accents to disguise themselves. They'd spent years learning to conceal their nationality for this trip.

"How . . . how could you know that?" asked Fiall.

"You'd be surprised how much some of us Numians know," Lucan said with a disparaging look toward Fiall. "Do you want to know how much more I know?" He held out the pieces of cloth. "I think you do."

Branna met Lucan's gaze. "Do you know what it is to blindfold a far-blood?" she asked.

"I do. I'm asking for your trust, as you are asking for mine."

She hesitated for a moment and then took the piece of cloth. When Fiall hesitated, she nudged him until he finally accepted it. They remounted, and Ren took up the reins of Fiall's horse. Branna and Fiall shared a look, and then put on the blindfolds.

"Anyway," Lucan continued, "you both have Tirian accents."

"What?" asked Fiall and Branna in unison. They had learned the Numian tongue flawlessly, without accent . . . or at least they thought they had.

"Yes, it's very subtle but definitely detectable. Don't worry, any-one else would think you from the province Ileria, or maybe Bah'ra."

This time Branna, as well as Fiall, lapsed into a brooding silence.

Lucan whistled low and long. "A true Tirian priestess . . . It's been many years since Numia has seen your like." Sadness tinged his voice. "It's been a long time since Numia has seen any priestesses at all."

She fingered her pendant. If only he knew the truth.

They traveled for another hour to a place where rushing water could be heard. Branna thought it must be a waterfall. They rode so close to the source of the sound that she felt wet spray. They went into an area that caused the horse's hooves to clop and echo. The ground seemed very uneven and mostly uphill. Up and up they climbed. Branna could smell the deep, rich scent of earth and the dusty odor of rock.

After what seemed like an eternity, they heard human sounds. Laughter, yelling, and the low murmur of conversation met their ears. Light reached under her blindfold, and cooking scents caressed her nostrils.

"We're here," said Lucan. Did he catch a tendril of her hair and work it back and forth between his fingers before he pulled the blindfold down to circle her neck, or was it her imagination?

His stubbled cheek brushed her earlobe. "You're free," he whispered. His deep voice rumbled through her, and something dark and pleasurable stirred to life within her. A shiver that had more to do with the touch of him than the cool temperature ran through her body. She drew a shaky breath and exhaled slowly.

He pulled away from her and said louder, "You may remove your blindfold, Fiall."

Branna and Fiall squinted against the light. When they could finally see, a large room made of rock met their eyes. Light shone brightly from celestial-fire lanterns that hung on walls that had been chiseled almost smooth.

Celestial-fire was a substance extracted in the mines of Pira. It was a viscid liquid that glowed with a clear, bright white light when touched with a flame, but gave off no heat or smoke.

A cooking area with a large open fire and a cauldron upon it stood to her right. A long table with many chairs stretched in front of the fireplace. Various barrels storing flour, oats, vegetables, beans, and smoked meat stood to the right of the cauldron. To her left was another long table, and around it many men and women engaged in a heated discussion. All around people sat, laughed, and talked. Some people even slept on bedrolls in the corners of the room. Off the perimeter of the room stretched long corridors.

Branna watched Lucan dismount and noticed the smooth muscles of his chest, arms, and thighs ripple under the fabric of his shirt and trews. Funny, she never noticed those things when Fiall dismounted from his horse. She bit her lip and stared down at Lucan in consternation.

He came to her and reached up, ready to pull her from the saddle. She let his strong hands close around her waist and lift her down. A whiff of spicewood soap, mingled with the rich scent of leather, hit her full in the nose as he placed her to the floor in front of him. Holding her gaze with his, he untied the blindfold, which was still looped around her neck. The back of his finger stroked her collarbone as he removed the length of material. The touch was subtle, but it made her shiver again. She pulled away from him, and he smiled.

"You are in the heart of our stronghold now," said Lucan. He made a sweeping gesture flowing into a half bow, her blindfold in one hand. "Welcome to Kern. We are the Opposition forces here in Numia. The people call us rebels. Our goal is to take Magnus out of power."

Fiall came to stand protectively by Branna.

"By bringing you here I was trusting that you are in accord with Opposition goals, knowing where you come from and about certain . . . atrocities that have been committed there," continued

Lucan. "Don't try and leave this place. There's no way you could ever find your way out, not even with your obvious abilities. The tunnels snake and lead straight into the depths of these mountains. There is a good chance you'll end up lost. Consider this your warning."

"So we're prisoners now?" charged Fiall.

"This is for your safety as well as ours," answered Lucan. "If you find you don't wish to stay here, I'll take you anywhere you want to go, though we would blindfold you for the journey. But I warn you, once out, you would never find us again. The Kernian mountain range is immense."

Branna merely smiled. Lucan smiled back at her. They already knew they were in accord.

"Why did you have to bring us here to tell us that?" asked Fiall.

"We don't know how powerful Magnus's pool of sorceresses are," said Lucan. Branna felt Fiall go very still at his words. He had not known about that. They had much to discuss.

Lucan continued. "To ensure the safety of this place, a—"

"—regio has been created," finished Branna in surprise. A regio was an area protected and concealed by magic.

"Yes," continued Lucan. "It protects what is said from going beyond Kern, perhaps traveling back to Magnus by some magical means. We suspect the sorceresses are not capable of far-hearing, but we don't know for certain."

Branna shook her head. "They are not. I'm sure of that. But it is good you took precautions anyway. Who created the regio?"

Lucan held up a hand. "Questions are for later. You need to eat and rest now. Ren, could you please make sure Fiall and Branna get some food? And would you please give them rooms with bathing pools?" asked Lucan.

"Of course," Ren answered.

Lucan caught the arm of a woman passing by. "Have any of the men returned yet from Strobia?" Lucan asked. "Has Morgan arrived?"

"Yes, my lord, a few. But I have not seen Morgan," she answered.

Branna jerked herself from the close examination she was giving the room. *My lord*?

"Have something to eat," Lucan said. "I'll come and talk with you later, but now I have things to attend to." With that he turned on his heel and left.

Ren led them to the long table and served them two steaming bowls of the rich stew that was simmering in the cauldron. Fiall and Branna fell to the food as if they were starving.

"I hope you know what you're doing," said Fiall between mouthfuls.

"Trust the Goddess, Fiall. This is *cinnunt* at work. We are with those who want the same thing we do. Did you receive my mental message telling you I was not in danger?"

"Yes, I did."

"Then why did you draw your sword against Lucan?"

Fiall cast his dark green eyes downward and did not answer. She decided not to press him. They'd each polished off two bowls apiece before Ren returned to lead them to their rooms.

They went down one of the corridors off the main cavern. Many celestial-fire lamps lined the walls, casting a light that flickered over the surprisingly even walls, ceiling, and floor. Many large wooden doors stood on each side of the hallway. Ren guided Fiall to his room and then escorted Branna to hers.

The room was small but seemingly comfortable. A bed took up most of the room, and a crude fireplace dominated the wall across from it. The fireplace appeared to have some sort of a flue cut into the rock to allow the smoke to escape. A small table and two chairs stood adjacent to the hearth. But what caught her attention most was the small pool of water at the far end of the room. She walked to its edge. A spring bubbled at the bottom.

"Feel the temperature," Ren said as he built up a fire. She knelt down and put her hand in the pool. It was warm.

"There are lakes, waterfalls, and heated springs all over within these mountains. Some of the rooms were designed to take advantage of the springs," he explained. "My lord must think you very special to give you one of these rooms."

"Why do you keep calling him 'lord'?"

Ren grinned at her and walked to the door. "I think that's for him to tell you. I'll let you rest now."

"Wait," she said, going to him. "I again apologize for what Fiall did to you back in Strobia."

The boy's grin widened. "Oh, it's all right. He is a good fighter, your Fiall. I admire that." Then his expression became serious and his eyes clouded. "But if he means my lord any harm, I'll have to take it up with him." Fierce loyalty and protectiveness threaded his words. "Lucan will be coming to talk to you soon, I'm sure." The door closed behind him.

Several minutes later a short, round-faced woman delivered a bundle of clothing, a cloak, and other things Branna would need.

Branna shed her dusty garments and stepped into the warm pool of water. She scrubbed, and then she soaked. When she finished bathing, she combed out her hair while sitting by the fire, deep in thought.

Lucan did things to her that no man had ever done. Never had she been so attuned to a man's body, the way he moved. Even Lucan's very breathing pattern was a source of fascination to her. It was disturbing on many levels. The priest was the one for whom she should have these feelings, not this rebel. She'd saved herself her whole life for the priest. She wouldn't lose her long-built-up sexual magic to anyone but him.

And Lucan was far from a priest. The man was hard-edged and slightly feral—a warrior, not a man devoted to Solan.

She wondered where the priest was right now. Did he sleep under the stars or beneath a roof? She wondered how she would find him. Closing her eyes, she offered a prayer to the Goddess that she would lead Branna to him soon. Time was running out. She could feel it slipping away. Events were coming together, congealing into a dark future for all the lands under Magnus's rule. If she didn't find the priest and the *Draiochta Cothrom* soon, she knew it would be too late to stop Magnus at all.

CHAPTER SIX

THE OFFICER STRODE DOWN THE CORRIDOR TO EMPEROR Magnus's meeting chamber, his boots clicking on the polished marble floor. He stopped in front of the thick oak door and stared at the two elaborate dragons carved into the wood. He took a deep breath, straightened his tunic, and then reached for the door knocker with a shaking hand.

As official messenger of the Northern Valorian Guard, it was his duty to bring communication from his superiors to Emperor Magnus.

His was not an envied position.

He knocked, and a deep voice told him to enter. He pushed the door open and descended the three steps into the room. "Emp . . . Emperor Magnus."

Dane Navius Magnus stood by the long, polished wooden table that dominated the room. His thick mane of white hair was unconstrained, flowing down his back. It framed vibrantly cold blue eyes. For certain, he looked like Malus, the God of the Underworld. Emperor Magnus took a sip of his red wine and then dropped the glass to his side with a look of impatience crossing his features. A fine black tunic, embroidered with dragons in silver stitching at collar and hem, covered his broad chest and fell almost to his knees. A silver torc adorned his throat.

The officer shifted his eyes from that cold gaze and swallowed hard at the sight of Crispus, the emperor's most trusted advisor, palace physician ... and torturer, who sat in an opulent velvet-covered chair at the table. He also held a glass of wine. A fire crackled in the immense gold-gilt hearth on the right side of the room, near the door that led to Crispus's work area. It was a place he hoped to never see, and he prayed his message would not send him there.

"Emperor Magnus," the officer began again, his voice trembling a bit. He wiped a bead of sweat from his forehead.

"Yes?" Magnus laughed thinly. "What? Do you think I would like to bite you? Go on, man, tell me what you came to say."

The officer took a deep breath and plunged ahead. "I bring tidings from the Northern Valorian Guard. The rebels have attacked them in the village of Strobia. Commander Armillon has been slightly wounded. They have lost men."

Magnus became very quiet and still. He took another sip of wine.

"Ummm ... unfortunately, the rebels managed to find a cache of tax revenue that the fiscal magistrate collected. They will probably redistribute it to the lower classes, as they have done in the past." The officer drew a breath. "We inflicted some damage on them also," the officer tried to finish hopefully. "We captured some of them."

They stood in strained silence for several long moments. The officer shifted his weight uncomfortably. Finally, Magnus spoke. "How many?"

"Eight, my lord. There's something else. There was a woman in the village. We believe that she's a sorceress, Tirian or Ilerian, we are not sure. She was definitely using magic. It appeared she was trying to cast some kind of beguiling spell on Armillon."

"Well . . . did you bring her here?" Magnus asked.

"No, my lord. One of the rebels captured her before we could."

The emperor stood staring at him. The officer noted uneasily that Magnus was growing increasingly red in the face. Magnus threw his glass to the floor. The tinkling sound of shattering glass and the splash of red wine on the marble filled the silence. The officer flinched and then stood stock still, suddenly very interested in the glass shards twinkling in the pool of red at Magnus's feet.

"Leave!" Magnus yelled.

He didn't need to be told twice. Scrambling backward, he tripped over the steps leading up to the door and fled.

Magnus turned and stared at Crispus. His advisor sat sipping his wine and staring into the fire speculatively. Delicate-looking hands, with long, thin fingers, grasped the wineglass. Magnus thought about what he did with those hands and shuddered. Crispus was in the business of inflicting slow and meticulous injury, ensuring there was no escape, either by loss of consciousness or premature death.

Crispus turned his storm-gray eyes on him. At nearly fifty years, he still had a child's face, complete with cherub's mouth and dimples—deceivingly innocent looking.

"Did you hear that?" Magnus asked him.

Crispus's eyes glittered. "Yes. But you must not allow yourself to become overly upset. These rebels are no more than a fly at the dinner table." He waved a free hand. "They are annoying, yes, but no threat, my lord. We simply need to swat them a little."

"We've been trying to swat these flies for a long while now," replied Magnus. "Obviously, we need new tactics. How do you suggest we go about that? These rebels obviously are not stupid, and they seem to be growing in strength. Every time we think we have them defeated, we find out we haven't."

Crispus nodded his white-blond head once, slowly.

"We have been unable to successfully infiltrate their organization," Magnus continued. "We've been unable to locate their stronghold or find even one turncoat within the rebel network." He put his fingers to his temples to rub away a budding headache. "I realize they are currently not a serious threat, but they rouse the passions of the commoners, and that, my friend, is dangerous."

Crispus took another sip of wine. "I agree."

Magnus gripped the back of a nearby chair. "I have always wondered if my nephew Lucan may be behind these attacks."

Lucan had been the only one to escape the day he overthrew Gallus. The guards who'd been in charge of bringing his nephew to the courtyard to be executed had paid for that escape with their own blood. Still, he did not see how Lucan could have possibly survived. He'd fallen a long way into the violent Agarian River, and he'd been wounded when he'd done it. If he'd survived, it was with the aid of the Gods. Indeed, the Gods would've helped Lucan. He'd been so damned devoted to them and their secrets.

Magnus squeezed his eyes shut in an effort to banish the memories. Killing his family was not something that had been pleasurable to him, as most seemed to think. It was a distasteful, if necessary, business.

If his father, King Dane, had done the right thing and made him his heir, instead of his younger brother, Gallus, none of it would have happened. His father had believed him too violent, too rash, and too unthinking to inherit the Dragon Throne. So he had passed over his elder son in favor of the younger. It had been an unbearable disgrace.

For years Magnus had soaked in that slight, that testament to his father's feelings about him. It had been simply too much to be borne in the end.

"My lord," said Crispus with a shake of his head. "It is impossible that your nephew lives. You should put that from your mind. If you must have the truth, there are many who would prefer to see you dead. There are many capable of leading a force of Opposition."

He nodded his head. "Aye, perhaps."

"Whoever he is, we'll need to be careful of him because he's the most dangerous kind of man."

"What do you mean?"

Crispus shrugged. "He has a cause he believes in."

Magnus grunted. "Aye . . . my downfall."

"Even though I don't think the rebels a great threat, it is true I am worried for your safety during your trip to Kastum," he continued. "It would be a good opportunity for them."

Magnus shook his head. "There is no way they could know of those plans."

"To leave the palace means you leave the safety of the sorceresses' shields."

"Yes, I know. But I won't alter my plans for them. I'll bring Nia with me in any case."

"And what of the sorceresses, Magnus? Why have they been unable to help us locate the Opposition?"

Magnus sighed. The sorceresses were a mysterious and powerful force, which not even he fully understood. It was important that he use a soft but strong hand in their manipulation. They were of the utmost importance to him and his ability to hold on to his conquered lands. They must be kept in a state of fear, certainly. However, it was important he did not paralyze them with it, or make them hate him so much that they would rather die than lend their help to him. He had constructed an elaborate mental labyrinth for them to exist in, built of fear and love, threats, and promises. The sorceresses he kept were his most important weapons. He could do nothing to alienate them. For losing them meant losing his power.

"I will see them," Magnus said simply.

"And your rebel prisoners . . . there are eight altogether, are there not?" asked Crispus hopefully.

"Aye. They're yours to do with as you please, as long as you wring information from them before they die."

His cherubic face lit up, making Magnus shiver.

"But first," Magnus continued, "I need to use them to set a trap."

M AGNUS STRODE WITH PURPOSE DOWN THE HALL TO-ward the sorceresses' chambers. There were twenty in all, handpicked by himself from Tir na Ban. They had a wing of the palace all to themselves, lush furnishings, the best food, the finest gowns and jewels, anything they wanted . . . so long as they did what he asked of them.

He turned the knob on the common room door. When he entered, the women scattered like surprised birds from a bush.

"Ladies," he said as he entered.

Nia, the only sorceress who would actually look him in the eye, stepped forward. "Lord Magnus. To what do we owe the pleasure of this visit?" She smiled, but as always there was something in her eyes . . . and beautiful eyes they were, Magnus continually noted. As well as a beautiful face framed by a gorgeous fall of hair of many different shades of golds and reds. Nia was ever the diplomat and appeared to be the appointed spokesperson for the rest of the sorceresses.

"My lady Nia. I would have a word with you."

Apprehension flickered in her eyes for the briefest of moments. "Of course, my lord," she answered.

"You know of the rebel forces, I would presume?"

"Yes, my lord. They have been causing you some trouble lately, have they not?"

"I would not say that they were causing us trouble. They are more like a minor irritation. All the same I would like to see them captured and punished. I wish to know where they're located. I would like to know who it is that leads them."

"And you wish for us to try to see? My lord, you have asked for such things before."

"Yes, and I know what you've always told me. You are unable to do this." Magnus turned and looked toward the other sorceresses, who had calmed and now sat in repose around the room. "But I don't understand. You can cast spells that make magic recognizable and put a shield up around this entire palace. You can even make me younger than the Gods themselves have decreed." Magnus turned back and stared at Nia for a long moment. His eyes darkened as he asked, "But you can't cast a spell as simple as I have asked?"

Nia shook her head. "My lord, you must understand the nature of magic. It simply does not work that way. We each have individual strengths and weaknesses. None of us are able to cast a tracking spell, and we've no one to teach us how. I'm very sorry, my lord."

Magnus stared at her for several moments before he spoke again. She did not avert her gaze and he respected her for that. "My lady Nia, we believe there is another far-blooded sorceress traveling with the rebels."

Her whole body snapped to attention.

"She attempted to use some sort of beguiling spell on Commander Armillon," he continued. "We were about to capture her when one of the rebels appears to have gotten to her before we could. If she is one of you, a Tirian, would you be able to track the rebel movements using her as a sort of beacon?"

She hesitated. "My lord, a sorceress traveling with the rebels makes no difference in our ability to track them. We could communicate mentally with another sorceress, but to do that we must have an intimate link with her, a personal object of hers, for example. Anyway, she is most likely Ilerian."

Magnus walked toward her until he was right in front of her face. He spoke with soft threat in his voice. "Nia, I really hope you're telling me the truth. You know what will happen if you ever lie to me, if you ever withhold your abilities from me. You and this group of sorceresses are responsible for the continued well-being of your families, your country, your people . . . not to mention yourselves. It is not a light charge, my lady."

She shivered. "You know, my lord, that we'll do anything you require of us . . . anything we are capable of doing, that is."

He took her hand in his and patted it. "Now, now, Lady Nia, I did not mean to upset you. You and the other sorceresses are doing a magnificent job. There's no reason to fear. You do a good job for me and I will provide you with anything you and the other sorceresses desire. Speaking of which, I would very much desire your company tonight at dinner . . . with me . . . alone. My lady, would you please do me that honor?"

"I . . . I would certainly enjoy that, my lord."

"Excellent," he said as he turned and walked through the door.

Nia sat down on a nearby chair and gripped the armrests to steady herself. She closed her eyes and sighed deeply.

CHAPTER SEVEN

LUCAN KNOCKED ON BRANNA'S DOOR. WHEN SHE OPENED it, his breath caught in his throat. Her long dark hair was swept up, and she wore a soft gown of rose-colored fabric. It enhanced her clear, cat-green eyes and made her skin seem even creamier.

"So we're to have our discussion at last." She turned away from the door and walked inside.

He took that as an invitation to enter and did so, closing the door behind him. "Yes, if you wish. That's why I have come."

She turned and regarded him in silence for a moment. Her cool, controlled façade of the unattainable far-blood was in place again. It was a marked difference from when she'd fallen back against him and gone to sleep on their journey to Kern. He'd enjoyed her sweet weight against him. "Yes, I very much wish to speak with you," she answered.

They took seats by the fire. She folded her hands in her lap. "Have your men returned from Strobia yet?" she asked.

"A few. They will begin to return in earnest by nightfall, I believe. There are other places in Numia besides Kern they will go." He'd tried to sound undisturbed. In reality he was very concerned about his men. This was one of the biggest offensives they'd waged thus far. He worried what kind of damage had been done to them. So far only a few of the less seriously wounded men had arrived. More were due to come in. No sleep in his future this eve.

If it had not been for the arrival of the Tirians, he never would have left Strobia. If many of his men were lost, he had no one but himself to blame. He would forever wonder how many he could have helped had he stayed. As soon as he finished here, it was back to the cavern room where the arrivals would congregate to swap stories and receive medical aid. He hoped Morgan would arrive soon. There had been no news of his second-in-command thus far.

"You have been very generous to us, Lucan. I wanted to thank you for your hospitality," she said.

"Well, we've never had such a distinguished guest. Having a priestess within the walls of Kern is a true pleasure."

Her hand went to her throat, and she rubbed her thumb over the moonstone pendant that adorned it. "I . . . I must be truthful with you, Lucan. I am not only a priestess of Tir na Ban. I am the high priestess, the Tirian Raven."

Lucan went silent, absorbing this new bit of jarring information.

"I know you know what that means," she continued.

He did. It was as though he sat conversing with Tir na Ban's queen. "I do," he said carefully. "It is a pleasure to meet you, Raven."

She looked down, a slight blush colored her cheeks. "Thank you."

"There are many stories about your people, but the country is so small and keeps to itself so much that many believe the stories to be merely for children . . . myths."

"Yes, we've tried to keep our country a secret," she answered.

"Aye . . . I know. Never has Tir na Ban even traded with other countries or engaged in any sort of commerce."

She went silent. Lucan could see the questions jockeying for position in her mind. "How do you know so much about my country, and about what being Raven means?" she asked finally.

"I know someone who also comes from Tir na Ban. He taught me much about the country and its culture. Before Numia's invasion, its priestesses and priests ruled the country. One tier below the priests and priestesses was the mage class, made up of sorcerers and sorceresses. That class dedicated itself primarily to magic, the priests and priestesses primarily to the Goddess. The Raven, the high priestess, is considered to be the Goddess incarnate and to have the most powerful magic in the land."

He leaned forward. "What I don't understand is why the Tirian Raven would come to Numia viritually alone, with but one warrior as a protector?"

She looked away with a pained expression on her face. "The population of Tir na Ban has been decimated. There was no one else to send. I ordered my men to stay behind to protect the remaining sorceresses and priestesses against the occupying Valorian force. I waited for years for the opportunity to escape. I am here because—" She bit off the end of her sentence.

"You need to find a man," he answered for her. "And not just any man, a mysterious and special one." He couldn't quite keep the weariness and undercurrent of sarcasm from his voice. He was so tired of information and dark secrets that had to be cajoled or bribed into the light.

She returned his comment with a sharp look, her eyes flashing. "Aye. Is that so hard to believe?"

He didn't smile. Mocking her was not something he wished to do. On the contrary, this woman was not to be taken lightly. "No. I understand you believe your Goddess is leading you in a particular direction. You trust her. You have faith she will lead you where you need to go to obtain the goals you feel you need to reach."

"Yes."

"Believe it or not, my lady Raven, I understand the concept of faith. At one time, I even had it."

"Where did it go?"

He sighed. "Oh, it died long ago, along with my family and my country."

She looked down and said no more.

Lucan thought to press her on the issue of the man she sought, but there would be time to learn more of her and her plans. Far more important was that she grew to trust him now.

She looked back up at him, spreading her hands wide. "What of this place . . . Kern? How is all this possible? The hot springs, the kitchen, the smooth walls and floors, the cavern room?" She finished in a wondering rush.

"My great grandfather, Marcus, my grandfather, Dane, and my father, Gallus, had this done over many, many years. It was to be a secret military stronghold. No one knew about it except the direct heirs to the Dragon Throne and a few other select individuals."

Shocked realization dawned slowly over her features as he spoke.

He continued on. "Secret caches of assets were also left. They fund all this. My great grandfather created Kern because he feared Numia might one day have to fight a tyrant. As you know well, his fears came true."

"Do you mean . . . ?"

He rose and bowed deeply. "Allow me to formally introduce myself. My name is Gallus Navius Lucan."

She froze. Her expression was of pure shock.

He'd known no easy way to tell her. Navius was the royal family's name. The same name Magnus held. Lucan could only imagine how much she hated Magnus, and he shared his blood. Rebel or no, she was in the stronghold of her enemy's nephew.

Branna stood and paced in front of the fire.

He rose and took her hands in his, stopping her in place. She would not look at him. Gently, he cupped her chin, turned her face up, and held her gaze. "I've said it before. I will say it again. I mean you no harm," he said in a soft voice designed to comfort her. He couldn't stop himself from noting her lips—full and red and slightly parted. They'd feel so nice beneath his, probably taste sweet. It was an odd thing to notice right at that moment, but he couldn't stop himself.

She went still and searched his eyes. Reaching out, he caught a tendril of her midnight-colored hair and wound it around his finger. He smiled in an effort to put her at ease and toyed with the idea of using those smooth strands to draw her face toward his and find out if her lips tasted as good as they looked. When she pulled away, her hair unwrapped from his finger like a long length of black silk. She sat down by the fire once more. "I'm sorry. I think I need more sleep," she said.

"I'll leave you alone now," he said, starting for the door.

"No, please don't go. I need answers more than I need sleep. I thought all the children of King Gallus were executed when Magnus seized power."

He sat back down with a sigh. These were painful memories better left in the past. "They were, Branna, all of them except me. I escaped and was almost killed in the attempt. My uncle assumed

I had died, but I fought to survive . . . only to take Magnus out of power and make him pay for what he'd done. I found a friend I knew was loyal to my father, the same Tirian I told you of before." He stared into the fire. "He nursed me to health and helped me build the Opposition. He told me of this place. All this has been fourteen years in the making, and it's time . . . past time."

He looked at her. She sat mute, watching him. "It is our goal to overthrow Magnus and give the country back to its people," he continued. "It's time to end the corruption, the killing, and the poverty. Besides my father, Magnus killed my mother, Jovia, my three older bothers, Cassius, Artus, and Maron, and my baby sister, Valentina. I was made to watch the executions. Believe me, Branna, I would've been happy enough to die had it not been for the prospect of revenge." It had been years since he'd uttered their names aloud, but to this woman, for some reason, he felt strong enough to do it. It actually felt good, like a weight had been lifted from him.

She leaned forward, studying his face. Then she reached out and traced the line of his jaw lightly with her finger. "So that's where it comes from," she murmured.

"Where what comes from?"

She smiled and spoke in a gentle voice. "The pain and wildness you hold deep within."

He tried not to do it and failed miserably. He caught her fingers and brought them to his lips, kissing them softly. She surprised him by allowing the intimacy. He flipped her hand over and, holding her gaze, laid his lips to her palm. Her eyes widened and her lips parted a bit, but she did not pull away. Taking that as encouragement, he pressed his mouth to the pulse at her wrist. He parted his lips and tasted it with the very tip of his tongue and felt it speed up.

Abruptly, she pulled away. "Don't touch me like that. You . . ."

She struggled for a moment as if trying to find the right words. "You . . . make me uneasy."

He raised an eyebrow. "Do I now? And in what way do I make you . . . uneasy?"

Anger flitted across her features before she mastered her expression. She looked down and away from him. "You . . . you . . ." She went silent, at a loss for words. She blushed and said no more, but she didn't really need to. He knew that she was attracted to him, as he was to her. Very intriguing, that.

"Forgive me, my lady. I take liberties I should not. It seems I cannot help myself for some reason." Lucan thought it odd she should react thus if she was attracted to him. He knew well that in Tirian culture, women were free to take whatever man they wished to their bed, barring a love or partner bond with another. He could not help but inquire. "Do you have a bond with someone in Tir na Ban?"

She glanced at him. "No, I have no one."

Perhaps he had misread her. Then he remembered what Arturo had told him about lovemaking and magic. Tirians used sexual energy sometimes for special spell casting or ritual. Perhaps that's why she behaved in such a demure manner. Perhaps she was saving hers for an event she foresaw in her future. Perhaps for the mysterious man? *Solan.* If that was true . . . lucky man, whoever he was.

She spoke quietly. "I trust you did not bring me here to occupy your bed."

Nice thought. "No, my lady. I would never presume such. As I said, I simply could not resist."

"But you will from now on." It was half order, half query.

Should he say yes? It might be a lie. "I will try," he said carefully.

It seemed to satisfy her. She remained silent for a few moments. Finally she spoke. "Magnus has decimated my entire country. He also killed my loved ones. Tir na Ban used to be a thriving, vibrant place. Then Magnus came with his Valorian and ripped its heart out." She turned and looked at Lucan. "But you know so much about Tir na Ban. There is no need for me to tell you this."

"Aye, Arturo told me much. But now I would like to hear about your homeland from your own lips."

She looked up, undoubtedly because Arturo was a Tirian name.

"Yes, he is the Tirian I spoke of. You will meet him tomorrow. Please continue."

"Very well. Tir na Ban is matriarchal. Most of the country's inhabitants, especially the women, have highly developed intuition and psychic skills. We also have high magic."

"The ability to alter the Universal Fabric."

"Yes. We had been doing a very good job of keeping our country secret from the rest of the world. We knew that we would be vulnerable to attack and that countries to our east were conquest minded. Since Tir na Ban is mountainous and very small, it was easy for us to stay hidden. But Magnus found out about us and came with his entire Valorian." She paused, pain flitting across her features.

Lucan could see it was a painful subject for her, but talking about it seemed to be a catharsis for her. "But he knew exactly where you were, what you were, and most important, how you could aid him, didn't he?"

She nodded. "First, he came dangling carrots in front of our noses, appealing to our greed, but he didn't understand the fundamental philosophies of Tir na Ban. If he had, he would've known that tactic was bound to fail. When it did, he chose the path of violence. He killed many . . . especially the men who were his greatest threat. We call that period of time the Terror, for that is truly what it was."

As Branna spoke, Lucan studied her. They were aligned in a way he could not fully understand. They shared the same goals and had memories and experiences that were much alike. He was looking in a mirror that reflected his pain, and it made him uncomfortable.

She continued. "He killed our priestesses, gathered up our sorceresses, and took them away. We never knew what became of them." Branna paused. "Except I know now. You told me back in Strobia. It's our worst fears come true."

Lucan remembered well the screaming of the priests and priestesses of Solan and the four Gods of the Elements. Magnus dismantled as much religion as he could in all the countries he ruled.

Silent tears rolled down her cheeks. "Magnus must be made to pay for what he's done. I want nothing more than to see him taken down." Determination glittered in her eyes.

"You and I have much in common, Branna," he said softly. He could not stay in the room any longer. Her pain was like daggers stabbing into his sorrow. He got up and left, closing the door behind him.

CHAPTER EIGHT

THE NEXT MORNING, BRANNA DRESSED IN A SLEEVE-
less gown of dark green. Two green enameled brooches in
the shape of dragonflies held the fabric together at the top of each
shoulder. Its cut was not unlike Tirian styles.

The dress hung low at the neck, revealing her collarbones and
the swell of her breasts. It clung to her waist and then flared gently
out to fall to her ankles. Her hair swung free and kissed her waist
as she walked toward the door.

She stepped out of the room and walked down the corridor
toward the main chamber of the stronghold. She wished to stop
at Fiall's room, but she had no idea which of the many doors was
his. Stopping in the hallway, she closed her eyes and concentrated,
sending out a thought-wave pattern he'd be able to pick up.

"Tsk, tsk, tsk."

Branna's eyes popped open. A stooped old man with a completely bald head stood staring at her out of one good eye.

"A daughter of Tir na Ban." He sighed. "It does my heart good to see one of you again. It has been so long . . . so very long indeed. I am overjoyed to see you, even though you're using high magic to send out a mental message. Even that little thing gives off a glow here in Numia," he said reprovingly.

She blinked.

The wizened old man laughed. "But I see you are confused. Allow me to introduce myself. I am Arturo ta Derianna, of Tir na Ban, at your service, your highness." He made a deep bow. "Raven."

"I am Branna ta Cattia. How do you know that I am Raven?"

"Ahh . . . you exude power from your very pores." Arturo took her arm. They strolled down the corridor toward the main chamber. "Not to mention you wear the moonstone crystal, and besides, I've already met your man, Fiall. He told me who you are," he continued, smiling. "Even now he's enjoying a bowl of hot porridge, though he wears a fierce scowl. I do believe he fears for your safety in this place and doesn't like losing control."

Branna remained silent.

"Oh, but how I'm babbling on and on. You must understand how happy I am to see you both. I'm an old man. I don't have much time left. Having Tirians near me is more than I could ever ask the Goddess for."

He was ancient looking. She thought he had to be near ninety-five years old at least. "You are the one who put the regio around Kern."

"Yes . . . my primary ability is far-seeing, and I have very little high magic. But the Goddess desired this place be protected, and so I formed the regio. You cannot find this place unless your thoughts are in line with that of the Opposition's."

"How long ago did you come to Numia?" Branna asked.

He laughed. "Oh, long before you were even born, dear. Goddess, it's been nigh eighty years now. I came when I was but a lad of sixteen." Arturo winked. "I came for adventure. I definitely got that."

"So you were not in Tir na Ban during the Terror then?"

Arturo went silent. Sorrow flooded his eyes. "No, my dear. But I felt it in my heart. I screamed and bled when my homeland screamed and bled. I saw it all." Arturo tapped his temple. "My gifts may have dimmed somewhat since I've been away from Tir na Ban, but not so much that it prevented me from experiencing the Terror right alongside my countrymen."

"I was eight years old," Branna said. "The Valorian slaughtered my parents. I watched them destroy the temples, decimate our places of study and worship, and take down our government. I never truly got to see the Golden Age of Tir na Ban. It was gone before I was nine."

He nodded. "Yes, so I saw . . . so I saw."

"The stories of the Golden Age live on, though. I was raised on them. Still there are Valorian troops there. Did you know that? A regiment lives there and keeps the fear alive and well. To make sure we don't organize against Numia."

Arturo halted near the entrance to the common room and released her arm. "Hmm . . . yes, I've felt that Tir na Ban has lived for revenge these long years. How healthy do you think it is to stew in such bitter juices for so long, my child? My young friend, Lucan, he has done the same."

"Ahh . . . you must be the lovely Branna. Our guest from so far away." A man about the same age as she, with hair the color of the sun, stood before her. His bright blue eyes twinkled, and he knelt smoothly to kiss her hand. He lingered over the back of it in a sensual way. When he spoke, his tone was suggestive. "My name is Varro. I wanted to introduce myself. Should you need aid or someone to show you around—"

Arturo sighed and looked annoyed. "Rise, Varro, and give the lady room to draw a breath."

The man straightened but didn't release her hand.

"That is enough, Varro," said Arturo.

Varro's eyes never left hers. "I simply wanted to offer the lady my help, should she require—"

"I'm sure you did," Arturo responded. "I'm quite sure my lady Raven will have more than enough help between Fiall and Lucan."

Something behind Arturo's words begged closer attention. She realized she was picking up on his far-seeing . . . involving her own future.

"Let go of her hand," said Arturo.

Finally, Varro released her hand.

Arturo guided Branna forward, away from Varro and toward the cooking area where Fiall and Ren sat.

"Remember, my lady . . . call upon me if you need anything . . . anything at all," Varro called after them.

Branna turned and smiled. "What an odd man."

"Mmm. Ordinarily he's not so strange as all that. Varro is a good and loyal man, but a beautiful face easily distracts him. I thought to try to cure him early of any thoughts he may have in your direction. You have your hands full already, I think." He walked off, leaving her alone. She frowned. He'd left before she'd been able to ask him what he'd meant.

She walked into the dining area. A scowl did mark Fiall's handsome face. Ren sat opposite her protector. The two stood as she took a chair beside Fiall.

"Good morning, Raven," Fiall said.

Ren sat back down and favored them with a lopsided grin. "You are from Arturo's country," he stated.

"Yes," replied Branna.

"How does high magic work, my lady?" he asked, awe saturating his voice.

"Well . . . you understand that everything is simply a template. Nothing is permanently set. Everything is malleable. All the world is your awareness reflected back at you, and with your mind you can change or create what you would desire . . . up to a point. Some things are the domains of the Deities of the One." The Goddess and all other Gods . . . even Angelyn's All-Father, who was a bloodthirsty god, were all Deities of the One.

"Like looking at your reflection in the lake and then poking your finger into the water to distort it?"

Branna smiled. "Kind of like that, yes," she murmured, distracted by Lucan, who walked toward the table with Varro at his side. Lucan wore black trews and a tan shirt, laced at the collar. Over the shirt he wore a leather jerkin, open at the top to reveal smooth skin and the beginning of his muscled chest. He wore tall, shiny black boots that reached to just below his knee, and his shoulder-length black hair was caught up in a queue at the nape of his neck. Blood dabbed him from foot to head. He'd been working with the wounded. They stopped, speaking in hushed tones. In Lucan's hand, an object glinted. He tipped his hand, showing it to Varro. It was a small eight-pointed star. Branna drew a surprised breath—the key to *Draiochta Cothrom*.

A woman set a bowl of porridge in front of her, startling her. Ren fell to his bowl as though starving.

"Are you all right, Branna?" asked Fiall. "You were staring at Lucan and all the blood ran from your face."

She spoke in Tirian so Ren could not understand what she said. "The rebel has the key to *Draiochta Cothrom*." She picked up her spoon and stabbed into the porridge. Here was the key. Where was the priest?

Fiall looked to Lucan and went as white as she must've been. "Will you tell him what it is? I'm sure he doesn't know," he responded in their native tongue.

She shook her head. "I've got to take his measure first." But she had to stop herself from getting up, running over to Lucan, and seizing the object from him. Out of the corner of her eye, she saw that Lucan had placed the key on a long chain. Now he looped it around his neck and pushed it under his shirt and jerkin.

The porridge tasted like ashes in her mouth. No, the Goddess hadn't led her astray . . . not at all.

Lucan came over to sit down beside Ren. They all said their good mornings. Lucan and Fiall's exchange was notably terse.

"The wounded from Strobia have begun to arrive in earnest," said Lucan. She noticed then how drawn his face was, how dark the circles beneath his eyes. He looked like he hadn't slept. "Some arrived late last night and still more this morning."

"What can we do to help?" asked Branna.

"Well . . . we have no other far-bloods here except for Arturo, yourself, and Fiall. Arturo has no healing ability. If you wouldn't mind—"

"But of course," answered Branna before he could finish his sentence. "My skills are your skills, without hesitation or question."

Fiall sat back in his chair and folded his hands across his chest. "However, my skills are not."

Lucan sat back in his chair, letting out a short breath. "I can't compel you to aid us, Fiall."

Fiall leaned forward and said sharply, "That's right. You can't."

"Enough, Fiall," snapped Branna. "I don't know what's causing you to act so strangely, but I'm becoming weary of it. I can compel you to aid those who are injured, Fiall . . . and I will."

Fiall sat back, chastened.

Branna felt a twinge of guilt. She had no wish for him to lose face in front of Lucan and Ren.

She placed her hand on his arm under the table and said softly, "If you were injured, maybe dying, would you not wish to be healed? Therefore, do you not wish to give your aid?"

"Aye," said Fiall. Then in a flash of anger, "But not if he bids it of me."

"Well, *I* bid it of you," she responded.

"Then I'll help, my Raven."

Lucan was clearly trying to suppress a bemused smile. Ren didn't bother to conceal his reaction. He smiled openly at Fiall's being put in place. Branna knew it was a rare thing for them to see a woman hold authority over a blooded warrior, but it was the way of it in her country and Fiall was well accustomed to it.

"Where are the wounded?" she asked Lucan.

Lucan rose and motioned for them to stand and follow.

He led them through a corridor and into a large, open cavern room. Many men lined the floors, and others treated them. There were all manner of wounds: deep cuts made by swords and long knives, broken bones, and wounds made from arrows that had struck true, through clothing and flesh and hitting bone. The salty, metallic scent of blood reached her nose. When their fear and pain assailed her, she sucked in a breath and threw up blocks against the emotion.

Despite his initial hesitation, Fiall moved into the mess right away, searching for a suitable wound to heal. Branna knelt beside a man who had a laceration that ran down his thigh. It was deep enough to reveal bone. She spoke softly to the man and set her hands to his wound. When she was finished the wound was partially knitted. His healing time would be cut in half.

When she looked up, Lucan's eyes were on her. His deep blue gaze penetrated her. There was a strange look in his eyes, but she could not read it. He made her feel tense. She looked away quickly, and when she glanced back, he'd left.

They spent the entire day with the wounded rebels. Some they were able to help, some were insensible and unable to give their consent or aid, and still others were already in the hands of the Goddess. By evening, her nerves were frazzled beyond repair. She had merged and meshed her energy with so many that day that her mind reeled from the effort she'd put forth.

She looked up and saw Fiall across the room. He knelt by one of the men and seemed to be in a deep discussion. She knew Fiall was also fatigued. Every line of his body shouted exhaustion. His scar stood out in harsh relief in his pale face. He'd also given everything he had.

Despite his clear reluctance to do what Lucan had wished of him, Fiall had fallen to the task efficiently. He was one of the few males of Tir na Ban to possess the power to heal, and the ability was strong within him.

She rose from the last man she would treat that day and brushed a tendril of hair away from her sweat-moistened forehead with the back of a bloody hand. Glancing up, she saw Lucan walking toward her. The true prince of Numia cut an impressive figure. He had a strong, confident stride and a gaze that . . . made her look away. Why was it every time he looked at her she felt like he saw through to her very core?

A S LUCAN APPROACHED BRANNA, HE STUDIED HER. She looked fatigued from her endeavors with the wounded. Tendrils of midnight black hair had freed themselves from where she'd secured them at the nape of her neck and clung to damp skin. Blood streaked her dress, arms, and face. Fiall had also worked very hard, Lucan grudgingly noted.

"I thank you from my heart for your hard work, my lady Raven," he said, placing a closed fist to his chest and inclining his head several degrees. "You've saved many from much pain and even death today."

She wouldn't meet his gaze but for a moment at a time. "I was happy to be of assistance, and I know Fiall was also."

Lucan glanced at Fiall, who was speaking with one of the men he'd healed. "I hope so."

"Fiall is not the man you've seen. I don't know who he is pretending to be right now. Normally he is ready to help any in need." She brought her gaze to his and held it.

"You look warm."

She sighed and brushed away an errant strand of hair. "Aye, I am a bit overheated and tired."

He hesitated for the briefest of moments and then said, "Come with me, my lady." He turned and walked from the room. Branna followed.

The far end of the corridor narrowed to an entryway big enough for a single man to slide through. The passageway remained narrow and continued for close to a quarter length. It was not an easy passageway to negotiate, but the end brought much reward when it led into a huge, naturally formed room.

When they entered the chamber, he heard her gasp of surprise. Tiny quartz crystal flecks embedded the walls and celestial-fire lamps flickered and moved over them, so they glittered like diamonds. A large lake spread in front of them, fed by a waterfall at the far end of the chamber. Unlike the countless hot springs found throughout the mountain, this water was cool. The source of the waterfall trickled down from the highest parts of the mountain, under the earth and rock, to reach this naturally made chamber.

"Only a few in Kern know of this place, and if you would like, you may swim here whenever it would please you. The water is cold but not frigid. I thought perhaps you would not wish the warm water of the bathing pool in your room this evening."

Branna closed her mouth, which had been open in awe. Lucan almost smiled. She had lost her cool composure for a moment. "Thank you," she managed to say.

They stood staring at each other for a few tense moments until she looked away from him. "Well, I'll leave you now," he said. "I must return to the care of my men." He turned to exit the chamber.

"You have much concern for their welfare, my lord. It is the mark of a truly great leader to care so deeply, but I see . . . I feel . . . that you take much on your shoulders—too much sometimes to be healthy."

He turned back toward her. "They fight for me and for the Numia that once was and hopefully shall be again. When I lose men, it pains me greatly, yes. Yesterday, I left Strobia before the battle had been fought. If I'd stayed, I wonder how many I could have saved."

She walked to him, stopping not a breath's space from him.

Every muscle in his body stiffened. He felt her body heat and the brush of her gown against his clothing. The scent of skyflower, faint now, teased his nostrils. *Solan.* This girl did things to him no woman had done in a long, long time.

He wondered if she could feel the desire he had for her and how hard he tried to tamp it down. It rode up like waves and crashed along his spine, rising like hot energy from the core of him.

"You're in need of a healing, my lord," she said. "A deep and emotional one. I cannot heal the soul, only the body." She reached up and fingered the braid at his temple. "But if I could, I would give you all the aid you require."

Lucan fought to keep his hands from her slim waist. He wondered what it would feel like to pull her against him and press his mouth to hers. She taunted him, even if she did not realize it.

He'd told her he would try to stay his hands from her, and so he would. In any case, he had men to see to—men that were hurt and dying because of him. Sorrow coursed through him. He backed away from her touch, toward the opening that led back to the main part of the stronghold.

"I must leave you now, my lady. Avail yourself of the lake at your ease," he said and then disappeared into the opening.

B RANNA WATCHED HIM GO. HE HAD SEEMED DISMAYED by her hand upon him, but she'd been unable to help herself. His pain was so deep and so achingly close to the surface at the same time. The man was light and dark all at once, sometimes the lighthearted man who whistled his way through the forest, caring and amiable, sometimes restless and dangerous seeming. Other times he was guilt-ridden by the charge that he had placed on his own shoulders: the protection and safekeeping of everyone he knew, if not the very nation of Numia itself.

She turned and looked at the sparkling water of the underground lake, wondering which Lucan was the true one. Which one had been the Lucan before his family had been killed?

Branna could venture a guess, and it made her hate Magnus even more, if that was possible. For to bring such darkness from so light a character as Lucan must have possessed was something truly tragic.

She drew the gown over her head, tossed it to the side, and waded into the water.

CHAPTER NINE

BRANNA TOSSED THE COVERLET AWAY AND SHOT FROM the bed. Agitated, she walked toward the bathing pool at the far end of the room. Every inch of her skin felt scraped with rough bark, and an uninitiated mental link scrabbled at the edges of her mind. She turned and paced back toward the bed, rubbing her upper arms in an effort to calm the urgent magic running over her skin and through her mind. She had to find out who was causing it.

She sat on the edge of the bed. Drawing a deep breath, she allowed color to swirl through her mind as she located the link and cleared it up. Images of men in shackles flooded her mind's eye. Packed in a large rolling cage drawn by horses, they moved down a tree-lined road. Valorian soldiers rode in formation on each side. Faces flipped through her consciousness until the visage of one man in the cage stood out and held steady.

He was perhaps twenty-five years of age, with dark brown hair curling to the nape of his neck and light blue eyes. He was a large man, muscular in the way of a warrior. The features of his face were chiseled and attractive, with full lips and a strong chin. She did not recognize him. She knew only that he was someone close to Lucan. Blood trailed down his forehead, and his dark green jerkin was dirty and ripped. One long gash, made by a long knife, marred his shoulder. His bloodied hands gripped the iron bars.

A city rose in the distance. Tall rain-washed granite walls and structures of various heights could be seen through the dust made by the cage rolling down the road.

The realization came like a blow to her solar plexus—these men were captured rebels from the battle in Strobia.

She reached for the first gown she could lay hands on and shrugged it over her sleeping chemise—no time to change. Barefoot, she threw the door open and hurried down the hallway.

She reached the common room at a dead run and searched out Lucan. She spotted him across the room that now bustled with activity. He gave orders at a rapid clip, and she realized he already knew about the prisoners. She ran up to him. "They're on their way to—"

He turned wild blue eyes on her. "They're on their way to Ta'Ror."

She nodded. "I've linked mentally with one in particular. He is a handsome man, with dark brown hair and very light blue eyes. He was about—"

"Twenty-five?"

"Yes, around that age."

"Morgan," he breathed, looking past her. "My second-in-command." His eyes fixed on her. "They must be freed, Branna. If they are not, Lord Crispus, a particularly nasty and disturbed man, will torture them. They won't be able to endure his treatment, and some of them may reveal information." He paused. "After Crispus has wrung all he can from them, he'll subject them to horrific deaths." Sorrow and guilt passed over his face like a fast-moving storm before he mastered his expression.

No, he wouldn't want anyone to see he felt responsible for their capture. Too bad it was apparent to anyone looking at his face.

His lips twisted in a wry smile. "We're getting better. We've never had a battle yet that was impressive enough for them to bother taking prisoners. They are noticing us."

"Hmm. A dubious honor at best, Lucan."

"Aye."

Fiall came up behind them accompanied by Varro and Ren. "So, when do we leave?" asked Fiall. "We need to free them, do we not?"

Branna turned amazed eyes on him. Did he actually sound cooperative?

Fiall saw her expression of surprise and fixed Lucan with a cold stare. "I may not like you, but I support the Opposition."

"That's good enough for me," said Lucan. "Varro, ready horses for the Lady Raven and her companion. Ren, make sure we've enough food to make it to Ta'Ror. We'll have to stay over one night near Pannonia." He turned and looked at Branna. "We leave within the hour."

S EVERAL FORCES OF THE OPPOSITION LEFT FOR TA'ROR to free the prisoners. Lucan separated them into smaller parties, and gave each group specific instructions. Smaller groups were safer. The fewer the number of travelers, the less attention they drew to themselves.

Branna, Fiall, Ren, Varro, and a few competent and trusted Opposition soldiers traveled out of Kern with Lucan by midmorning. The sky above threatened rain, and Lucan hoped for the sake of his imprisoned men that the heavens held it off. He gave a silent and quick prayer to the God of Water that it might be so.

Branna, the only woman in the party, rode next to Fiall and kept up the fast pace as well as the men. She had chosen to wear trews, short boots, and a bulky woolen shirt for the journey. The trews held her legs in a close embrace, and the effect jarred Lucan. He hadn't been able to keep his eyes from her before, and he wouldn't be able to today.

Lucan shook his head in an effort to rid himself of the notion of her. Distractions . . . He needed to concentrate on the task at hand. To let himself become distracted by a pretty face could mean death for his men.

They rode until it was dark. The moons were hidden behind heavy cloud cover, and rain still threatened. The damp smell of it hung heavy in the air. When he dared push Branna and the men no further for their safety and that of the horses, they stopped and made camp. They built a fire for the purposes of warmth only, having nothing to cook over it. Ren pulled food from the saddlebags and passed it around. The light fare consisted of flatbread baked with herbs and a bit of smoked fish—simple, nourishing, and portable food for traveling.

Ren settled in beside him and, as always, attacked the food with a hearty appetite.

Lucan watched as Branna sat beside Fiall and leaned against him. The Tirian warrior twined an arm around her and caught Lucan's gaze upon them. Fiall narrowed his eyes in an expression that almost seemed . . . competitive.

Ah. So that was the way of it. That explained why Fiall was hostile. Interesting, Branna seemed oblivious to her protector's deeper feelings for her.

He couldn't blame Fiall for his admiration of Branna. If Lucan had time for women, she'd be a candidate for conquest. *Solan*, he didn't have time for women, and he still couldn't manage to restrain himself where Branna was concerned.

Lucan knew well of Tirians and their free attitudes toward the physical expression of love. There was little chance Branna was a maiden, and he could imagine what she would be like to bed. She would be as confident and magical in that area as she was in every other aspect. He would lay coin . . .

What was wrong with him?

He had men out there in the night near Ta'Ror. They were cold, frightened, mistreated, and facing torture, and he was thinking about a woman.

He finished the last bit of his flatbread. "Go to sleep soon," he ordered in a voice made gruff from anger at himself. "We leave as soon as the sky lightens in the morn or the cloud cover breaks, whichever comes first." He turned his back to the fire, drew his blanket over himself, and tried to sleep.

B RANNA AWOKE TO DARKENED SKIES. SHE'D ACTUALLY slept, she realized with surprise. The connection between herself and Morgan had ceased, for the time being at least. It was a good thing because it had provided her with some much-needed rest. It was a bad thing because she did not know how Morgan and the others fared. If Morgan had lost consciousness, that could account for the break. But a million other things could also cause a mental link to cease.

The magical gifts of the far-blooded were forever unpredictable and inconstant. Some had strong gifts in varied areas, while others had only a few weak ones. Psychic connections could be forged and lost for reasons as varied as the weather or something that was eaten for dinner.

She was one of a lucky few of the far-blooded. She had very strong skills in sending and receiving mental messages, psychic linking, and healing. However, there were always trade-offs. Her skills in far-seeing and emotional sensing were lacking, and how she wished she had Arturo's skill in far-seeing now. She would like to know what Arturo foresaw for these poor men they sought. The old Tirian mage hadn't been able to see anything before they'd left. His gifts, too, were inconstant.

Branna shifted on the thin traveling blanket she lay upon and tried to let sleep catch her once more. She was able to sleep often now for some reason. Her insomnia seemed to be either disappearing or giving her a well-deserved break. Her ability to sleep had coincided with meeting Lucan. She'd not yet determined why that was, but the fact that Lucan had the key to *Draiochta Cothrom* was perhaps the reason. The book itself was undoubtedly in Magnus's possession. He'd taken it long ago from Tir na Ban.

She would not let Lucan out of her sight while he carried the key. The Goddess had led her this far. The key was within her reach. The priest could not be far behind. Perhaps Morgan was a priest? Maybe that was why she'd linked so strongly with him. She would have to ask Lucan, though Morgan didn't look like a priest. He seemed more like a blooded warrior than a clergyman.

A low sound caught her attention. She turned her head toward the source of it and saw Lucan on the other side of the camp. He gripped the blanket as though it were a rope he'd been thrown as he drowned. Another sound of suffering escaped his lips, and Branna scrambled to her feet and went to him.

His black hair lay around his head like tangled silk. A thin layer of perspiration sheened his face and chest. He was caught in the maw of a terrible nightmare.

She knelt, placed a cool hand to his chest, and said his name in a soft voice. He didn't stir. She said his name a bit louder, and he opened his eyes but appeared unseeing. Before she could utter a protest, he pulled her down against him, twining an arm around her waist and holding her close.

Branna was too surprised to move, not that she could have moved anyway. He had her in a fierce hold. The words of indignation poised on her lips died an easy death when she realized he still slept. His eyes drifted closed, and his breathing quickened for a moment, then returned to the deep, easy rhythm of untroubled sleep. Having her near him seemed soothing to him for some reason. Her presence drew him into sweeter dreams.

Without awakening him, she managed to move herself into a more comfortable position. She worked her way onto her back so she could rest her head against his chest. The solid length of him pressed against her. It was nice. She let her eyes close, and she relaxed in the crook of his arm. She felt safe.

At least, she felt safe until he shifted to his side with a contented sound and one of his hands drifted to trace the line of her left side up from her hip and then move over her breasts and down to her stomach in a possessive way. In his dreams he slept with a lover, she guessed. The warmth of his hand bled through her trews and shirt as he rested it on her lower abdomen. Her eyes opened and her breath caught. The touch of his hand on her ignited some little-known flame deep within.

Then Lucan shifted closer to her, pulling her over on her side and against the full length of him. His mouth found her throat and nuzzled there for a moment, his lips finding the sensitive skin below her ear. Branna thought her heart would stop. Her eyes fluttered shut as heat rushed through her.

Sweet Goddess . . . How could a person's throat be so sensitive?

At last he quieted and rested on his side. His breath found a regular rhythm, and he slipped to deeper sleep, the nightmare now banished.

Branna, however, did not sleep. She was aware of every single inch of his body and of hers—conscious of where their bodies touched and of the space where their breath met and mingled in the chill autumn air.

His sensual mouth was just a short space from hers. If she pressed her face forward, she could brush her lips across it. Her heart pounded in her chest at the thought. She bit her bottom lip, while staring at his. The temptation proved too great.

She tilted her head to the side a bit and brought her face close to his. His warm breath, scented with the herbs that had been baked into the flatbread, teased her lips and nose. She brushed her lips against his.

With a smile, she pulled away from him. Letting her eyes drift shut, she floated away on the warm clouds of deep sleep.

L UCAN AWOKE AND SAW THAT BRANNA LAY IN HIS ARMS. He had no idea how she'd ended up there, and at the moment, he didn't care a bit. She was there and that was all he could have wanted in the world. The slightest trace of a smile graced her rosebud of a mouth. Her long, dark lashes were swept down upon her rosy, vanilla-silk cheeks.

He had his arm thrown over her waist, and her arm rested on his hip. Just about every part of their bodies touched. Her breasts pressed through the fabric of her shirt. The graceful arch of her hips flared from her narrow waist and melded into long, strong legs. He raised one eyebrow in speculation.

How many distractions could one man take before he started to think that perhaps distractions weren't all that bad?

Her lips were full and parted in a way that seemed to beg for him to press his lips to hers. If he leaned his head in just a bit closer he could kiss her, and she would never even know. It wouldn't hurt anyone for him to just take a little taste . . .

He let his lips brush hers. That one innocent action sent a searing wave of want through him. He battled with himself for a moment. How easy it would be to part her lips and demand a deeper kiss to awaken her. How easy it would be for him to cover her body with his own and see if she desired more from him than a simple kiss.

He'd said he'd try to resist her. *Solan*, he didn't realize how hard that would be.

She roused and he pulled back. Her eyes came open, and she drew away from him in surprise, sitting bolt upright. "Lucan."

He rose up on an elbow and watched her color. It was a pretty sight.

"You were having a nightmare," she explained. "I tried to wake you from it, and you pulled me against you and wouldn't let go. Having me near seemed to calm you, so I just slept that way."

"Ah." He gave her a half smile. "Forgive me."

"N . . ." She swallowed hard. "Not at all," she said with a nervous shake of her head.

Had this situation, his nearness, caused the composure of the Tirian far-blooded sorceress to slip? Interesting . . . very interesting, in fact. He regarded her in silence, considering the implications.

"Don't do that," she said.

"What?"

"That. Don't look at me like that. Your eyes go a deep blue and your lips . . ." She trailed off and looked away, embarrassed.

"My lips . . . what?" He couldn't keep the smile from his voice.

She blushed even harder.

Lucan sat up and spoke in a gentle tone, banishing all laughter from his voice. "I'm sorry I make you uncomfortable. I honestly don't mean to." Though it was fun all the same.

She didn't look at him. It was time for a topic change to ease her discomfort. "I have one particular nightmare over and over," he said.

Branna went silent for a few moments, and when he looked back at her, her eyes were intent upon him. Her cool verdant gaze seemed to hold all the green, growing mystery of the forests. Lucan thought for a moment that the magic she possessed could almost heal him.

She moved closer. "Would you let me in for a closer look at you?"

"Do you mean a magical look? A mental look?"

"Yes. That is, if you don't mind."

Lucan didn't know if he minded or not. He'd never had anything like that done before. He knew she'd done something along those lines when they'd first met, but this sounded more involved. He shrugged in a noncommittal way.

She drew up close so they faced each other, crossed her legs, and brought her hands a couple of inches from each side of his head. He could feel the heat of her palms radiating out and hitting his temples. Her eyes drifted out of focus, and she seemed to look through his body.

The examination she performed on him was less obtrusive than he'd expected. He felt a slight pressure on his temples, but that was all.

Her facial features were calm, relaxed, and beautiful. Lucan soon found himself drawing a finger down the curve of her lips and chin in his imagination. Then her mouth tightened and her body went tense. Her eyes moved back and forth rapidly, as though she were dreaming with them open. She drew her hands back from him with a gasp and pushed herself away, burying her face in her hands.

"Goddess . . ." she breathed. "Oh, sweet Goddess . . . Mother of us all."

Concerned, he touched her shoulder. "Branna, what is it? What did you see?"

Her shoulders shook a little, and he realized she was crying. She wept for him, for something she'd seen way down deep within him. Lucan knew what it was, the only event of his life that could cause such a reaction.

She turned toward him, her eyes glistening with tears. "I saw it all, Lucan. I saw your family . . ." Her voice trailed off.

Aye, he knew. He'd seen it too. It had been many years ago, but still the images haunted him.

"I wanted to see what pained you so," she managed to get out. "I'm sorry."

He pushed a hand back through his hair. "Aye, so am I . . . so am I."

She moved closer to him and touched his arm minutely with light fingertips. "My parents were also killed by the Valorian, but I never had to live through the pain of seeing it happen. I was spared that horror."

But she sounded so far away. At the brush of her fingertips against him, he was transported somewhere else entirely.

Branna lay in an unnatural position, unmoving—skin sallow, her hair dull and fanned out on the grass. He leaned over her, took her in his arms, and knew she was gone.

With effort, he banished the image, and his eyes focused once again on her. He'd had a glimpse of the future. Such prescient images had not haunted him for many years now. The far-blooded Ilerian gifts bequeathed to him by his great grandmother were now much diluted by Numian blood, but he retained a breath of the ability to far-see. He blinked and tried to steady himself.

Branna moved away, still wiping tears from her cheeks.

In his vision he had felt a strong sense of guilt. Was he the cause of her death? Would it be a situation he put her in that somehow caused her demise? Perhaps it would happen as a result of his attempts to use her in his quest to unseat Magnus? Lucan sighed. It could not be allowed. No more blood could be permitted to stain his hands.

Sweet Solan! He'd been an initiate of the God of the Overworld so many years ago and still the marks remained.

Above them, the threatening clouds finally let their moisture loose in the form of a light rain. With effort, he forced a smile. "Branna, it's almost daybreak. Perhaps we should find our blankets, hide beneath them so we don't get soaked, and try to sleep a bit before it is light enough to ride."

She regarded him in mute misery for a moment. He knew the images that now crowded her mind, and he wished he could help her clear them, but he had his own frightening images to grapple with now. Now he had images of Branna lying crumpled on the grass and the remnants of his own painful emotion to go along with them.

She nodded her head and moved across to where she'd been sleeping, until the sweet length of her had found its way, miraculously, into his arms. He watched as she lay back down and pulled a blanket over herself.

He collapsed back onto the ground and stared up at the sky. The light rain fell from the darkened heavens and splashed onto his face.

Her scent still hung in the air. Skyflower.

CHAPTER TEN

T HEY LED THEIR HORSES OUT OF THE THICK FOREST
and Ta'Ror rose in front of them like some enchanted city
that existed only in the realm of imagination. Branna could not
help gaping. A tall city wall of weathered gray stone rose around
Ta'Ror. Beyond the wall, buildings of many different shapes and
sizes towered. Some were built of wood, others of bricks made from
various types of stone. Some had entire walls and fluted columns
made from fine sheets of crystal. Many of the buildings sported
tall turrets as though they were palaces themselves. Still others had
pitched roofs or domes.

It was far too beautiful a place for Magnus to live. Indeed,
Branna knew he was ensconced in his palace on the other side of
the city, near the ocean. Her heartbeat quickened at the thought.

Branna shivered. She'd relived Lucan's experience through his eyes last night and understood him better because of it, but the cost had been high. Never would she be able to erase those violent images from her mind.

Lucan had been the last one to be executed. Through a trick of *cinnunt* he'd managed to escape the Valorian that held him. His flight from the palace had been harrowing, but it had been nothing compared to the plunge he'd taken from the cliffs of Ta'Ror into the icy Agarian River.

Aye, she shared Lucan's nightmares now.

Someone touched her arm and she jumped. "We approach," said Fiall.

Branna looked up and saw they'd neared the western city gate. Lucan had long since sent Varro and the other Opposition off to enter through a different entranceway. They'd no wish to call undue attention to themselves with a large party.

The gateway bustled with activity. Valorian soldiers lined the entrance, but these were times of peace, and their inspection of the incoming citizens was not an exacting one.

She, Lucan, Fiall, and Ren melted into the river of humanity that sought entrance into Ta'Ror. Lucan came up on Branna's right side and pulled the hood of her cloak over her head. "Hide your face until we are well beyond the gates, my lady," he said under his breath. "We don't know whether or not these soldiers were in Strobia to see your lovely dance performance."

Lucan hung back until she, Fiall, and Ren were much farther ahead than he. She supposed he worried he too could be recognized from Strobia and did not want to endanger them.

Branna pulled the edge of her hood over her face but could not help glancing sidelong at the Valorian soldiers as they passed them. They were dressed in full regalia, wearing vests of hardened leather over their blue military tunics. They each wore a heavy protective helm. Upon their vests and their thick leather gloves blazed the emblem of the Dragon Throne of Numia, a gold and green dragon.

The soldiers stopped people here and there and asked them to state their business in Ta'Ror. Lucan had already instructed them in what to say should they be pulled aside.

Branna simply hoped it wouldn't happen.

They were almost to the gate when two of the Valorian stepped out and came toward her. Her horse shied and she cringed, but the hand of the Valorian soldier fell on the reins of a stranger's horse beside her. The Valorian yanked the man off his mount, threw him to the ground, and began kicking him, calling him a thief.

Lucan made it to her side within the space of two heartbeats. He reined up beside her, looking down at the Valorian's prisoner. "All right, my lady?"

The two Valorian hefted the now moaning man to his feet, and they staggered forward under his weight, toward Branna's horse. Lucan maneuvered his horse between the Valorian and her mount, his arm stretched out in a protective gesture. One of the Valorian looked up at Lucan in a considering . . . and menacing way.

"I'm fine. Stop calling attention to yourself," she said only loud enough for Lucan to hear. "You'll have us killed before we even get into the city." She gave him a sharp look, squeezed her horse into a trot to get through the gate, and then slowed. He caught up to her. Fiall and Ren followed behind.

"I was trying to protect you," Lucan said when he came up beside her. A hank of dark hair had fallen across one blue eye. She tried not to let that distract her.

"Well, you can't protect everyone all the time, Lucan," she said under her breath. "You are the pri—" She bit off the end of the word, realizing her mistake. "You are too important to endanger for silly things such as that."

His full lips parted in a smile. A dimple she'd never noticed before indented his left cheek. "I don't consider you silly. Actually, I think you're worth my life, so I beg to differ, my lady."

At a loss for words, she turned her horse away and urged it farther into the city. "Protecting her is my job," she heard Fiall growl at Lucan as she rode away.

L UCAN LED THEM THROUGH TA'ROR IN RECORD TIME. The inside of the city was every bit as magnificent as the outside. Teeming with humanity, carriages clattered down the cobblestone streets, flanked by people both astride and afoot. Shops of every imaginable type stood open for business, and the smell of meat pies, horse, and aged leather wafted on the air.

An impressive Valorian presence patrolled the city. Sometimes Lucan took them far out of their way to avoid coming into contact with soldiers. That was fine with Branna. She'd had enough Valorian at the city gates, but she knew soon they'd be meeting up with more. Valorian would be unavoidable when they attempted to free the captured Opposition.

She'd not felt anything more of Morgan, and it worried her.

Deep twilight had fallen by the time they neared the palace on the eastern side of the city. They stood at a busy intersection, in the shadows of the buildings.

Branna recognized the structure from Lucan's memories. It rose in a mass of dark gray stone, with many turrets and thick ramparts. Many Valorian soldiers guarded its tall gates. Beyond the gates lay a huge expanse of green grass and gardens before the rich gold-gilded entrance of the palace. She knew that on the other side of the palace was a barbican that opened up beyond Ta'Ror's city walls to the grassy plains and the Arbonne Forest beyond. Farther lay the Agarian River and eventually the ocean.

Lucan came up beside her. "I brought you here to show you where they would be keeping any prisoners," he said. He pointed to a building to the left of the palace. "Without using high magic, can you tell me if it's shielded?"

They were taking a chance by standing out in the open and speaking this way, but Branna was near positive the sorceresses were not capable of far-hearing or far-sensing, so they'd deemed it safe enough. They had no choice, anyway. Branna sent her awareness out and touched the building with her mind. She knew right away. "No, it's not shielded."

Lucan looked surprised. "Are you sure?"

"Aye, no shields, but"—Branna sent her awareness in farther—"there are no prisoners either."

Lucan went silent for several moments. "Are you sure?"

She nodded.

"What games are they playing?" he said to himself.

Fiall and Ren had been listening to the conversation, and now Ren approached them. "Perhaps they were expecting us to come for the prisoners?"

"Aye . . . it's a trap," said Lucan.

Branna concentrated on the building. "I think you're right, Lucan. I feel a presence in that building, but it's not Opposition, it's Valorian." Branna turned to Lucan. "They would suspect you have magical aid now, would they not? Because of what happened in Strobia? They know a sorceress could easily determine if there was a shield present. However, using mental means to determine whether or not there is Opposition in the building requires much more skill. They cannot be aware I can accomplish that."

"They must have taken the shield off the building in the hopes we'd think the prisoners were there and enter it—then spring a trap," answered Lucan. "Could you locate the captured Opposition somehow?"

"Maybe. If I can find somewhere quiet and have some time to mend the broken link between myself and Morgan."

"They won't be expecting us to be able to locate the men. That means it might be easier than we thought to free them," said Lucan.

Fiall came up next to Branna. "I can help her mend the link."

A flash of lightning lit the sky above them and thunder boomed. A light rain began to fall. "All right," said Lucan. "It's time we sought shelter anyway."

Lucan led them away from the palace and back into the city. They stabled their horses and continued on foot. Soon, they came to a very poor part of the city. The smell of unwashed bodies and hard living assaulted Branna's nostrils. She peered around the edge of her hood. The windows of the houses and apartments were broken and grimy, and many had timeworn and torn curtains hanging in them.

Lucan led them to a house that had a chipped and faded frieze upon one of its walls. Branna could just make it out in the rain-drenched early evening gloom. It was a picture of a young girl with flowers in her hair dancing in a field. Once it had been a vibrant, happy piece of artwork, and now it brought tears to her eyes.

"Sal'vi." Varro answered the door at Lucan's knock and ushered them in.

"We stopped by the palace before coming here," said Lucan to Varro. He told him what they'd found.

Branna entered with Fiall at her side. It was one large room with a woodstove in the back. A fire burned, adding to the light created by the candles scattered around. The windows were covered over with a thick coating of grime. Many trunks scattered the floor of the room. Branna guessed they contained supplies the Opposition might need. Men were reclined in various places, talking and playing cards. The other Opposition had arrived before Lucan's party. Ren went to sit with a few who were rolling dice on the floor.

"Is there not a place near the ocean where they keep prisoners?" asked Varro.

"There are many such places in those woods. The Arbonne is a large and unforgiving forest," said Lucan, running a frustrated hand through his hair. "And time is running out. Soon Lord Crispus will be starting to . . ." He trailed off, unable to form the word.

"Extract information?" Varro finished.

"That's one way of saying it."

"So, what are we going to do?" asked Varro.

Branna interrupted them. "We are going to clear out a corner of this hovel and give Fiall and myself some time to mend the link. Then we are going to go find those men and release them." She sounded more confident than she felt.

Lucan and Varro shared a look that seemed to speak of all her fears. Then Varro moved to clear the men out of the far corner of the room.

Fiall took Branna's hand and led her to it. They sat on the floor facing each other. Her hands rested on Fiall's upturned ones.

"I don't possess the power you do in this area," Fiall said. "I'll join my magic with yours, in an effort to make it more powerful, but I'll let you do the searching."

Branna felt a gaze upon them. She glanced over her shoulder and saw Lucan looking at them from across the room. His steady blue gaze was like a hand touching her in intimate places, a solid caress over her bare skin. His interest in her was not unpleasant or unwanted . . . nor was it unrequited. She drew a shaky breath.

"He looks at you all the time," Fiall said. "I like it not."

She did not meet his gaze. "He is curious, merely."

"Aye . . . curious," he muttered.

"Join your awareness with mine, Fiall. We must work quickly."

The flash of irritation Branna had sensed from Fiall faded.

He merged his consciousness with hers. It went from a trickle to a stream to a flood. She opened her mind to him and let it join with hers. Then, combined, she sent it forth, toward the palace.

She went through the streets of Ta'Ror, down alleyways, and around corners. When she reached the palace, she hit the shields the sorceresses had placed there and could not go within. She went around the structure, onto the green, grassy plains she'd seen in Lucan's memories, deep into the Arbonne Forest beyond. She sent her awareness all the way to the ocean and found nothing. Discouraged, she brought her consciousness back through the woods, this time much slower. Mentally, she called to Morgan.

Nothing.

Again she called and received a whisper of a response echoing through her mind. The image of a tall, broad-shouldered man standing near a tree flashed, then steadied. It was Morgan. He looked whole and unharmed. She'd found his disembodied awareness in the world that laid just a little past the realm of dream but not quite as far as Vallon, the place between lives. He crooked a finger at her, motioning for her to follow him.

Together, they flew through the forest to the edge of the sea. On a cliff overlooking the water below, Valorian swarmed. In the same iron cage on wheels that Branna had seen before was Morgan's unconscious body. Seven other prisoners stood and sat in the cage, all looking worn and defeated. Like Morgan, some of them had been beaten into submission, but Morgan was the only one unconscious.

Morgan's disembodied awareness turned to her. He was fading now, going farther toward Vallon, where she could not follow. "Point of Sorrow," he said, sounding far away. They needed to get to him soon or he'd slip all the way to Vallon.

A Valorian soldier came up to the cage, walking through Branna's projected awareness. He hit the iron bars with his steel scabbard and laughed. The sound of the metal hitting metal was deafening and it jarred her. She came back with a jolt and yanked her hands from Fiall's.

"What is it?" Fiall asked. "Did you find them?"

Her head pounded. She placed her fingers to her temple and tried to rise, but she was weakened from what she'd done and collapsed back to the floor. She felt strong hands on her waist. Lucan helped her to stand. She leaned against him, absorbing the heat radiating out from his chest.

"Aye, I found them," she said in a shaky voice.

She felt the whole of Lucan's body relax. "Thank Solan."

"Do you know where the Point of Sorrow is?" she asked.

"Aye. That's where they took them?" asked Varro.

She stepped away, now steady enough to stand without aid. "They are in a cage, exposed to the elements, upon a cliff called the Point of Sorrow."

"They probably planned to wait for an Opposition retaliation against the prison at Ta'Ror. They were probably planning to bring them back to the prison after they'd captured us," said Lucan.

"But it's not going to work that way, is it?" asked Ren from afar.

"No," said Lucan. "We're going to ruin their plans." The men cheered.

"Yes, but I've got bad news," Branna said. "Morgan is badly injured. If we don't get to him soon, he will slip to Vallon."

Lucan stalked away from her and then paced back in a gesture that reminded her of a caged cat. Concern marked his face. "Can he hold on until morning? It's dark now, and there is cloud cover. There is nothing we can do this eve." Emotion was thick in his voice.

"I know." She hurt for the heavy sense of responsibility she felt within him. "Honestly, Lucan, I don't know how long he can hang on. As it is I cannot even heal him. He is unconscious."

Lucan let out a low, colorful string of curses. "There is nothing to be done for him then."

"We'll leave as soon as there is light," said Branna.

He rounded on her. "We'll do nothing of the kind. You and Fiall will stay here. If we are successful, you will travel back to Kern." He paused. "If we are not, well then, you will travel on to wherever it is you were going before we met you." Sadness tinged his eyes.

Branna had different ideas. She advanced on him, her voice rising with every step she took. "You won't leave us behind, rebel. We are here for the same reason that you and the Opposition exist. You won't prevent us from reaching our goals because of some silly, misplaced sense of responsibility for Fiall and me."

Branna came within a breath's space from him. She stood, rigidly staring up at him and he down at her. A muscle in his jaw twitched as he clenched it, but she did not back down. She noticed the entire room had gone silent. She realized suddenly that no man dared raise his voice to Lucan, much less a woman.

Now aware that every eye in the room was upon them, she stepped back. He stepped forward. For a moment it was as if they danced. "It is you I feel responsible for," he said in a low voice. "You, my lady, who haunt my dreams. You, I wish to protect."

His breath stirred the fine hairs around her face. She dropped her gaze from his intense stare and studied his jerkin, at a loss for words once again. The smooth, sun-kissed skin of his chest above the top of his half-opened jerkin was bared to her eyes.

She looked back at his face and cleared her throat. "I can aid you. I have the ability to provide you with a shield when you fight. Also, I'll be able to divine certain things about the enemy. While we are bound by the Goddess's law against harming others, we are able—"

"I am aware of your gifts, but I feel that for your protection it is better you stay here for now."

"What's wrong? Do you believe us of no value?" asked Fiall from behind. Sarcasm dripped from every syllable.

Lucan stepped away from her and smiled, but it didn't reach his eyes. His voice was thin. "I have been building the Opposition since I was sixteen, Fiall, and we didn't begin to make even the tiniest of impressions on Magnus until five years ago. So, please, excuse my incredulousness that you two have come expecting to turn the tide and overthrow a man who has been entrenched in this land for the last fourteen years."

"We follow the Goddess, Lucan," Branna said. "We follow *cin-nunt*. We know that we'll be victorious if we listen and act as she wishes. You have no faith, as most Numians. Of course, I forgive you your incredulousness. In fact, I pity you." She saw Lucan stiffen and realized her words were untrue. She had a flash of Lucan kneeling in the woods, his face turned skyward. She realized she'd said the wrong thing. "I didn't mean—"

Lucan's spine went rigid. "I know what you meant." He stared at her for a long moment and then cursed under his breath in a manner that spoke of defeat. "Fine, you come with us, but you will do as I say and stay out of danger's way."

It would have to be enough for now. She nodded her head in acquiescence.

"I have a plan," said Lucan.

CHAPTER ELEVEN

T O PASSERSBY THEY LOOKED LIKE TWO VALORIAN SOL-
diers escorting a female prisoner down the road that ran
along the outside of Ta'Ror's city wall. Sandria had fashioned many
of the Valorian uniforms for the Opposition long ago. They'd been
stored at Kern and at the house in Ta'Ror in case they needed them.

Lucan glanced at Branna. He knew she'd slept as little as he had
the previous night. Deep smudges marred the skin beneath her
eyes. He placed a hand to the back of his neck and rubbed. The fact
that they'd slept on the floor hadn't helped. Every muscle in his
body was stiff, but he knew his unease had more to do with their
upcoming endeavor than a lack of sleep. Solan would have to be
with them today. Branna rode beside him, and he didn't want her
there. The far-seeing he'd had of her was still fresh in his mind. He
did not need yet another person to worry about.

She shot him a look of high irritation. "I cannot tell you how horrifying you look in that," she said, shuddering. "But for as bad as you look, Fiall is even more frightening."

Lucan looked over at Fiall, who rode on Branna's opposite side. The Tirian warrior had been silent ever since they'd made him don the costume. He stared straight ahead with a dangerous look in his eye. Lucan did not like wearing these clothes either, but he'd do anything to save his men.

"Be quiet and try to look like a menace to the city," he said to Branna. "You'll see Fiall is managing it very well. Follow his example."

His comment had the desired effect. A smile tugged at the corners of her mouth.

He and Fiall could easily pass for Valorian. Branna, however, was a far stretch for a dangerous-looking criminal, but they'd done everything they could to give that illusion. Her wrists were bound to the pommel and her ankles tied to the cinching of the saddle. Because it would be dangerous if she had to flee, they'd used knots that pulled free with a good tug. Her trews and the edge of her shirt were ripped, and her dark hair was unbound and tousled. Dirt was smeared across her cheeks and chin. They'd had no trouble getting out of the city. So, despite Branna's noncriminal appearance, they were convincing enough.

They neared the end of the road where the cobblestone gave way to dirt and eventually disappeared. Beyond lay the Arbonne Forest and the Point of Sorrow. They entered the Arbonne and let the shadowed mystery of the forest swallow them whole.

About halfway to their destination, a shadow moved on their right. Another flitted past them on the left. Branna drew a sharp breath of alarm.

"What is that?" Fiall asked, drawing his sword.

"Sheathe your blade," said Lucan. "It is merely the Opposition. They are ensuring we get to the Point of Sorrow unmolested."

Glancing around with unease, Fiall replaced his sword.

"Once we get there, some will fight at the camp, but others will draw the Valorian away to weaken and disorient them so we may complete our task."

They saw the first soldier two quarter lengths from the Point of Sorrow. One of the camp's perimeter guards rode toward them in full regalia. His mount sported a forehead covering with the Dragon Throne emblem upon it. Lucan's hands tightened on the reins as he watched him approach.

"Sal'vi, I am Valorian Rochius," he said, placing his closed fist to his chest and inclining his head.

Lucan did the same. "Sal'vi, Valorian."

"What is this?" the soldier asked, indicating Branna.

"We come from the north," he replied. "We brought this woman to be imprisoned at the palace, but the officials instructed us to bring her here."

Rochius's eyes flicked over Branna. She cast her eyes downward. The soldier smiled and moved his horse near hers. He reached out and cupped her chin. "What could this pretty little thing have done that was so terrible?" His hand strayed to the top of her shirt as if he meant to open it.

Wordlessly, Fiall drew his sword and placed the point of it to the man's throat. Rochius's eyes snapped with fury, but he drew his hand back.

"She's suspected of witchcraft, Valorian Rochius," Lucan said quickly. "We found her near Ebru. She's for Emperor Magnus, and he'll have the head of any man who touches her. He is only protecting you." He turned to Fiall. "Sheathe your blade, Valorian," he ordered.

Fiall hesitated for a moment and then complied.

"She's possibly an Ilerian sorceress," Lucan continued. "That was why they bade us bring her here. They didn't want her anywhere near the prison because—"

"Aye, I know why they didn't want her there," the soldier broke in.

"I am not a witch," Branna spat. "You've mistaken me for some other woman."

"Aye. Sure we have, Ilerian spawn of the Underworld," Lucan retorted.

"Why is she not blindfolded, Valorian?" asked Rochius.

"Blindfolded?" Lucan asked, playing dumb. He knew well what the Valorian was about to say.

"*Solan's blood!* Everyone knows you have to blindfold a witch to keep her from using her abilities." Rochius dug a long strip of material from his saddlebag and threw it at Lucan.

Lucan reached over and placed it over Branna's eyes, tying it at the back of her head. "We are new to the Valorian, please forgive us. We were only conscripted a month ago."

Rochius gave them a long, slow look of appraisal. "Cursed inexperienced soldiers making more work for everyone else," he muttered under his breath. "All right, follow me," he ordered with a poisonous look at Fiall.

The soldier led them through the trees and into the temporary encampment where Valorian soldiers swarmed. The sound of the surf met his ears, and seabirds swooped down from above, looking for any food the men may have dropped on the ground. The cage that held the prisoners stood at the edge of the cliff.

Rochius pointed at the cage. "Those are the rebels they captured at Strobia. We thought we'd just pitch them over the side if they caused us any trouble." He laughed and spat on the ground. "Rebel slime," he muttered.

"I don't think Lord Crispus would approve of that," Lucan said.

"Aye, I know. They have to be in one piece before they can be broken." He hooked a thumb at Branna. "What do you want to do with the chit? If you don't want her touched, you better not put her in with that lot," he said, indicating the cage.

"I'll take care of the witch," said Fiall, speaking for the first time.

"Aye. Well, put her by the cage and see she's bound properly." Rochius sniffed and cast one last look at Branna that seemed to take in every detail of her from head to foot and undress her at the same time. Lucan's hand went to the handle of his sword. He knew that look. That was the look of a man who'd have a woman, no matter the cost. That one would have to be watched.

Rochius moved away, going to the huge fire that burned in the center of the encampment.

They went to the cage, and Lucan and Fiall dismounted. Lucan tried not to be visibly concerned with the rebel prisoners. He untied the bonds at Branna's ankles as Fiall worked on the ones at her wrists. Out of the corner of his eye he could see the men recognized him, but they showed no obvious signs of it. He could also see Morgan on the bottom of the cage. The men had propped him up and had stanched the flow of blood from his shoulder wound with ripped pieces of their own clothing. His face was swollen and beaten to a bloody pulp. Morgan was the only one unconscious, and he had the worst of the wounds.

Two Valorian soldiers stood guard near the cage door. They acknowledged Fiall and Lucan with a nod of their heads. He knew they had the keys. Lucan jerked his head, indicating Morgan. "What happened to that one?" he asked them.

"He was recalcitrant and difficult to manage, the worst of the bunch. We had to beat him into submission," said one.

Aye, Morgan would be, Lucan thought.

They pulled Branna from her mount. She put up a mock fight against them, and they made a show of getting her under control and binding her ankles and wrists. Lucan slipped the blindfold up for a few moments so she could get a look at the prisoners. She gave Morgan a quick appraisal. As he tied her bonds to one of the bars of the cage, she looked at Lucan. Her expression conveyed hopelessness. His heart dropped to his stomach as he pushed her blindfold back into place.

When she was secure, Lucan and Fiall moved away from her and stood with their backs to the cage.

"Now what?" Fiall asked out of the corner of his mouth.

"We watch and wait," Lucan replied under his breath.

They didn't have to wait long. Signs of commotion on the opposite side of the camp spread like wildfire all the way to the edge of the cliff.

"Rebels!" yelled one of the two guards at the cage in alarm. He drew his sword and balanced on the balls of his feet, unsure whether or not he should remain to guard the cage or go to fight.

Aye, thank Solan for rebels, thought Lucan. They were attacking the camp even as they stood there watching. Soon, one force of rebels would draw some of the Valorian away from the camp. Another contingent would stay behind and fight.

The highest-ranking Valorian officer let his horse prance. He looked surprised.

The Opposition fought with their hearts and souls, and the Valorian fought from of a sense of duty or, oftentimes, simple fear. One rebel was worth three Valorian in a battle because of it, though the rebels were almost always outnumbered. The Opposition had the advantage now because the last thing the Valorian had been expecting was an attack at the Point of Sorrow.

The cage guard who'd drawn his sword finally ran into the fray. "Soldiers, what are you just standing there for? Do something," the other yelled at Lucan and Fiall.

"You're right," Lucan said, turning to the man. "We have things to do." Lucan advanced on the Valorian, drawing his sword as he stalked to him. He placed the edge of his weapon to the soldier's throat. The Valorian was so shocked he didn't even draw his sword. His hand went to it belatedly, but the slight pressure Lucan applied to the blade at his throat stilled the action.

"Rebel," the Valorian breathed, his eyes narrowing.

"Aye, you're a quick one," said Lucan. "Now give me the keys to the cage."

The man didn't move. Commotion swirled around them, but Lucan didn't take his eyes from the Valorian. The battle was growing near. He needed the keys now.

"Fiall!" Branna cried in alarm as a Valorian fell from his horse to the ground near her feet, his blood spilled by a rebel hand. Fiall ripped off her blindfold and drew his sword. With two deft motions, he cut Branna's bonds at her wrists and ankles. Then he swung around just in time to meet the blade of a Valorian soldier.

"I've no wish to cut down an unarmed man," Lucan said to the cage guard. "But I will if I have to."

Still the man didn't move toward the keys. He only cast Lucan a poisoned glance.

Lucan twisted the blade until it drew blood. "Do you think I would hesitate to spend the life force of one who helps to bleed Numia into a slow death every single day? I wouldn't, Valorian, believe me. Now give me the keys."

The man's hand went to his belt. He drew the keys from a pouch that hung there and tossed them to Lucan. Lucan tossed them to Branna. She went to the cage and unlocked it. Opposition prisoners poured out.

"Now go!" said Lucan to the soldier. He lowered his blade and turned away. The Valorian did what Lucan knew he would do. He drew his sword and brought it toward Lucan with a battle cry. With one turn and a twist of his wrist, Lucan slashed the man high on the upper shoulder of his sword arm. The soldier crumpled to the ground and relinquished his weapon.

Lucan turned and met an oncoming Valorian.

B RANNA HOISTED HERSELF INTO THE CAGE AS THE PRIS-oners pushed their way out. She located Morgan and knelt by him. One of the Opposition also remained, concerned about the fallen man. She put a hand to Morgan's cold cheek and felt his pulse. He was alive, but he needed care if he was going to stay that way.

"We've got to get him out of here," she said to the man. "Can you help me?"

"Yes, my lady. Of course." His eyes flicked to a horse that roamed riderless outside the cage. "Can you secure that mount?"

Branna nodded.

"Get that mount, remove the saddle, and I'll lift him on."

Branna got out of the cage and inched her way toward the horse, taking care to avoid the fighting. She grabbed the horse's reins and undid its cinching with fingers made surprisingly sure and deft from fright. The saddle fell to the ground. Branna understood that with the saddle, there wouldn't be enough room for herself and Morgan both.

By the time she had the beast to the door of the cage, the man had gathered up Morgan. He draped him over the back of the horse, belly down.

He jumped down from the cage and took a sword from the hand of a fallen Valorian who lay on the ground. "I'd ride south, my lady, and I'd ride like the wind," he advised.

Branna nodded and mounted behind Morgan's unconscious body. She placed a hand to his back to steady him and spurred the horse hard into a flat-out run toward the tree line of the Arbonne. Her heart felt lodged just south of the back of her tongue.

The horse ripped its way through the trees. Branches slapped at her, twigs caught in her hair and tore at her clothing and exposed skin. She felt warm blood dribble from a scratch on her cheek. She bent close over the back of Morgan's body and let the horse lead her, daring not to slow her pace nor look behind her. Anyway, Branna already knew she was being followed. Every inch of her body told her that.

And she knew it wasn't anyone who meant them well.

Desperate, she altered her path to the west and rode blind. She didn't have the knowledge Lucan had of the Arbonne Forest. In that way, she had a distinct disadvantage because whomever it was that was following her did know these woods.

She risked a glance back through her tangled hair. A sole Valorian rode behind her. The hair on the back of her neck stood up. One Valorian seemed much more ominous than many.

"Ai'yah!" she yelled, trying to push the horse to an even faster pace.

Her breath caught in her throat. A steep cliff rose in the distance, blocking her route. She veered to the left and raced along the length of it, but it seemed to never end. An enormous fallen tree came into view, too big for the horse to jump. There was no way around it.

She was trapped.

She reined the horse back hard in an attempt to halt it before it ran straight into the trunk. The horse let out a high sound of desperation and almost dumped Branna and Morgan off in its effort to stop. The beast came to a screaming halt only a breath's space from the tree. The animal breathed hard through its nostrils and was lathered with sweat.

The sound of pounding hooves behind her grew louder. Branna whirled the horse to face the oncoming rider. Her hand found her athame, which was hidden at her waist in the folds of her shirt. The rider approached and pulled his helm off. He wore the satisfied smirk of a hunter who'd just trapped his prey. Branna recognized him as Valorian Rochius.

His horse approached hers, and she brandished her blade out in front of her.

"Oh now," he said, his lips twisting into a smile. "That's a pretty blade, chit." He drew his long knife and tilted it so its silvered edge glinted in the daylight filtering through the leaves of the trees above. "But I have a bigger one."

"Stay away," she warned. Her hand went to Morgan in a protective gesture.

"It's not the man I want," he said. "But I think you know that already."

He inched his mount forward until she was trapped between the cliff and the fallen tree. She spurred her horse forward in a futile attempt to push past him. He caught up the reins of her horse, slid off his mount, and holding the reins of her horse in hand, reached for her.

She brought her athame down hard, catching him in the fleshy part of his upper arm. He cried out in pain and released her, but his hand did not stray from the reins of her horse as she'd hoped. He reached up and grabbed the handle and, grunting, pulled it out. Blood welled from the wound and soaked his tunic. He tossed the blade to the ground and raised his eyes to hers. The look he gave her chilled her to the bone. "You'll pay for that."

He wrapped sweaty hands around her waist, pulled her from

the horse, and pushed her against the fallen tree trunk. She fought against him. Her nails ripped at his face, drawing blood. He fell away from her, clutching his cheek.

She took the opportunity to flee, but he caught her, toppling her to the muddy forest floor and straddling her. She brought her hands up to strike his face, but he caught them and restrained her. His hands found her throat and squeezed. She could bespell him if only he would look in her eyes . . . if only she could focus. A strangled sound escaped her lips.

"What are you? Are you a whore for the Opposition, woman?" he asked. When she didn't respond, he shook her by the throat. "Answer me!" he yelled.

"No," she rasped.

"No? Well then, you'll be a whore for the Valorian." His mouth searched for hers. She twisted her face away as his hot, sour breath fouled the air. He moved his hands from her throat to her waist, and she coughed, trying to draw air into her starved lungs.

Tears stung her eyes as she knew bitter defeat. She was glad she'd worn trews. It would make his job that much more difficult, but there would be no way to avoid giving what this man wanted to take from her.

CHAPTER TWELVE

THE SOUND OF AN OBJECT SLICING THROUGH THE AIR and hitting something solid reached her ears. Rochius grunted. Through the haze of tears in her eyes, Branna saw a surprised look on his face. He slumped down on top of her. Immediately, strong hands pulled him off and pushed him to the side. An arrow stuck out of the back of the man's neck.

She blinked away tears, and Lucan's face came into focus. He reached down and gathered her up, helping her to her feet. He held her against him, his hand stroking the back of her head, running down the length of her hair. "Are you all right?" he asked.

She nodded because she couldn't speak. Then her legs went out from under her. He caught her before she collapsed and eased her to the ground. He came down into the fallen leaves with her and drew tendrils of hair away from her face. She tried to stop her tears and failed. His hand went to her throat, tracing the bruises she knew were already blooming.

"I saw him leave on your trail," said Lucan, "but I couldn't follow him right away. I couldn't find a horse." He drew a breath. "*Solan!* If I'd been any later . . ."

She raised her eyes to his. Her throat was clogged with emotion, with the relief that he'd come at all. She couldn't form words.

"I'm sorry. I'm sorry I was . . ." he began.

She shook her head, and tipping her face to his, she laid a line of kisses along his jawline. It was the only way she could tell him thank you without speaking. It stilled the flow of his words. He looked down at her, his arms tightening.

She swallowed hard. "Morgan," she managed to push out.

"Aye, Morgan. We must get him somewhere safe and by a fire to get him warm."

She nodded.

"Then let's go." He released her and they stood.

I T WAS TOO DANGEROUS TO GO BACK TO THE HOUSE IN Ta'Ror. Instead, Lucan brought Branna and Morgan to a home in the smaller city of Pannonia where he knew an Opposition sympathizer would take them in.

Lucan stood in the kitchen of Hartus's cottage and gazed at the old, stooped man who sat across the room. Hartus remembered back to the days of Lucan's great grandfather. He'd been just a boy then, but he remembered well Numia's golden years and had told Lucan all the stories. And Hartus knew Morgan well.

Hartus cleared his throat. "Morgan has a wife in Angelyn, doesn't he?"

Lucan nodded. "Aye. He hasn't told me much about her, nor of his life in his homeland, but I know he loves her very much." He respected Morgan's privacy, but he sometimes wondered what his second-in-command had to hide.

The old man shook his head sadly and stood. "Morgan did not have to come to Numia to fight," he muttered.

Lucan smiled. "He was a soldier in the Angelese Guard, Hartus. You could not keep him from the fight for anything. Morgan, and other Angelese, know the Numian Opposition's fight is their fight too."

Branna had cleaned and dressed Morgan's wounds, and Lucan had persuaded her to change out of her muddy clothing and into a pair of trews and shirt borrowed from Hartus. They'd found another sword gash on Morgan, besides the obvious one in his shoulder. The other ran along the length of his lower back.

Branna sat with Morgan's head in her lap on the floor in front of the fireplace. The light flickered and licked its way over them. Lucan watched as she drew the blankets up to Morgan's collarbone and placed the back of her hand to his cheek. She bent her mouth to his ear and whispered something Lucan couldn't hear. If Morgan hadn't been in such bad shape, he'd envy him her ministrations and unwavering attention. The truth was, he didn't know if Morgan would live . . . and that tore his heart asunder. Lucan sank into a nearby chair and closed his eyes as a sudden wave of grief washed over him.

"I tried to go to him in the place beyond dreams," said Branna.

Lucan opened his eyes and looked at her.

She shook her head sadly. "But I couldn't find him."

"He is in Solan's hands now."

Across the room, Hartus also watched Branna with Morgan. He slapped his thigh and clucked his tongue. "Fire-juice!"

Lucan looked at him.

"Morgan could never resist Pirian fire-juice." A grin spread over his wrinkled face. "I'd lay coin fire-juice could bring him back to us."

For a moment Lucan wondered about the stability of the old man's mind. He shook his head, at a loss for words. "I don't think—"

"I have lived a few years more than you, eh? And I have seen a fair bit more than you have. Would it harm him to try?" Hartus asked.

Lucan shrugged his shoulders. "No."

Hartus rose and hobbled over to a cupboard. He extracted a bottle and knelt at Morgan's side. Branna looked at the old man uncertainly when he placed the bottle under Morgan's nose and waved it.

Of course Morgan didn't stir. Lucan cursed himself for hoping even a little.

Hartus placed his fingertips to the mouth of the bottle, tipped it end up, and wet them with the liquid. Then he drew his fingers across Morgan's lips. He stood and hobbled back to his chair.

Branna watched Morgan for several long moments and then sighed when he did not stir. She tucked the blanket around him more securely. In the process, she arched her throat, showing the lurid black-and-blue bruises in the firelight.

Lucan clenched his fists. The sight of that Valorian on her had caused the pure and simple desire for violence to rip through him. He'd felt deep satisfaction when his arrow had hit its mark, though Rochius had escaped into death far too easily. He'd deserved a more drawn-out end, and Lucan would've been more than happy to provide it to him.

He relaxed his hands and hung his head. *Sweet Solan.* He felt a far cry from the man he'd once been . . . but then, peace had never been destined to be his. The short time he'd had it seemed like a dream.

Even now Lucan prepared himself to finally come face-to-face with his uncle. He knew Magnus would soon be traveling to Kastum to attend a series of trade meetings. If their plans worked accordingly, Lucan would be there to meet him with the edge of his blade.

It was a desperate scheme, but he had no choice but to execute it. Even now Magnus planned the greatest offensive ever against Ileria. It looked as if the country would likely fall. Ileria was the last stronghold of free magic. If Ileria fell, Magnus would strip and plunder the land, just as he'd done to Tir na Ban. He'd imprison Ileria's mages and sorceresses and control all magic. He'd be too powerful to overcome.

It couldn't be allowed.

The Opposition had sent many envoys to Ileria asking them to form an alliance with the Numian Opposition, but the fear of splitting their troops and weakening their defenses had caused them to refuse every entreaty. Now, with the new information the Opposition possessed about Magnus's plans, Lucan hoped Ileria's government would finally see the wisdom of an alliance. One more envoy had been sent, and Lucan hoped this time they would be successful.

"Morgan!" cried Branna.

Lucan bounded out of his chair and to Morgan's side in a heartbeat.

Morgan roused a bit and opened his eyes a crack. He grimaced as if in severe pain and groaned deep in his throat. His tongue stole out to taste his cracked bottom lip. "I . . . I taste fire-juice," he croaked.

Lucan looked at Branna's amazed face. A smile spread across

her mouth. Behind them, Hartus could not suppress a raucous cry of triumph and a heartfelt laugh.

Lucan placed a hand on his shoulder. "I thought you were gone forever, friend."

"It takes a lot to kill an Angelese," Morgan rasped.

Lucan laughed.

"You can have all the fire-juice you want, Morgan," Branna said, running the back of her hand down his face. "Just as long as you help me to heal you."

Morgan opened his eyes a little wider. "You," he breathed. "I . . . remember you."

"Shh. Save your strength," Branna admonished in a gentle voice.

"I . . . saw you in the . . . forest. I thought you were one of Solan's celestial goddesses that had come for me." He tried to smile and winced. "I . . . wanted you to help the others."

She smiled and shook her head. "I'm no celestial goddess. I'm simply a sorceress who wants to heal you."

Lucan looked at her. Her loose dark hair cascaded past her shoulders and created a curtain around Morgan's head. This woman wasn't simply anything. She was enigmatic and sensual, power and beauty—everything he found fascinating and compelling.

"Will you consent to a healing, Morgan?"

He nodded.

"I may not be able to heal you completely. Your wounds are varied and deep. I can help you to heal yourself. I can bring you back to a place where natural healing can take place quicker. We can do another healing on the morrow. All right?"

Morgan nodded again.

Branna carefully removed the dressing that covered his shoulder wound, placed her hands on the deep slash, and let her eyes drift out of focus. The telltale shimmering began.

Across the room, Hartus gasped in surprise. He'd likely never seen magic before.

When she finished, Morgan's wounds were not completely healed, but they had knitted together. "Help me to turn him," Branna said to Lucan.

Morgan bellowed in pain as they flipped him to his stomach. Branna attempted to heal the wound running along his lower back and got the same results—almost healed, but not quite.

They shifted him comfortably to his back, and Branna put her hands to Morgan's bruised and swollen face. The less serious wounds there healed completely under her ministrations, leaving his face smooth and unmarred.

She pulled the blanket up to Morgan's chin. "Rest now," she said, smoothing his dark brown hair over his brow.

Morgan reached up and touched her face. "You were the dancer in Strobia."

"Yes," Branna replied.

"Thank you. If it was not for you, I'd be in Vallon now."

"If it wasn't for Hartus," she corrected, "you'd be in Vallon now." She looked to the old man and smiled. "I'm sorry I doubted you."

Hartus stood and brought the bottle to Morgan, who reached out and took it gratefully. "Ah," Morgan said, sighing. "The beverage of the Gods." He sat up a bit and took a long drink.

Branna stood on shaky legs. She staggered and caught herself on the back of a chair. Beaten down with fatigue and worry, she couldn't even stand. Lucan stood and went to her. In one smooth motion, he lifted her into his arms before she could protest.

"I can walk on my own. I'm fine!"

"No, you are not fine. You are exhausted and need to sleep."

Her arms twined around his neck, and he couldn't help enjoying the feel of it. Her head dipped a little in a gesture he took for acquiescence. Probably, she was simply too fatigued to argue. He bore her light weight to one of the beds that lined the one-room cottage and laid her down upon it. Sighing deeply, she settled her head against the pillow. He drew the blanket to her collarbones, and his fingers strayed to the bruises on her throat.

"Why do you not heal these?" he asked. "Are you too busy taking care of everyone else to bother with yourself?"

"I cannot. Fiall will be able to heal me, but I cannot heal myself."

"I see." His fingers lingered, gently caressing her skin. He wanted her pain to go away, and he felt helpless to do anything about it. He wanted to drop his head and kiss away the bruises.

She drew a shaky breath. "I'm running out of time, Lucan. I can feel it slipping away, and I don't know why."

He drew his hand away. She sounded bereft, lost. "What do you mean?"

"I can feel something is happening, but I don't know what it is. Fiall and I came here to find someone, to do something, but time is running out. Magnus is planning something that will negate my plans."

"An attack on Ileria, Branna," he said right away. "I would make a guess that's what you're picking up on. It's the largest one yet that he has managed to prepare. Ileria will fall."

Her eyes widened and grief flooded them. Her voice shook when she spoke. "Ileria fall? Magnus will do to Ileria what he did to Tir na Ban."

"Aye. We're working to stop it from happening."

She closed her eyes. "That's why I feel time slipping away."

"Sleep now. We'll speak of this more tomorrow." He watched until her breathing deepened and he knew she slept.

He turned and saw Hartus also tucked into bed. Lucan sat by Morgan. His second-in-command had his eyes closed, and Lucan thought he slept until he asked, "Who's the woman?"

"A Tirian priestess, the Tirian Raven, in fact. Her name is Branna."

Morgan nodded his head. "Aye, the Tirian Raven and a whole lot more."

"What do you mean?"

"Oh, come now." He chuckled and then fell silent.

"What, Morgan?" Lucan pressed.

He opened his eyes. They were two vibrant blue slits. "It's even in the way you say her name. It's clear you care deeply for the woman."

Lucan resisted the urge to laugh. "I may feel lust for her, but lust is merely lust and not anything close to what you're suggesting."

"Love . . . that's what I'm suggesting."

Lucan let out a surprised laugh. "Being injured has given you the tongue of an old woman sitting at her spinning wheel, Morgan. What has gotten into you?"

Morgan smiled. "I know you don't believe in love. When so many people you've cared for have died, it's a difficult thing to believe in."

Silence overcame Lucan.

Peering up at his face, Morgan let out a light laugh and then let his eyes drift shut. "Sometimes there's no choice, my friend," he murmured.

"No, Morgan, you are seeing things where there is nothing. Branna is an exceptional woman. That's true. But I have no feelings for her beyond that of the admiration any man would have."

"Ah, you see . . . there it is again, every time you say her name."

"Then I'll stop saying her name." Lucan let out a frustrated sigh. "There is always a choice."

Morgan shook his head. "No, friend. Believe me. I know. Sometimes things happen and it's all we can do to hold on against the force of them. I was pushed into marriage with the daughter of my worst enemy. I never thought I'd love her." He smiled. "It shows how much I knew . . ." He trailed off and a few moments later began to breathe the breath of deep sleep.

Lucan spied the bottle of fire-juice that Morgan still had in a loose grasp. He plucked it from his fingers and took a long swig.

Ridiculous.

Morgan obviously had some sort of head injury that had affected his judgment. They'd have to impose on Hartus for a while in order for him to recover enough to travel. They had a few days before they had to be in Kastum anyway.

M AGNUS'S YELL OF RAGE ECHOED THROUGH THE PALace at Ta'Ror. The servants in the kitchens stopped kneading the bread dough at the sound. The workers in the palace gardens ceased their pruning as his enraged voice poured forth from open windows. The guards at the door of the room where Draoichta Cothrom lay tightened the holds on their war staffs. In their sitting room, the Tirian sorceresses cast looks of deep concern at each other.

"They what?" yelled Magnus, rounding on the official messenger of the Northern Valorian Guard. He'd brought the news of the escaped Opposition prisoners.

"M . . . m . . . my lord. They somehow knew we were keeping the rebels at the Point of Sorrow. They hit us in three waves. One attacked us straight on at the camp. Another rebel force drew part of the Valorian into the Arbonne Forest, dividing us. A third wave attacked the camp and the separated Valorian. A couple of them posed as soldiers escorting a woman they claimed was a prisoner. We now believe the woman may have been the escaped sorceress from Strobia. They were the ones to obtain the keys to the cage and allow the escape."

Magnus studied the messenger. The officer shifted uncomfortably and muttered a prayer to Solan. The messenger's eyes darted to Lord Crispus, who stood in the back of the chamber in the shadows.

Magnus knew what he was thinking. Crispus was the nightmare of the palace, more feared than even him. Everyone knew that to see Lord Crispus for the healing of a wound or illness was far more dangerous than the ailment itself. Crispus had a nasty penchant for inflicting pain. He took pleasure in it. In fact, it was said he took perverse pleasure in it.

The officer shuddered as though hearing Magnus's thoughts.

Magnus shot forth, grabbed his jerkin with both hands, and lifted him off the ground. "They were very organized, weren't they?"

The officer nodded.

"They were very knowledgeable too, weren't they?"

The officer nodded again.

"Do you know why we weren't as organized or as knowledgeable?" Magnus shook him. "Hmm? Do you know why that is? Why our mighty Valorian Guard was undone by an unruly bunch of rebels?"

The officer shook his head.

Magnus dropped him, letting him collapse to the floor. "Then I have no use for you."

The officer picked himself up and made his way toward the door.

"Halt!" ordered Magnus. "Someone must pay for this! Does the captain of your regiment still live?"

"Nay, my lord," said the officer.

"Then who is the second-in-command?"

The officer closed his eyes and swallowed hard. "I . . . I am, my lord."

"Ah." Magnus clasped his hands in front of him. "Well . . . it would seem we would need someone to be made an example of, wouldn't it? After all, the troops need a reason to give their all for me. Fear is as good a reason as any."

The officer backed toward the door.

Crispus stepped from the shadows. "I'd hoped to work within the next couple of days, my lord. All my instruments are sharpened. All my equipment is prepared."

"No!" cried the officer.

Magnus shrugged. "Why not? Excellent notion, Crispus."

The officer turned and ran for the door, but Magnus took several wide strides and closed one powerful hand on his shoulder before he reached it. He swung the man around to meet Crispus, who slapped manacles on his wrists. The officer whimpered.

Crispus let out a short, cold laugh. "Magnus, the mettle of your Valorian officers is lacking. This one won't last but the afternoon with me." He pouted a bit. "The rebels would have been much stronger. They would have provided far more enjoyment."

The officer let out a bloodcurdling scream.

Magnus pulled his handkerchief out and stuffed it into the man's open mouth. "Oh, be still," he said in irritation. "It will be over before you know it, and we'll string you up in the courtyard for your regiment to see."

The officer breathed heavily through his nose, his eyes wild.

Crispus took the man by his upper arm and led him toward the secret door in the back of the room. The door led to an underground passageway that connected the palace with the separate building of the prison. It was there, in the bowels of the palace prison, where Crispus did his work. Lord Crispus stopped and turned toward Magnus. "When do you leave for Kastum?"

"In two days' time," Magnus replied. "I await Nia even now to discuss the details with her."

"Take care, my lord," said Crispus before continuing on with his prisoner. The officer pushed the handkerchief from his mouth with his tongue and screamed. Crispus shoved the man through the doorway at the back of the room and down the stairs. The heavy door closed behind them, muffling the man's cries.

At the same time, the guard admitted Nia. Her beautiful gaze found Crispus's secret door and rested on it. She missed nothing. "Nia," Magnus said, coming toward her and taking her hands in his.

"My lord."

"Oh, but your hands are cold!" He rubbed them vigorously between his own. "The palace is too draughty a place for a woman as warm-blooded as you."

"Forgive me, my lord, but I fear my hands are not cold because of the temperature within the palace." Her eyes met his.

His breath caught in his throat. *Solan*, but she had pretty eyes. "Then why are they cold, and what can I do to warm them?"

"You can show mercy to those whom you feel have let you down," she said in a quiet but steady voice.

Magnus went silent for a moment and then released her hands. He turned from her. "My men have failed, Nia. It is necessary I display my displeasure with them." He turned and fixed her with a steady gaze. "And make no mistake, I am highly displeased."

"You knew the rebels would try and free the Opposition prisoners."

"Of course! The Opposition is not cowardly, and they are far from stupid. They knew well what sort of information we could have extracted from those men. Don't worry, I'll capture more, and next time they won't escape."

"You meant to lure the rebels to the prison to capture them."

"Aye, but they found out the prisoners were not being held there," Magnus said. "Somehow, they knew they were being kept at the Point of Sorrow. They knew it was a trap, and they turned that knowledge to their advantage."

"You have a leak within your ranks."

"I don't think so, Nia." Magnus fisted his hand. "I think it is the sorceress. She must be traveling with them. Perhaps the woman is an Ilerian. If so, the Ilerians might know of our upcoming plans to attack them." That would mean they'd have to move quicker in their attack plans. The Ilerians could not be allowed to form an alliance with the Numian Opposition.

"If it is the sorceress, Ilerian or not, she is powerful," said Nia.

"So I am beginning to learn." Magnus struck his open palm with a fist. "I would have her for Ta'Ror!"

Nia looked away from him. "Aye, she would make a good addition to your power base."

Magnus placed his hands on her narrow shoulders. "But you . . . you will forever be the first and best sorceress in my eyes." His index finger found her chin and tipped her face to his. "You're forever the most magical and powerful sorceress to me."

Something unidentifiable moved in her eyes, and she stepped away from him. "I thank you for your confidence, my lord."

"Enough of this talk!" Magnus turned on his heel. "I've a surprise for you." He went to the back of the chamber, drew forth a small box, and placed it in her hands. "For your upcoming trip to Kastum."

Nia opened the box and pulled out a necklace of delicate golden Pirian star-stones. She cast her eyes down, and her manner remained subdued. "My lord, you are too generous."

She was such a modest woman. How he wished he could kiss away the serious set to her lips, but he dared not push her. He preferred she rouse to his charms on her own.

He took it from her fingers and placed it around her throat, fastening it at her nape. His fingertips traced the chain to her collarbones and rested there. "A beautiful woman deserves beautiful things," he whispered in her ear. "Can I count on your cooperation in Kastum, Nia? Will you keep your emperor safe?"

"Aye, my lord, of course."

CHAPTER THIRTEEN

Branna drew her cloak around her shoulders and made her way down the street toward the chapel of Sor'chen, the Numian God of Fire. She needed time alone to think.

Ileria could not fall.

Not one more country could be allowed to suffer, and Magnus could not absorb all of Ileria's magic. With such a large power base, he would be undefeatable; no one would be safe from him. She had to find the Book of *Draiochta Cothrom* and the priest soon. She just didn't know how to accomplish that, and time was running out at a rapid pace.

Had the Goddess forsaken her?

She shook her head. No. Impossible. This was how *cinnunt* worked. She'd dreamt of performing the Ritual of the Balance since she was a child. She knew it would come to pass, in all its beauty and its horror. The ritual would bring glorious and magical things to the planet, but so would it bring sorrow. The ritual brought equilibrium in all ways—never the sweet without the sour.

Branna drew a deep, calming breath. She couldn't allow herself to think of that. She simply had to permit things to unfold as they would.

So far they'd had much good fortune. Hartus had been a wonderful and gracious host. That morning he'd heated water for her to bathe in and found her a kirtle spun of gray wool to wear when she was finished. In the bath, she'd scrubbed her skin until it was bright pink, in an effort to rid herself of the taint of Valorian Rochius.

Morgan was recovering nicely. Later today she'd perform another healing on him. She didn't know if she could help him any further, but it was worth a try. He was strong of mind, body, and spirit and would mend nicely without her help.

Fiall would be arriving soon. She could feel him tracking her even now.

Lucan was . . . Lucan. It was amazing how intensely the man made her feel—passion, anger, lust . . . definitely lust. And he wasn't even the man she sought. He wasn't the priest. He was a lot of things—the rightful heir to the Dragon Throne and Opposition leader. He was heat and light and dark all at the same time. He was enough . . . more than enough.

But he wasn't the priest.

She reached the chapel and pushed the door open. Heat flowed past her and poured onto the street. Heavy wax candles sat on every available space. A roaring fire burned in a large hanging cauldron in the center of the room.

She closed the door behind her and entered. The chapel was empty. Taking a chair in front of the fire, she let the heat of it penetrate her. Something moved behind the cauldron, and she realized a man stood there. He moved into the shadows and then took a step toward the fire. The light illumed glossy black hair framing a face with an intense blue gaze.

She smiled. "Lucan." Strange how she felt content to see him when she'd wanted to be alone. "I would not have expected to see you here."

"Really? I would've said the same of you." He smiled. "This is not exactly a temple of the Goddess."

"No."

He glanced around. "I can only imagine what your temples must look like in Tir na Ban." His eyes clouded. "Or rather what they must've looked like before the Terror."

"They were full of crystal that reflected the sunlight, and flowers, lots of skyflower, for that is the bloom of the Goddess. They were not enclosed but open, like your temples of Akal, except there were no roofs on our temples. The forests were allowed to grow into them over the years so eventually they became one with nature."

"They sound beautiful."

"Perhaps, when this is finished and we rebuild them, you can come to Tir na Ban and see one."

A doubtful smile played on his lips. "Perhaps."

"Do you think me optimistic?"

"I think you idealistic. I was that way once too, but now I can barely remember that time."

"You have trouble keeping faith."

His eyes darkened. "Aye, I do. Once . . ." He trailed off, glanced away, and lapsed into silence.

She stood and crossed the space between them. She couldn't help it. The heat from his body radiated out, touching hers. It called to her. She wondered what it would be like to have that heat wrapped all around her and within her. She wondered how his bare skin would feel against hers.

"A time? A time when you had faith?" she pressed. She moved close enough that she could touch him.

He reached out, caught a tendril of her hair, and pushed it behind her ear. "Aye, but I was young then, and the world had not seemed so dark."

She had an intense desire to catch his hand and bring his palm to her lips. She fisted her hand in the skirt of the kirtle to prevent herself from acting on the impulse. "It is Magnus who is dark, not the world."

"Your experience yesterday didn't make you think that perhaps it is more than simply Magnus?" His hand strayed to caress her throat. "Don't these bruises give testament to a dark world?"

She glanced down and away from him. "Perhaps."

Lucan drew a hand back through his hair. She'd noticed he did that when he was frustrated. She'd begun to know well his gestures and ways of being.

He raised his hand, lowered it, and then raised it again. Finally he reached out and touched her cheek. She couldn't stop herself; she closed her eyes and turned into his palm, letting her lips brush the place where his hand met his wrist. He shuddered and took a step closer to her.

She didn't know why she wasn't backing away, protecting herself. She just didn't want him to stop touching her. He let his hand stroke down the length of her hair, rubbing it back and forth between his fingers.

"So, are you still looking for that mysterious man of yours?" he asked.

His voice was a silken caress. She shivered. His nearness was an intoxicating thing and she could barely think. "No."

"No?"

She shook her head in an effort to clear it. "I mean . . . yes, I am still looking for him."

Lucan dropped his hand from her hair and went silent for several long moments before he finally spoke. "Maybe you could tell me exactly who it is you're looking for. Maybe I can help."

She bit her bottom lip in speculation. It was worth a try, though she doubted Lucan had any ties with the religious orders of Numia. But now that she knew she could trust him, there was no reason for her not to tell him of her dream and the Ritual of the Balance. "I am looking for a pr—"

The doors of the chapel swung open. She turned to see Fiall and Ren. Fiall strode straight to her and knelt on one knee, bowing his head. "My Raven." His voice shook. "I have failed you."

"Fiall—" she began.

"No, I have failed you. At the Point of Sorrow I did not feel your need or that you were in danger. I tracked you to the cottage of Hartus, and he told me what had occurred. I am your protector and I . . ." He looked up, caught sight of her throat, and drew a sharp breath. "It was worse than I feared."

"Fiall," she said, reaching out and laying her palm against his warm cheek. His scar glowed thin and white in the firelight, and his dark brown hair curled at the collar of his shirt. "You cannot be expected to be at my side every moment. I don't expect such from you. You are brave and a wonderful protector, and I don't know how I would manage without you. You are more dear to me than I could ever possibly tell you."

"As you are to me," Fiall whispered.

Lucan turned and looked into the fire. Ren went to stand beside him, and they began speaking in hushed tones.

"Rise, Fiall," said Branna. "You act more like a servant than a friend, and you are friend to me, aren't you? Not a servant. You are the brother of my heart."

Fiall took the chair beside her. "Tell me what happened."

"I was followed and attacked, but Lucan cut the man down before he could do anything truly terrible to me."

Fiall's brown eyes darkened. "Lucan aided you?"

"Yes."

He hesitated, the firelight reflecting off his silver shield necklace. Then he stood and walked to Lucan. "I owe you a debt of gratitude for your protection of Tir na Ban's Raven. That was my responsibility and I failed in it. Without your aid—"

"I protected Branna, not Tir na Ban's Raven. You owe me no gratitude. We all must look out for one another."

Fiall bristled. "I protect Branna as well! I've known her since she was a child. I have done so all our lives."

"I don't dispute that."

Alarmed by Fiall's sudden burst of anger, Branna went to him and placed a comforting hand on his forearm. "I don't think Lucan meant to offer you insult."

Lucan's blue eyes found hers and she held his gaze. "I think we can both agree that Branna is far too valuable to lose," said Lucan in a low, soft voice. A tremble went through her at the look in his eyes. There was heat there, and something that went beyond lust—true caring. She knew her own eyes reflected his feelings back at him.

Fiall pulled away from her and turned wild eyes on her. "I . . . I cannot bear this."

She took a step toward him, and he backed away. "Bear what, Fiall?"

Fiall hesitated for a moment in agitation, and then he went for the exit. Pushing the heavy oak doors open, he disappeared into the bright sunlight.

"You must excuse him," Branna said, still staring after Fiall. "He's had a hard time with all of this. It's been difficult for him, coming to the land of Tir na Ban's oppressors. He was treated . . . very cruelly by the Valorian in our homeland on numerous occasions."

"That's not why he acts that way," said Lucan. "I'm surprised, with all your abilities, that you don't realize that Fiall cares for you."

Branna whirled. "What do you mean?"

"I mean he *cares for you*," he repeated with emphasis.

"It is quite clear to all that Lucan speaks the truth, my lady," added Ren. "Clear to all except you, I think."

"No." Then a million different memories rushed through her mind. Times when there had been deep tenderness between them. Had the look in Fiall's eyes come from more than a sense of mere kinship? The full implications sank in. She gasped with the realization that Lucan was correct. How could she have been so blind? She looked up and met Lucan's gaze.

He nodded. "Aye."

"Goddess." She sat down on a chair. It changed everything between herself and Fiall. Branna felt betrayed. It was as though she'd lost her best friend. The man she thought she knew better than anyone else in the world was someone she suddenly couldn't fathom at all.

Worse, all the feelings she had for Lucan, all of them, Fiall had been picking up on. She hadn't masked her desire for Lucan, thinking she had no reason to. She'd been cruel without knowing it. That was why he'd fled the chapel when he did. He couldn't bear to feel what she felt for Lucan, while all this time Fiall had been masking his own feelings for her.

"Lucan told me Morgan is recovering, my lady," said Ren. "When do you think he will be fit to travel?"

Branna was glad to have something else to discuss. "I will perform another healing on him today. If he accepts it, he could travel by this evening or tomorrow morning. If he does not, it will be a few more days."

Ren let out a sharp breath. "Let us hope your healing takes. We are to be in Kastum soon."

"What is in Kastum?"

"We're—"

Lucan shot Ren a look, and the boy fell silent. "Something we've had planned for a long while," said Lucan in a tone that brooked no further inquiry.

She smiled, but she knew it didn't reach her eyes. "That's very vague, Lucan."

"Yes." Lucan said with a smile to match hers. "It is. Shall we leave you to the chapel? I must go see to Morgan."

So . . . Lucan endeavored to conceal something from her. She would let it go for the time being. That would be a battle for the near future. "Yes, thank you."

CHAPTER FOURTEEN

BRANNA WATCHED MORGAN WALK TOWARD LUCAN. MORgan placed a hand to his lower back and winced. He was yet a bit weak but regaining his strength in a hurry. It jarred her to see a man of his strength laid low.

They'd stopped in a clearing to rest on their way back to Kern. As they left Pannonia, Branna had overheard a discussion between Lucan and his second-in-command when they thought she was not near. Lucan had pressed for Morgan to return to Kern and take time for his recovery, but Morgan would not back down. He was going to Kastum no matter the cost.

She sat down on a mound of sweet-smelling grass and watched Varro and Ren walk into the woods toward a stream. Morgan and Lucan stood talking in hushed tones a distance away from her.

Fiall knelt beside her. His dark brown hair was secured in a queue at the nape of his neck. "May I heal you of your bruises now, Raven?"

He'd been distant ever since he'd come to the chapel of Sor'chen in Pannonia. She felt uneasy around him, unsure how to act knowing what she now knew. "Yes, please."

He placed his hands to her throat, and for the first time ever in her life, she flinched from his touch. He drew his hands back and hesitated before replacing them. Naked pain flashed through his deep brown eyes. "Are you well?" he asked in Tirian.

"Yes, of course," she lied.

Letting his eyes go out of focus, he looked beyond to the Universal Fabric, and the shimmering began. His hands grew warm against the skin of her throat, then cooled. Instead of drawing away when he was finished, he cupped her chin in one hand and forced her eyes to his. His fingers dug into her flesh, but the look in his eyes stilled the exclamation of discomfort on her tongue. Desperate heat blazed there, mingling with something far more disturbing. Love. The kind of love that surpasses mere friendship.

"Branna," his voice broke on her name.

He must have seen deep dismay on her face, but she couldn't mask her feelings. She did not know how to answer the question that Fiall seemed to be asking with his gaze and his body. Every single bit of him seemed to be straining toward her, wondering if she might ever return the affection he had for her.

"Forget the priest and the Ritual of the Balance. I won't lose you to another man, and I won't let the ritual take you from me. Come away with me now and end this. We could be very content together, you and I," he said in Tirian. His voice was a low, soft caress, but it didn't make her feel as Lucan's voice did.

She pulled from his grasp. Many different emotions flowed through her, anger not the least of them. She needed to remain calm.

Mastering her expression, she spoke in Tirian. "Fiall...I would never be content to forget my duty to Tir na Ban. I would never be content to let Ileria fall and be ravaged, or for Magnus to hold un-questionable power. The only thing that can stop those things from happening is the Ritual of the Balance. I cannot simply forget it." Her voice rose, her anger suddenly eclipsing the dismay and fear she felt. "We came here to perform the ritual, do you not remember?"

"No. I came here for you, not to perform the ritual. I came to be near you." His tone was angry and his almond-shaped Tirian eyes jumped with fire.

Branna opened her mouth and then closed it, at a loss for words.

Fiall stared at her, expecting her to say something. When she didn't, he expelled a frustrated breath. "So you have appointed yourself caretaker for Numia, Pira, Angelyn, Bah'ra, Tir na Ban, and Ileria. You will sacrifice yourself or your priest consort to the Ritual of the Balance for them?"

"Gladly."

"Why? What do you owe these countries, these peoples? What have they done for you?" Bitterness laced his voice, and the skin around his eyes pinched with lines of pain. "They did not come to Tir na Ban's aid when Magnus's Valorian invaded. They did nothing as Numian soldiers raped our priestesses and killed our people."

She also harbored sorrow that no nation had come to their de-fense, but she would not let those feelings rule her.

Looking at Fiall, feeling a deep emotional kinship with him, she desired to soothe him. She reached toward him, but he knocked her hand away. "Answer me!"

She turned her palms up and gestured in a beseeching way. "Don't you see, Fiall? If there is something I can do to prevent Mag-nus's Valorian from raping any more priestesses, killing any more people, I will do it. I will do it no matter the cost."

Fiall stood and looked down at her, hands fisted, shoulders hunched. "I won't lose you. You mark my words now, Branna. I will not."

"I DON'T WANT THE PRIESTESS TO KNOW OF OUR PLANS to leave for Kastum," Lucan said. He did not want to say Branna's name because of what Morgan had told him at Hartus's cottage in Pannonia.

"She is not unintelligent, my lord. I'm sure she already knows we are planning something of great importance," answered Morgan.

"Well, that's all she has to know." Lucan flirted with the idea of telling Morgan about the vision he'd had, but he decided against it. It was as if speaking it aloud would make it real. "You and Ren must make ready to leave with me soon. It is better we leave from here than Kern. Varro will travel on with the Tirians and guide them to Kern. Then he will meet us in Kastum tomorrow."

Morgan's mouth twitched. "As you wish, my lord."

"What are you thinking?"

"I'm thinking you won't lose her so easily. That is a woman who gets what she wants. After having spent some time with her, I know she wants Magnus as bad as you do . . . maybe more. Seems a pity to deny her. Just think if someone was trying to keep you from an opportunity to see Magnus defeated. Imagine how you would feel."

Morgan's words gave him pause. He'd want to see anyone who kept him from Magnus in their grave. "Aye. Well . . . I will have her safe. That is the most important thing."

Morgan raised an eyebrow.

"Don't say it, Morgan!"

He smiled. "All right, I won't say it."

"Don't think it either!"

Morgan's smile widened. "Ah, but that is a realm in which not even the rightful heir to the Dragon Throne, the prince of Numia himself, can command." He inclined his head a degree. "Do forgive me if I am unable to comply, my lord."

"I have no time for women, Morgan. No time for distractions."

Morgan merely smiled.

Lucan made a sound of frustration and turned. He spotted Branna and Fiall and went toward them. It was not until he was too close to turn back that he realized he was interrupting a serious conversation. They spoke low and in Tirian. He approached them and inclined his head. "My lady . . . Fiall." Branna seemed relieved at his presence.

Fiall turned toward him. Anger sat in the hunch of his shoulders and glittered in his eyes. "What do you want now, Dragon Prince? In what other way can my Raven endanger herself for your pleasure?" Sarcasm laced his tone.

Lucan's jaw locked.

Branna scrambled to her feet. "Fiall, I think our horses need tending. Would you mind seeing to it?"

Fiall stood for a moment, his gaze steady with Lucan's, then moved away. He did not go to the horses but into the woods.

Branna watched him go, concern showing in her eyes.

"Branna," Lucan said finally, "we'll part with you now. Varro will bring you and Fiall back to Kern."

She opened her mouth, but he cut her off. "I won't argue over this as we did in Ta'Ror. You will stay behind this time." He turned and walked away.

She ran after him and touched his arm. "I did aid you in freeing the rebel prisoners, did I not?"

Lucan stopped and turned. "You know you did, and for that I'll always be in your debt. But you are yet recovering from what you endured at the hands of that Valorian soldier. You need to stay at Kern and rest."

"I'm fine. You're just using that as an excuse."

Lucan took her gently by the shoulders. "You arrived at a very critical time. We have many things planned right now. They've taken months and months to prepare. They are very dangerous things—"

"How dare you treat me like a child!"

Lucan sighed. "The truth is that if we suddenly changed the plans we've worked so hard on and included you, they might fail. You could be identified as sorceress and taken, killed, or sold into slavery. I don't want any of those things to happen."

Her eyes were alight with green fire, and her hair shifted loose on her shoulders, sending up a cloud of skyflower scent.

Solan.

All he wanted was to pick her up and carry her into the woods, pin her against a tree and sheath himself deep inside her. He wanted her bare skin sliding over his, her sweet tongue brushing his. He wanted her moving under him, over him.

Grasping a tendril of her hair in his hand, he held it for a moment. He let it slip like a silken shadow through his fingers, before turning and walking toward his horse.

Morgan swung up onto his mount. "My lord, we're ready."

Ren and Varro had returned from the stream. Ren was also astride and waiting for him. Lucan mounted his horse and without a backward glance, rode away with his men.

B RANNA WAS LEFT WITH THE WARM FEELING OF HIS hands on her shoulders, and memories of the actual look of caring in his eyes. Still, it took her a heartbeat to make her decision.

She would not allow Lucan out of her sight as long as he wore the key to Draoichta Cothrom around his neck.

Varro walked over to stand beside her. "My lady, where is your companion?"

"He went into the forest."

"We should also be on our way if we wish to make Kern by nightfall."

She shifted her gaze from his. "I cannot go after Fiall, Varro. I'm . . . definitely not someone he wishes to see at present."

"If I go find him will he take my head off?"

"No." She smiled. "Not *your* head."

"All right then." He turned and disappeared into the trees.

Branna ran to her horse and mounted. Finding Lucan's trail, she also disappeared into the trees. She felt guilty about leaving Fiall behind, but she knew telling him of her plans would only result in an argument. She put up a strong mental block against her protector so he would not be able to track her. His presence would only complicate matters.

She traveled behind the men until the sun hung low in the sky. Then the trails broke and the riders separated. Lucan split his men often to prevent tracking by Valorian patrols. Branna stopped cold. Which trail should she follow?

She had to invoke a tracking spell. She let her eyes drift out of focus and felt for the connection between herself and Lucan within the Universal Fabric. A long, powerful golden cord stretched between them. Along its length white and gold flecks of strength, compassion, respect, even love, sparked and swirled. An indigo spot appeared far down the cord and grew nearer and larger until it hit her, sending a wave of warm energy over her that rocked her in her saddle. She broke the spell with a gasp. Without a doubt, she and the prince had a strong connection.

She took a deep breath and looked down at the separated trails. Lucan's glowed golden. Still somewhat disoriented, she followed it. After a while, she heard whistling and knew he wasn't far. Branna slowed her pace and smiled.

After the sun had gone down, she saw the glow of a campfire ahead. She halted her horse and dismounted. He'd stopped for the night. She couldn't start a fire of her own for fear of being discovered, but soon the promise of heat drew Branna near Lucan's fire.

She pulled the hood of her cloak over her head and peered into his camp while hiding in the bushes. He lay up against a rock with his eyes closed. His shirt was open, and firelight played over his face and bare chest like a lover's hands.

Branna couldn't help wondering what it would be like if instead of firelight, it was she that covered his body. In her imagination, it was she that warmed him with her hands and mouth instead of the fire. It was her fingers instead of the breeze that tousled his hair and pulled at his shirt. Her lower body tightened.

She'd never had this kind of an attraction to a man. Always it had been her priest that pulled at her, the promise of the one who would be her consort for this lifetime . . . at least for a little while. But Lucan . . . Lucan was a man to whom she could easily lose herself. He had the power to take the sexual magic she'd built up. One kiss and Branna knew she'd be lost. He represented danger to her because of it, but there was nothing for it. She couldn't shut off her desire for him.

A night bird called behind her, startling her. When she looked back, Lucan was gone. She glanced around anxiously. Then, out the corner of her eye, she saw a shadow move. Before she had a chance to scream, the shadow leaped and knocked her to the ground. Her ordeal with Rochius came back at her with vengeance—throwing her into a panic. Branna struggled, kicked, bit, and hit. Then she realized it was Lucan and went limp. "Lucan!" she yelled.

He had her pinned by her wrists. He stopped trying to restrain her and took a good look at her face, hovering over her for a few moments longer than Branna thought was necessary. A jolt of shock mixed with something else went through her as she noticed how close his mouth was to hers. His breath teased her lips. He smelled of leather and spicewood soap.

He pushed away from her and stood in one lithe movement. "What are you doing here?"

Branna pushed herself up onto her elbows. "You . . . you . . ." she stammered breathlessly. She paused, trying to compose herself after having him so near her. She hoped he thought her unease was due to surprise, not because she was drunk on the scent and feel of him.

She started again, sudden anger propelling her as she thought about how he'd tried to leave her behind. "You don't know how important it is that I help you do whatever it is you're doing in Kastum. If you ever have a chance to send Magnus to the Underworld, I want to be there." She rose to her feet as her voice rose in volume. "I represent Tir na Ban, and my country has a stake in the undoing of Emperor Navius Magnus!"

Lucan stood looking at her with his shoulders hunched forward, like a wolf with its hackles raised.

Branna took a step toward him. "And I don't like your silly, patronizing attitudes couched in chivalry." She advanced toward him until she stood in front of him, her index finger pushed into his chest. "So, where you go . . . I go! And I especially take issue with your concern for my welfare—" She bit off the last word, not understanding why that had come out of her mouth.

Lucan tipped his head at her quizzically, then, like lightning, he grabbed her wrist, taking her finger from his chest. "Fine. I won't show concern then."

He released her wrist, turned, and walked to the campfire. She followed him. He placed more wood on the fire without looking at her. "Where's your mount?"

"Not far. I'll get her."

Lucan whistled and the chestnut mare trotted into camp. Then he sat in front of the fire and stared into it.

Branna sat down beside him.

"I want to take Magnus down more than I want anything else in the world," said Lucan. He turned and looked at her, his eyes darkening. "Anything else."

She stared at him. Darkness partially shadowed his face on one side, and firelight illumed the other half. Determination and something else, some restless, unnameable element moved in and out of his blue gaze. She reached out and placed a hand on his upper arm, wanting to soothe him and not understanding why.

He shifted up onto his hands and knees and pressed her down on the ground beneath him. He covered her with his body, straddling her. Branna lay stunned for a moment and then tried to wiggle out from beneath him. He caught her gently but firmly by pressing against her hips with the inner part of his knees. She let out a gasp of surprise. His black hair hung in his eyes, masking them. "You're an empath, aren't you?" he said in a low, rough voice.

She nodded.

"Can you feel what I feel for you, my lady? Can you sense how much I want you? I want you so much I have to stop myself from touching you, from finding the edge of your skirt and pushing my hand beneath it."

"Lucan—"

"You endanger me, my lady. You distract me. I want you and fear you at the same time." His mouth descended on hers, but he did not kiss her. He let it hover over hers, brushing his lips lightly against it. His breath smelled of mint. "Perhaps most of all, I fear for you," he said against her lips.

She closed her eyes and a breeze brushed over her. When she opened them, he was gone. She got up, stared into the fire, and did not sleep until the night was half gone.

CHAPTER FIFTEEN

BRANNA AWOKE TO THE SOUND OF LUCAN PUTTING the saddle on his mount. Drowsily, she sat up. He drew an apple from his saddlebag and tossed it to her. "Breakfast," he said.

Her teeth bit through the smooth skin and into the flesh of the fruit. It filled her mouth with sweet and tang. She was ravenous. "Is that a stream I hear?" she asked around a mouthful.

Lucan pointed to the left. "Down there."

She scrambled to her feet and went in that direction. Branna devoured her apple on the way to the stream and then discarded the core for the birds. She knelt and hung her head over the water. Her black hair hung forward in an opaque curtain, obscuring her face.

She cupped water in her hands and splashed it over her eyes. Then cupped more and drank it, savoring the feel of the cool, sweet fluid sliding down her throat. She worked her fingers through her hair and braided it, tying the ends to secure it. Then she rose, shook out her skirts, and went back to the camp.

She immediately went to her horse and mounted. She turned the beast to face Lucan, who was already astride—tall lean, hard, and handsome in his rugged, rough-edged way. She gazed at him, and he sat looking back at her with his star-stone eyes.

In Lucan's eyes she saw her single-mindedness and purpose for existence reflected back at her, and then . . . something more. Branna broke the gaze, disconcerted by what she thought she saw.

"Let's ride," she said with vehemence.

They rode out fast and kept up the pace for the entire journey.

"When I said you'd arrived at a critical time, I meant it," he said after a long silence. "We are on our way back to Kastum." He paused. "Magnus will be there. It will be the first time he has left the safety of the palace since we've had the numbers and the strength to possibly succeed in attacking him. Magnus almost never leaves the palace at Ta'Ror. As you know, there is a spell of protection around it. It makes it near impossible for us to attack."

"Yes, the shield."

"Aye."

Branna was silent, absorbing what she'd been told.

Lucan turned in his saddle. "Are you all right?"

"I feel bad about not bringing Fiall along. This . . ." She sighed. "This could be it."

Lucan reined his horse alongside hers. "Don't get your hopes up too much. I'm trying not to. Magnus isn't stupid, and he doesn't take chances. We've got a small chance of killing him, or taking him captive." He drew a breath. "And a large chance of ourselves being killed or taken captive. Which is why . . ." Lucan pushed a hand through his hair in a gesture that screamed frustration. "Why I didn't want you to come along."

"I told you—"

"No, Branna," he cut her off. "I don't want to see anything happen to you." He smiled. "But you're not the kind of a woman who'll listen to a man, are you? Even if it's for her own good."

Branna simply stared down at her horse's mane.

At twilight they reached the top of a hill. In the distance lay Kastum. It was a trading port, and the busy harbor showed ships coming, going, and unloading their wares. Branna recognized the blue-green waters of the Glasmor Sea. Tir na Ban also shared shores with this great body of water.

Lucan dismounted and went to stand at the top of the hill. "We have spies enlisted in the Valorian Guard. One of them has gone fairly high up in the ranks." Lucan turned and flashed white teeth at her. "Magnus has no idea of the kind of knowledge we have. He'll be here in Kastum for the next few days to attend trade meetings. He cannot stay in his palace all of the time, and he knows it. Even now some scorn him for staying safe behind his fortress walls and hiding behind the skirts of his sorceresses. We have a chance here," he said in wonderment. "Even if it is only a slim one."

Branna sat atop her mount looking down at him. His back was rigid with determination, and he cut an impressive figure standing on the hill. Every inch of him was princely, despite the worn leather trews that sheathed his legs and the peasant-spun woolen tunic that covered his broad chest and shoulders. Snowflakes began to fall, and a cold wind blew. It was time to find shelter for the night.

She dismounted and sent her awareness into the town, seeking out Magnus. She found his dark, hard presence easily . . . and something else too, an anomaly attached to him, guarding him. Reds and golds shimmered and swirled around her. Exploding lights crowded her mind. They grew in intensity and grasped Branna's consciousness. She couldn't pull away. Dark magic swept over her skin, enveloping her in a prickling sensation that spread over her body. Her knees gave out from under her and she collapsed to the ground.

When she came back to consciousness, she found herself cradled in Lucan's arms. "He's here," she said right away. "But there's something else here too. Something I've never known the likes of. Some kind of violent magic. It wouldn't let me go."

Lucan held her against his warm chest. The feel of him made her even more lightheaded. She drew a ragged breath, half wishing he would let her go and half wanting to wind her arms around him.

"It's all right, you can tell me later."

"It was Tirian magic. I know at least that much, but . . . it was Tirian magic perverted—meant to harm anyone trying to access Magnus mentally. I have never known a far-blood to use magic to harm. The Goddess forbids it. This magic has been tainted by fear of the highest degree."

She swallowed hard. "Lucan, this could be very dangerous. I don't know how to deal with dark magic like this." She sighed in defeat. "Now I don't even know what to expect."

Lucan smiled down at her. She pushed herself up and away. "What are you smirking about?" she asked, irritated.

"Now you're like the rest of us. You don't know what to expect. Branna, Solan and the Gods of the Elements wove the skein of your life before you were even born. It is the *Parcae* in the old tongue . . . the Fates."

Branna caught and held his gaze. "*Cinnunt*," she answered in her own tongue.

T HAT NIGHT THEY RENTED ROOMS AT AN INN. IN THE morning, Lucan procured a table in the corner of the inn's common room and ordered some hard bread, cheese, and watered-down ale.

The Messenger was not one of Kastum's finest inns. Even in the morning light, the acrid smoke from the cook fire filled the room, burning Lucan's nostrils and fouling the air. Candles made from animal fat sputtered on the tables and cast a wan light in the dark room. The inn's primary attraction was that it was a place one could go unnoticed. Anonymity was valuable.

Lucan watched Branna descend the stairs from her room. Yesterday, they'd bought her a new gown, colored a light green that matched her eyes and with long sleeves to guard her from the chill. She'd caught her silken hair up in a twist on the back of her head.

He'd meant what he'd said to her the night before last. She did distract him. He did want her . . . and he did worry for her life.

Solan, she was a headstrong woman. But Lucan knew well how different things were in Tir na Ban, where the women held the strongest of the magic and, therefore, the power, and the men were the brawn that protected them.

She inched her way past the inn's rowdy and disgustingly fragrant occupants on the way to the breakfast table. A sailor leaned forward and caught her by the waist as she passed, pulling her toward him.

Lucan stood, his hand on the hilt of the long knife he wore at his waist. But Branna freed herself by stamping the heel of her boot solidly on the man's instep. The sailor exclaimed loudly in pain and released her.

Lucan smiled and sat back down.

"I think these men have been away too long from society and forgotten their manners," Branna said primly in her accented Numian as she approached the table and sat down.

"I think it's beautiful women they've been away from for too long," Lucan replied and smiled as Branna colored.

"Well, whatever it is, I'll be happy to be quit of this place." She pushed her plate away, shuddering. "These men have been far too long away from mouth paste as well. That one's breath smelled like dead socabeast."

Lucan pushed the plate back to her. "You must eat."

Branna eyed the piece of bread for a moment before she picked it up and gnawed. "So what are the plans?"

Lucan sighed. "Well, some of us will take the place of some of the guards and officials. Then some of us will push our way in to take Magnus. While that is going on, some of us will be fighting the Valorian stationed around Kastum." He was deliberately vague.

Branna raised an eyebrow. "Sounds very involved."

"Now don't be sarcastic. Everyone knows what they have to do. Everyone simply needs to do it correctly and on time."

"And in which 'some of us' do you fall?"

"The one that goes in to take Magnus."

"Of course."

"I have another identity. His name is Marius Flavius Ammon. Ammon is a wealthy businessman from the east who trades spices from Pira. I have worked for years to complete that illusion. You'd be surprised how easy it is to become part of the higher portion of Numia's citizenry when you have some money to throw around." Lucan grinned. "Ammon will be attending today's meetings."

Branna raised an eyebrow in curiosity, but she did not comment. "How will I be helping today?"

Lucan leaned forward. "Well now, interesting question, that. You weren't in the original plans, were you? I would like to say you are in the *some of us* that stays at the inn in her chamber and waits until it's over."

She opened her mouth, a protest ready on her tongue.

"But that wouldn't work because you'd just follow anyway," Lucan continued sweetly. "And under no circumstances can you be in the *some of us* that does anything, and I mean anything, even remotely magical because there are Valorian swarming all over this town, not to mention many people who would love to have a pet sorceress to call their very own."

She folded her arms over her chest. "So what then, pray your lordship, am I to do?"

He sat back and studied her for a moment before speaking again. Overnight he'd thought much about the part she had to play in this. The vision had been haunting him ever since he'd discovered she'd followed him. His need to protect her battled with his desire to let her aid the rebel forces. He understood too well her need for vengeance. That was why what he was about to do would pain him greatly.

"I have been thinking about this all night, and I think I have a place for you." Lucan stood and walked to her. He reached out and motioned for her to rise. She took his hand with curiosity shining in her eyes. When she stood, he picked her up and threw her over his shoulder.

"Put me down!" she ordered.

Lucan ignored her and headed for the stairs. The occupants of the inn hooted and howled lewdly.

"Teach that wench a lesson," yelled the owner of the foot Branna had stomped.

Lucan kicked open the door to his room and tossed her down on the bed. She struggled against him, and he subdued her. His body covered hers, and he could feel her hips against his, her breasts brushing his chest. Her hair came loose from its twist and spread over the bed beneath her. He suppressed a ragged groan. All he wanted to do was let his mouth find hers, let hands find even more of her. He pushed up and away from her and went to the door. She probably wouldn't welcome that right now.

"Your part to play today is being safe and sound in your room at the inn . . . with the door locked so you cannot follow," he said.

She sat up, her hair in wild disarray around her face. "I thought you understood my need to do this! I trusted you, Lucan!"

His stomach contracted with guilt as if she'd punched him. "This is no place for you, Branna. I won't see you come to harm. I'll see Magnus brought to justice for you, for me, for Tir na Ban, and for Numia."

Branna came off the bed at him. He stepped out the door and closed it behind him. She beat on it with her fists, and Lucan thanked the Gods her words were muffled by the thick oak. He slid the key into the lock and turned it.

He leaned his head against the door. The night before last he'd said he wouldn't show concern for her, but it was a promise he couldn't keep. "I'm sorry," he said to the door, then walked away.

B RANNA PACED THE ROOM, CASTING MURDEROUS LOOKS at the door. She hadn't stopped scheming about how to get out of the room since Lucan had thrown her down on the bed.

The room had no windows, so she couldn't get out that way. She glanced around at the sparse furnishings—a dresser, a chair, and a bed. No help there.

She could try to get someone on the other side of the door to open it for her, but in view of the patrons of this particular establishment, Branna thought that idea somewhat risky. The individual might want to be repaid in a way she was not willing to accommodate.

Was there something she could use to pick the lock?

Branna went to the dresser and opened drawers, frantically looking for something to use. At the bottom of one drawer, she found a thin bit of wood. She seized it, ran to the door, and stuck it in the lock. Then she realized she didn't have the first clue how to pick it. She fumbled around, poking here and there. The wood broke off. Branna stared at the broken bit of wood still in her hand, then threw it across the room in frustration. Defeated, she went and sat on the bed.

Suddenly she knew how to get out of the room. She had some skill in the mental manipulation of objects. Not much skill, but maybe enough to help her unlock the door. She went again to the door and sat down. Concentrating on the lock with her mind, she entered it and saw how it was constructed. She saw exactly the place that needed to be pushed and which place needed to be pulled. With her mind, she tried it.

Nothing.

She drew a frustrated breath. This had never been a skill she'd been able to master. Very few far-bloods had it. Again and again she tried with methodical patience. Finally, she saw the tumbler within the lock and caught it with her mind, hearing a satisfying click. She withdrew her awareness from the lock and opened her eyes. A residual shimmering hung in the air around her. She waited until it was gone and tried the door. Success! She left the room and made her way to the street—a plan already percolating in her mind.

Kastum was a city unknown to her, and within it she had to find the costume maker, Sandria. She could not use any magic to locate the woman. That would elicit shimmering. Instead, she used her naked intuition.

Her boots clicked on the cobblestone as she made her way to where her horse was stabled. Once astride, she headed down streets and alleys, feeling her way toward the costume maker's house. Eventually Branna wandered into an area she recognized and was able to retrace the steps she and Lucan had made to Sandria's home. The same old woman Lucan had given money to was still on Sandria's street.

Surprise marked the costume maker's face when she opened the door and found Branna there. Sandria looked her up and down and tipped her chin at her. "What do you want?"

Branna got right to the point. "I've gold crowns. If you help me with my needs, I'll pay you well."

Sandria looked uncertain.

Branna became impatient. "The rebel is not the one I'm looking for. I've no designs on him." It was true . . . well, partially true.

The costume maker gave her a long, appraising look. "Every woman has designs on that man. Don't fool yourself."

Branna shook her head but wouldn't meet her gaze.

Sandria stepped closer to her. "He refused my bed the night you two came here. He never refuses my bed." She braced her hands on her hips and nodded at her. "You've some hold on him."

"I've no hold on him. Sandria, truly, I need your aid." She looked at her meaningfully. "It's for a cause we both believe in."

Sandria stood staring at her for several long moments before stepping back and motioning her into the house. Branna stepped over the threshold, and Sandria closed the door behind them.

"If what you need is for the Opposition, girl, you don't have to ask me twice," Sandria said.

Two hours and five falcon-head crowns later found Branna dressed in the finest gown she'd ever seen, let alone worn. It was made of watered silk in the palest shade of rose. The dress was tight at the waist and then gathered and fell to her feet, which were clad in the softest of doeskin slippers. The dress bared her shoulders fully and the décolleté dipped, showing the swell of her breasts to best advantage. It was the height of Numian fashion, and that was the look she needed to pursue her plans.

Sandria had done her hair, piling it high on top of her head in a mass of twists, swirls, and coilings. It dripped with false indigo star-stones.

The costume maker had also carefully painted her lips a light shade of red, blushed her cheekbones pink, and lined her Tirian eyes with kohl. Branna felt like a rich child's doll.

She wound a cape around her shoulders and thanked the woman. Then she stepped out into the street, headed for the stables that sheltered her mare. Sandria had given her another thing she'd needed . . . the location of the trade meetings.

CHAPTER SIXTEEN

B RANNA RODE SIDESADDLE TOWARD THE MAYOR'S
sprawling residence. Four gigantic pillars graced the front of
the white building, shading a large porch. The four-story house
had more windows than she could count. At the front, stable boys
in house livery rushed around taking horses from arriving guests,
and servants ushered the attendees through the double doors.

This was the first day of the trade meetings, and all of the region's most important business people had come for it. Somewhere
between these walls Magnus waited for her blade.

That thought halted the butterflies in her stomach and spurred
her on. She rode straight up to the front door and let a serving boy
take the mare.

She approached the Valorian guarding the front door, her head
held high. "I'm here to see Marius Flavius Ammon."

"What possible business could you have with Flavius Ammon?" the Valorian asked with lewd insinuation.

Branna's eyes snapped with anger. "I am his wife."

The Valorian looked surprised. "His wife? Excuse me, madam. I had no idea he was married."

Branna straightened her skirts and thought of a comment that would reinforce the supposed difference in their ranks and make him uneasy. "Well, you wouldn't know, would you, since you are a soldier and he a wealthy businessman? You don't exactly sit around chatting, do you?"

The soldier blushed. "Flavius Ammon is quite friendly with us, madam, but, please, excuse my impertinence."

She sniffed. "I don't. Now let me through and call my husband to me this instant." Branna pushed past the soldier and into the building's foyer. Her hands shook with nervousness, and she wound them into her cape to hide them.

The soldier followed. "Right away, Madam Flavius."

Branna glanced around. The floor of the foyer was marble. Paintings of men that had long since died hung on the walls. She assumed they were the former mayors of Kastum. An expensive-looking vase brimming with fresh blooms of amberdine sat on a table to her right.

"Wife? I have no"—Lucan turned the corner and stopped in his tracks—"time for this." He walked toward her with doom in his eyes. "Madam, don't you realize wives don't accompany their husbands to business meetings?" He said it sweetly . . . through a clenched jaw.

She smiled. "This one does."

If it were not for Lucan's eyes, Branna might never have recognized him. His face was clean shaven, except for a false moustache that adorned his upper lip and a small goatee he'd fixed to his face.

He'd caught his hair up under a wig several shades lighter than his natural color, and his eyebrows had been altered to look much bushier. A dusting of silver in his facial hair and the hair at his temples completed the transformation.

He wore a collarless shirt with buttons down the right side and a pair of silken trousers—the fashion for the Numian merchant class. A sword hung from his belt. Numian men wore decorative swords. However, Branna knew Lucan's weapon was not just for show. Its handle was wrapped with leather, and she knew the mark of the Dragon Throne glittered underneath it.

Lucan turned to the Valorian and grimaced, but Branna suspected he was actually trying to smile. "She's so adorable. She simply cannot stand to be apart from me. We're newly wedded, you know."

The Valorian nodded as if it suddenly all made sense and went out the front door and back to his post.

Lucan turned to her and said under his breath, "How did you get out of the room?"

"Never lock a sorceress in a room and never keep a Tirian from her destiny. Those are your lessons for the day," she whispered back angrily. A man passed through the foyer, and Lucan and Branna nodded to him and smiled.

"Walk with me, madam. We need to have words." Lucan looped his arm through hers. "I don't even want to know how you managed to find that dress or have your hair done," Lucan muttered. "But"—he swept his eyes down the length of her—"you look perfect."

"It's amazing what a few coins can do." She smiled at a man passing by.

Lucan pulled her into a dark alcove, pressing her against the wall so she was but a hair's breadth from him. Her nostrils filled with the scent of spicewood soap. If there was a smell she'd like to die smelling, that was it.

His breath caught, and he swore softly. Without warning, his mouth descended on hers. The feel of his lips, gentle yet demanding, tore her breath away. Her mind awhirl, she barely registered the rough sensation of the fake moustache. She made a sound in her throat, closed her eyes, and returned his kiss.

His body pressed against hers, and she could feel his chest, hard and soft at the same time, against her own. His hands found her waist and encircled it. She traced his upper arms with her hands, feeling the muscles that bunched there. She should be pulling away, but she couldn't. It felt so perfect to be in his arms and have his lips on hers.

His tongue brushed hers. She noted somewhere under her pleasurable haze that he tasted of mint.

He broke the kiss and pulled away. "Forgive me."

She swallowed hard. She didn't trust herself to speak. Feeling boneless as she was, she barely trusted herself to stand. She shook her head.

"You've put yourself in much danger by coming here," he whispered. "Magnus is in the main meeting room. He's brought a sorceress with him. I must go soon. You will have to entertain yourself. This is not Tir na Ban. You won't be allowed in with the men."

Branna nodded.

"When the festivities begin, try to stay out of the way."

She glared at him.

A young man in servant's clothes passed by the alcove, did a double take, then came toward them. Despite his disguise, she recognized Ren immediately. "My lady," he said as he bowed to her. He gave her his signature lopsided grin. "I'm not at all surprised to see you here." He turned to Lucan. "Lord Flavius, you are wanted in the meeting room now. Everything is set to begin."

"Should you become separated from me today, Branna, meet me back at the Messenger." Lucan left with Ren at his heels.

Branna watched them walk away, fear and tension tickling her stomach. What should she do now? She closed her eyes and prayed to the Goddess for direction.

A strange humming began in her mind. She opened her eyes in confusion, stepped from the alcove, and walked down the corridor toward the sound. The humming grew louder. She rounded a corner and came face-to-face with a woman. The sound intensified, transforming into an unbearable screaming. Branna clapped her hands over her ears. The woman looked at her curiously and then made a motion with her hand. The air around her shimmered for a moment and the screaming stopped.

"So you are the sorceress that got away," the woman said, her eyes narrowing. "You are no Ilerian," she stated in Tirian.

Branna froze. She'd given herself away by reacting to the mental signal that this woman, Magnus's sorceress, had placed for other sorceresses to hear. She'd fallen into a trap.

"I cannot understand a word you're saying," Branna replied in Numian.

The woman reached out and caught Branna's necklace, fingering the crystal raven. "Really?" she said, arching an eyebrow.

The woman wore a girdle that encased her slim waist and dripped with real star-stones interspersed with tiny bells that tinkled as she moved. The woman's reddish-gold hair tumbled over her shoulders, framing a face with full lips, high cheekbones, and the classic, almond-shaped Tirian eyes.

Those Tirian eyes widened, and she dropped the necklace, sudden realization marking her face. "You are the high priestess? You are the Raven?"

There was no reason for subterfuge. "Yes," Branna replied in her native tongue. She searched the woman's eyes for some hint of recognition. This was one of the lost sorceresses of Tir na Ban, abducted so long ago—a countrywoman. Branna needed to be careful nonetheless. This woman may well have been turned toward Magnus's agenda, having lived so long in Numia. Also, the perverted magic she'd felt yesterday had not left her mind.

"What is your name?" Branna asked, holding a hand out to her.

"Nia," she said as if in awe.

"I am Branna ta Cattia." When Nia didn't take her offered hand, she dropped it.

Nia's eyes widened. "Ta Cattia? Cattia ta Sorcha?"

"Yes." Her grandmother's name had been Sorcha.

Nia cast her eyes downward. "I knew your mother well."

"I have come to free you and the others who were taken during the Terror."

Nia shook her head, as though waking from a dream. "It's too late." She placed her fingers to her temple, as though receiving a mental message. She turned and began to run down the hallway.

"Wait!" Branna cried and started down the hall after her.

L UCAN TRIED NOT TO STARE AT HIS UNCLE. HE STILL could not believe that after all these years he was actually in the same room with him. Magnus had aged since last he saw him, but not as much as he should have. The sorceresses were doing something to keep him younger. That meant Magnus would stay in power far longer than nature would decree. Perhaps that was why he had not yet concerned himself with producing heirs.

Magnus's long white hair was tied at the nape of his neck. He tented his fingers on the table in front of him. They glittered with rings that had once belonged to Lucan's father. Lucan's hands shook in sudden rage, and he put them under the table.

"In response to those who've expressed concern about trade with the province of Pira, I have implemented a new rate for their mineral exports. I trust you shall have no more complaints of high costs in that area," Magnus stated.

Lucan sighed as the men around him expressed their approval. The province of Pira was already impoverished because of Magnus's trade policies. The people there were starving and enslaved by the gem and mineral mines.

Lucan let his gaze fall on Lord Crispus. He sat ever at Magnus's right hand. He remembered Crispus well from the palace at Ta'Ror. He was part Ilerian and had been Arturo's apprentice. Crispus had never been able to train his Ilerian magic to heel, and his inability to tame his own magic had distorted him. Since he could not control his gifts, he'd turned his hand to controlling beings weaker than himself—the palace dogs, unfortunate serving girls, and wounded prisoners—tormenting them in sick, stomach-churning ways.

Once Gallus and Arturo had discovered the violent manner in which Crispus vented his frustrations, he'd been banned from Ta'Ror. Magnus had brought him back, letting Crispus hone his tainted tendencies into a high art of torture. Aye, Crispus was a right dangerous man—intelligent, cruel, and half insane.

The meeting ended with the participants quite happy. Lucan watched them leave. One benefit of having Ammon as an alternate personality was finding out who the corrupt businessmen were. Unfortunately, Lucan was about to lose that mode of gathering information. Ammon was about to out himself, ending years of successful subterfuge.

Lucan stood up and approached Magnus. "My lord," he began. Crispus turned toward him as he spoke. "I would have a word with you . . . in private. I have a proposal to make that I don't think you'll want to miss."

"Flavius Ammon, is it not?"

"Yes, my lord."

"Can you not say what you would here?"

"No, my lord," Lucan whispered. "Truly, we need privacy for what I have to say."

Magnus began walking toward the door. Crispus broke in, "Flavius Ammon, Emperor Magnus has no time for this now."

Lucan's heart sank. If he could not lure Magnus into a room alone, it would be much more difficult to execute his plan. He needed some time alone with Magnus, before the Valorian guard and Magnus's sorceress discovered what was happening.

"There is a time limit for my proposal," Lucan called after him. It was not untrue.

Magnus stopped and turned. He went silent for several long moments before speaking. "Very well then."

Crispus motioned them into a room on the left. Lucan had been counting on an appeal to Magnus's greed to carry them through this part of the plan.

Magnus and Lucan entered the room. Immediately, Lucan removed his wig and peeled off the false moustache and goatee. "What is your propo—" Magnus began. Recognition blossomed on Magnus's face. "Lucan . . ." he breathed. "I thought you were dead."

Lucan had wanted to take him by surprise, and by the look on Magnus's face, he'd done it. He tossed the disguise to the floor and slowly began to unwrap the leather from the handle of his sword, baring the emblem of the Dragon Throne.

"Here is my proposal," Lucan said. "You give me back what you stole from me so I can right the wrongs you've done to Numia and its provinces, and in doing so you go to the Underworld for your crimes that much lighter." Lucan raised his sword and took a step toward his uncle.

Magnus unsheathed his own sword, and Lucan saw that his blade was not merely for show either. Warily, they circled each other. "You should have stayed dead," Magnus said, smiling. "Now I'll finish what I failed to do fourteen years ago."

Lucan raised his sword. "I think not. I've come a long way since I was your pupil."

"So have I."

They engaged.

CHAPTER SEVENTEEN

Branna followed Nia down the hallway and up a flight of stairs. Battle sounds spilled out of a large room with double doors, along with both Valorian and rebels. Nia ran straight into the fray.

Branna followed, hugging the wall and trying to stay clear of the men who were engaged in swordplay. Morgan fought a Valorian across the room. They locked swords, and the soldier forced Morgan down onto the long table that dominated the room. Morgan, in a sudden swell of strength from his powerful body, pushed up and freed himself. Another Valorian approached him from behind, readying his sword for Morgan's back. He turned just in time to block the blow and fell the man, then whirled and caught the first soldier in the midsection.

Lucan's voice came from a room off the main chamber. Branna made her way there. Nia stood just inside the doorway, her eyes out of focus and her hands fisted at her sides. The air shimmered around her as she cast a shield spell for her lord. Lucan went at Magnus, but his sword bounced off him. Magnus laughed and attacked Lucan with a renewed vengeance.

One of Lucan's men, who'd seen that Nia was keeping a protective spell over Magnus, ran at her with his sword raised.

"No!" Branna cried. She flew at Nia, knocking her out of the man's way. They tumbled on the floor together in a tangle of arms and legs, causing the shield spell to break. The rebel came at them both, not realizing Branna was on the side of the Opposition.

"No!" Lucan's voice rang out. "Stay away from her," he ordered the man. The rebel backed away.

"What, nephew?" Magnus taunted. "Are you distracted by a bit of skirt?"

Lucan's sword clashed against Magnus's blade, and he pushed him back a step. "I'm not distracted at all . . . Uncle."

Branna used brute force to keep Nia pinned to the floor and her arms at her sides. "What do you do?" She glared down at the struggling woman. "You aid the man who caused the downfall of your homeland? Do you forget Magnus is the man who killed your country people, your kin, my mother, Cattia? What sort of spell have you put yourself under?"

"Let me up!" cried Nia. The sorceress freed one arm and brought it up to strike at Branna. Instead, she grabbed the pendant at Branna's throat and pulled it free. Nia went still and stared at it dangling from her fingers. "If I don't do what he wishes, the other sorceresses will die and the Valorian will cause more suffering in Tir na Ban."

Branna relaxed her grip on the woman. That was what had kept Nia loyal to such a monster. Fear and the weight of responsibility had perverted the magic Branna had felt the night before. Nia took the opportunity to bolt upright and push Branna back.

"I have no wish to hurt you, but I must do as I am bid," Nia said, standing. "Don't attempt to interfere again, or I shall hurt you. My magic does not heed the Goddess's law anymore."

The air shimmered as Nia renewed her concentration on the shield spell.

Branna stood up and entered her own spell, shooting a hand toward Lucan. The shimmering around her grew bright. "The Raven chose me because my magic is strong, Nia, stronger than yours."

Magnus found an opening and swung his sword at Lucan's chest. It would have been a deathblow, but it hit Branna's field of protection. This time it was Magnus's turn to curse. Magnus turned toward Branna, his eyes narrowing. He hefted his sword and came at her.

She took a step backward but did not run.

"Branna!" Lucan yelled. He catapulted himself over a chair that lay on the floor and intercepted Magnus before he could reach her. They fought at a stalemate; while both shields were in place, neither one could maim the other.

"If I were you, I wouldn't make such assumptions about the strength of my magic, Raven," Nia said. A humming began in Branna's ears. It grew in intensity until it was screaming. Branna cried out and clapped her hands to her ears in an effort to make it stop even though the sound was within her mind. She tried to hold on to the shield spell and not pass out. Keening in pain, she fell to her knees. With a sob, she loosed her hold on the shield spell.

A Valorian took aim at her head with his sword, but Morgan pulled him off balance before he could swing. The sword sliced the air above her head. Morgan caught the man in the stomach with his blade, then he pulled her to her feet and guided her away.

Morgan grabbed a large vase from the floor and used it to shatter the glass of a window. "I'm sorry, Branna," she heard him say near her ear. Then he pushed her . . . hard. She fell through the air and landed with a thump in the thick amberdine bushes below. She lay for a moment in shock from the fall and thankful the screaming had stopped. Rolling over, she freed herself from the bushes and stood up. With twigs and leaves caught in her hair, she stared at the building. Valorian and rebels engaged on every floor. There would be no way for her to gain entry into the building.

"No!" A helpless sob escaped her, and she doubled over in fear and grief. How could Lucan hope to defeat Magnus with the shield spell in place? She'd failed him.

In front of her, a first-floor window shattered. A Valorian soldier scrambled out of it and came at her. "You . . . stop! The emperor would like to speak with you."

Branna picked up her skirts and ran, the soldier fast behind her. He reached out and grabbed her hair, pulling her to the ground. Pain ripped through her scalp, and she kicked, screamed, and fought. Remembering something Fiall had taught her, she brought her knee up hard, solidly connecting with the man's groin. The Valorian grunted, rolled off her, and curled into fetal position. Branna scrambled to her feet and ran as fast as she could away from him. She wasted no time getting back to the Messenger.

The city was in chaos, and the dining room of the inn was empty save for a few hardened men who, apparently, found the bloodshed in the streets nothing new nor of interest. Branna's dress was soiled and ripped, and her hair had come down with false star-stones still clinging to it.

Branna found a table in the corner and nervously worked the star-stones out of her hair. In hopelessness, she dropped them to the establishment's floor. Tears stung her eyes.

Afternoon turned to evening and the fires were lit in the dining room. Branna had heard that the Valorian and the rebels were deadlocked in a battle that neither side seemed able to turn in their favor. The Opposition held its ground only because many of the citizens had taken to the streets in their aid.

Finally, after evening had turned to night, a weary man entered the inn. He stumbled forward, his dark hair lank and falling into his eyes. Dark blood crusted his forehead and chest. The fine merchant's clothing he wore was ripped and dirty. He braced himself on his sword as he limped.

Branna stood and ran to him. She embraced him, going up on tiptoe to rub her cheek against his. With all the occupants of the inn watching, she wound her arm around him and helped him up the stairs.

LUCAN LAY ON THE BED WITH HIS EYES CLOSED. HE wanted to sleep, but there was no time. "We must go, Branna. The rebels won't take Kastum today." He tried to stand.

She pressed him back down onto the bed. "You are in no shape to go anywhere right now."

Her hands went to him, unbuttoning his bloody shirt and sliding it off. She ran cool fingers across his chest, arms, and back, ascertaining if there were any grievous injuries. Lucan knew she'd only find minor ones. Her warm breath teased the hair on his chest as her hands went to the drawstrings of his pants, undoing them. She slid them down and off, leaving him in only his undergarment. When she ran her hands along his legs, her long hair brushed his thigh.

Lucan didn't feel the pain of his injuries anymore. He only

wanted her to keep her hands on him. She touched him gently but dispassionately, as a physician might, but the blush of her cheek betrayed her. She enjoyed touching him as much he liked having her hands on him . . . even under these circumstances.

"I must find some water, soap, and rags," she said, her voice shaking a bit. "You have nothing life threatening, only a few wounds warranting a healing, but all your injuries should still be cleaned." She stood and went to the door. She turned. "Where is Ren?"

"I lost him at the mayor's house. Morgan stayed near him."

"What of Magnus?"

Lucan turned his head to the side in shame. "I lost him. There is more fighting ahead because I failed to take the head of the beast."

"You could not be expected to defeat Magnus and his entire Valorian in one day, Lucan."

He turned his gaze back to her. "The sorceress stopped aiding Magnus after you'd gone."

"Really?"

"If you hadn't been there she wouldn't have stopped casting for him. She was disturbed by your presence."

"She nearly killed me with her twisted magic."

He smiled. "Aye . . . and Morgan almost killed you by pushing you out of a second-story window."

She laughed. "'Twould have been better than death by mental screaming."

"Thank you for being there, Branna. If you hadn't shown up, Magnus would have kept his shield, and I might not have lived to fight another day."

"More important, the world would have lost a very great and special man." Her expression hardened. "Even though he locks women away in their rooms when they won't obey him, and—"

"Kisses them when they're not expecting it?"

Branna simply blushed, turned, and left the room. She returned with everything she needed and proceeded to wipe a wet cloth over the nicks and cuts decorating his neck, arms, chest, and abdomen. She performed a healing on the sword cuts marking his torso, thigh, and head.

Gingerly, she blotted away the blood on his temple, very intent on her work. Lucan smiled. Her beautiful mouth was held in a straight line, and all her muscles were tense. He longed to take her in his arms and kiss her to distraction.

Sweet Solan . . . she smelled good. He leaned forward, inhaling her scent. She started to pull away. Before he could stop himself he caught her around the waist and drew her to him.

She braced her hands on his shoulders.

He spoke near her mouth in a voice made rough by desire. "Was my kiss really so distasteful? You seemed to enjoy it."

"I—"

He cut her off by brushing his lips against hers, needing to taste her. Her chest pressed against his, and he felt the rise and fall of her breasts as her breathing quickened. Her breath tasted sweet. Teasingly, he moved his mouth over hers, barely kissing her. He wanted to prolong things before he parted her lips and took her in a deeper kiss.

Faint sounds came from the streets outside. Valorian soldiers knocked door-to-door, demanding to search homes and establishments for any remaining Opposition. He pulled away. "Do you hear that?"

Branna listened, her eyes widening.

"We need to leave," said Lucan. He swung his legs over the side of the bed and stood. Quickly, he drew his clothes on and then held his hand out to her. There was no time to delay.

Branna stood, but her knees buckled and she had to sit back down again.

"Are you all right?" he asked.

She nodded. "I'm ... I'm fine," she stammered. She stood and followed him out the door and down the stairs.

CHAPTER EIGHTEEN

THE DARKNESS WORKED IN THEIR FAVOR. THEY DARTED from shadow to shadow, making their way to the stables to get their horses.

Any disorientation Branna felt from Lucan brushing his lips against hers was gone by the time they reached the street. The cold wind slapped the very breath right out of her. Equally chilling was the fact that Valorian now scoured the streets for Opposition. But the taste of Lucan on her lips had not yet faded despite all that.

Just as she turned a corner, Lucan grabbed her around the waist and pulled her into the shadows. Not five feet away, four Valorian rode by on horseback. They waited for the soldiers to travel a distance down the road. The feeling of Lucan pressing his body against hers brought the kisses they'd shared back to her in a flood. His breath came fast and harsh, and his arms enveloped her. She closed her eyes as his scent invaded her nostrils—leather and man. It sent waves of longing crashing through her.

He put his mouth near her ear. "I want you to stay close to me, Branna," he whispered. "So close I can feel your heartbeat." All she could do was nod.

When the Valorian were gone, Lucan took her hand and they stepped out from the shadows. They watched to make sure no Valorian were within or around the stable, then crossed the street and entered. Something moved on their left and before Branna could even draw a breath to scream, Lucan had drawn his long knife and placed it against the man's throat.

"Morgan." Lucan lowered his knife. "Is Ren with you?"

"I have some bad news." Morgan stepped forward into a swath of moonlight. Intense fatigue etched his handsome face . . . and deep sorrow. He looked much older than his twenty-five years. Branna knew then what he would say. She'd seen that look on so many faces, so many times. It was the look of someone who'd lost a thing dear to them.

Morgan looked toward the ground and Lucan's eyes followed. Ren lay in the hay at Morgan's feet. A low sound escaped Lucan. He knelt and took the boy into his arms.

"He attempted to take Commander Armillon, of all people," Morgan said wearily. "I couldn't get to him in time."

Lucan picked the boy up. Ren lay limp against him; blood covered his face and arms. In the moonlight, Branna saw Lucan's face set like a steel mask. "Let's ride."

THEY RODE HARD AND FAST AWAY FROM KASTUM. LUcan was unapproachable. He rode ahead and did not say a word for the entire journey. His shoulders were stooped as if under an unbearable weight, and he kept Ren cradled in his lap.

They finally stopped near an abandoned temple of Solan. Branna felt they'd gone very far out of their way. They'd ridden nearly straight south when Kern lay to the north, but neither Branna nor Morgan mentioned it.

They buried Ren near the temple, in the easternmost part of the grounds. They carried rocks to place on his cairn, and Branna adorned Ren's grave with autumn flowers and long twigs of fragrant trees. She said a prayer to the Goddess for his safekeeping . . . the boy with the fire-streaked hair, clear brown eyes, and lopsided grin. As they stood next to Ren's cairn, Morgan and Branna shared a concerned glance over Lucan's bowed head.

They made a small fire, not large enough to call attention to themselves, near the temple.

The night seemed to last forever. Branna doubted dawn would ever come. She searched the skies for some sign of morning light, but there was none to be found. Even the Sisters were almost totally hidden by cloud cover, making the skies a fathomless black.

Morgan finally fell asleep three paces to her right. His breathing came harsh and exhausted. Branna feigned sleep. She knew Lucan was still awake, staring into the fire. She could feel him near her, even when her eyes were closed.

She heard him get up and leave the camp. Rolling to her side, she saw him retreating into the woods with his sword in one hand and a torch in the other.

L UCAN HELD THE TORCH IN HIS LEFT HAND. IN HIS right, he grasped the Dragon Blade. The sword seemed to burn his hand every bit as much as the torch had the potential to. All he wanted was to get rid of the length of steel.

He knew where the lake was—could find it in his sleep. As he came out between two tall oak trees, it was there, spreading before him like a gift from the Gods themselves.

But then, the Gods never gave gifts.

He placed the torch in the holder he knew would be there. He'd placed torches in that holder many times in his life.

Lucan didn't hesitate. He wrapped both hands over sword's handle and hefted it out into the open air above the lake. With a mixture of horror and satisfaction, he watched it sink below the surface of the water.

To his right, a figure swathed in pale pink bolted from the woods. Branna dove into the water after it. The smooth water closed over her head with nary a ripple. She emerged like some ethereal spirit sent from Solan, dragging the sword behind her. She walked to him and, with effort, sunk the tip into the ground before him.

She was dripping wet and spoke breathlessly. "It's not a light charge, but you are the only one worthy enough to take it up. You are weary, I know. But there will be peace when you are through."

He could feel the difference in their ages suddenly. He was only eight years older than she, but it felt like a chasm. She stood before him with the fire of youth in her blood, ready to take on all obstacles, believing in the absolute power of the *Parcae*. She believed that good always defeated evil. Blood and corruption had long since vanquished such idealistic notions from his mind.

His gaze dropped to the sword. The dragon glittered on the handle, staring at him balefully with its one green eye. He reached out and traced it with his finger.

"This was my father's sword. It was smuggled out and brought to me after he'd been killed. It has plagued me ever since," he said. "The Dragon Throne is a seat I never wanted."

"Lucan, I have knowledge you don't possess. It's past time I imparted it." She wiped strands of wet hair from her eyes. "It may ease you." He could see her warm breath hit the cold air as she spoke.

Lucan took off his cloak and put it around her shoulders. "Let us go where you can be warm and we can talk, and I'll show you the seat I would have preferred."

He took the Dragon Blade and the torch from its holder and led her through the woods, into the back of the main temple of Solan.

It had been a place of beauty once. At one time there had been gold inlaid in the walls. Now, the temple, and all the temples of Numia, had been looted. The Valorian had pillaged, prying the very gold veins from the marble. They had raped the priestesses, murdered the priests, and sent the students away. There was to be no religion in Magnus's vision of Numia, no Gods to detract from his glory. They'd done the same in the provinces, destroying the temples of the Gods of Pira and Bah'ra, the All-Father of Angelyn— all the Deities of the One. Magnus allowed only a few chapels scattered throughout Numia and its provinces, just enough to keep the people from staging a revolt.

Lucan heard Branna's breath catch as they entered the structure. Their footsteps echoed as they neared the center of the room. The walls cut the wind, and since they were hidden, he could build a large fire that would warm her.

Lucan went to gather wood and brush outside. When he came back, Branna had discarded her wet clothing and wrapped herself again in his cloak. The thought of her sweet bare skin next to his cloak made pleasure settle in his loins. He placed brush into a large bowl carved from a stone pillar in the center of the room and set his torch to it. The fire flamed up and the brush crackled.

He fed the wood to it until it was roaring. Then he laid her gown out to dry.

She stood in the center of the room, looking around her. "This is where you would have preferred to be? You wanted to be a priest of Solan?" She did not wait for him to answer. "Then you are him," she said in a wondering rush of breath.

"Who? Who am I, Branna? Perhaps you can tell me, because I don't know. I was the fourth son of a king and was never meant to rule. It was Cassius who would have become king, and Artus behind him, and Maron behind him. The chances of my ever finding the Dragon Throne were slim. I was meant to be here . . . a priest. It was against my father's wishes. He wanted me to follow in the footsteps of Magnus and become commander of the Northern Valorian for Cassius. It was ever a bone of contention between us." Lucan shook his head sadly. "It was here where I found my freedom. The mysteries of Solan were always more suited to me than the sword."

"Then you must have been an impressive initiate, because your skill with a sword is better than I've ever seen. You are a better warrior than even the men of Tir na Ban."

"Not good enough. I wasn't good enough to save Ren."

She closed the distance between them, stood in front of him, and found his gaze. The firelight licked her face. "I have known many boys of Ren's ilk, and I understand Ren's need. He needed to fight the Valorian. Nothing you could have done would've stopped him from doing so. Had you forbade him, he would have found another way."

When Lucan would have turned away from her, she reached her hand out and caught his arm. "He knew full well the danger of what he did. It is not your fault, nor Morgan's fault, that he is gone," she said.

He looked down at her. Her hair, still damp, spread like a raven's wing over the cloak, and her eyes glittered with emotion—emotion she felt for him, for Ren. "Branna, you are what my soul needs," he told her in a soft voice. Her breath caught and she went very still.

He slid his hand around to cup the nape of her neck, his fingers tangling in her hair, and took her mouth the way he'd wanted to in Kastum, deep and possessively. She returned his kiss with every bit as much passion, and it caused waves of desire to roll through him. His teeth nipped her bottom lip, and she folded herself into him, giving up every bit of rigidity, and parted her lips under his. His tongue met hers, tasting her sweetness.

Sweet Solan. He could feel the curves and hollows of her body under the cloak. If he reached his hand within, she'd be his to caress. Lucan groaned at the thought and intensified his attentions at her mouth, even as he rose and stiffened for her. She made a small sound of pleasure in her throat that nearly undid him. Lucan pressed himself against her so she could feel his arousal.

With every trespass she allowed him, he became bolder. He parted the cloak and let it hang precariously on her shoulders. Her skin was soft and warm. He wound his hands around her waist and drew her close to him, deepening the kiss. Then he let his hands stray to caress her back, her stomach, her breasts. Her nipples hardened when he ran his thumbs over them, teasing them. Branna responded to his touch with a quickening of her breath. He put his mouth to the pulse at her throat. It fluttered against his lips.

CHAPTER NINETEEN

B RANNA DID NOT MERELY FEEL LUCAN'S MOUTH ON
hers, or his hands moving over her body.

The essence of him went through her like a bolt of rich, silken energy, permeating everything she was. Her body, along with her emotions, responded to him in a way that was wholly foreign to her.

She had found her priest, her consort, at long last.

The first flickering of power, her magic, rose from within her, ready to reach up and out of her and consume them both. Light clouded her mind, and her consciousness split. Her body was with Lucan, but her mind . . . fell. No, not fell, flew through the air. Darkness surrounded her, and wind rushed past her as something catapulted her from a source of light. Beside her she felt a presence—Lucan. She couldn't see him. She simply knew it was him. The essence of him went through her like a silken rope, tying them through a millennia and beyond. The bond they shared held them close—through birth, death, and rebirth—always connected . . .

Branna gasped and pulled away from him, her eyes wide with surprise. She'd never expected this . . . never. It had the potential to change everything. She couldn't meet his eyes. Morenna's stars . . . how could such a thing be? Gripping the edge of a stone pillar, she tried to calm herself. Lucan was not simply her consort . . . oh no . . . nothing as simple as that. How could the Goddess be so cruel?

Branna pulled the cloak around her. Her eyes darkened as she turned to him. "I . . . I need to tell you some things."

Confusion marked Lucan's face. She wanted to drop the cloak and go to him. She wanted to bring him to lay with her on the floor of the temple and offer herself as woman to a man, but what she'd just discovered precluded all that.

She steadied herself before speaking. "You have an object in your possession, an eight-pointed star. You wear it around your neck on a chain. It is a key, Lucan. One you must have obtained somehow from Magnus. This is very important key. It unlocks *Draiochta Cothrom*."

Lucan looked bewildered. Branna knew his confusion was more from her abrupt departure from his arms than what she'd just imparted. He fished the key out from under his shirt and showed it to her. "You speak of this?"

"Yes."

He shook his head. "I have heard stories of that book, *Draiochta Cothrom*, but they are for children. It is called the Book of Magical Balance in Numian. There is no truth to these tales."

"Like many things of Tir na Ban, the legends are often more true than not. It is a very powerful book that was once kept in my homeland. Magnus found out about the book and its power. That is why he came to Tir na Ban first, before conquering any other country, to take the book. It was a threat to him, you see. The book contains a spell that will equalize and disperse magic over these lands."

He looked doubtful. "What do you mean, equalize and disperse?"

"Over the years certain truths have been realized by both Tir na Ban and Ileria. One of these truths is that our world is made of layers of energetic wave patterns. We are a part of the fabric they create. When that is understood, it is short step to tap into them, change them. It is these acts which people call high magic. Magic is simply the ability to alter the Universal Fabric."

Simply... Branna realized belatedly that Lucan would not think it so simple.

He drew a breath, held it, and then expelled it. "What does the book do?"

"The spell in *Draiochta Cothrom* alters that fabric, makes magic accessible to many people, instead of just those who have come to the truths on their own. The ritual would grant magic to people all over Terrestra."

"Magic in everyone's hands?" His eyes darkened. "That would cause chaos of incredible proportion."

She paced back and forth as she spoke. "That is what the priestesses of Tir na Ban always believed. That is why, even though it was the will of the Goddess the spell be performed, it was not. The book was kept secret and guarded by Tirian warriors. Magnus knew if the spell was worked and many others had magic, his own power would be diminished. He knew he would not be able to hold his empire if he did not control all the magic, and that the priestesses of Tir na Ban would work the spell in order to defeat him."

He drew a hand through his hair. "You wish to find the book and work the spell?"

"Yes."

"What is the good in swapping one chaotic force for another?"

She stopped in front of him and shook her head. "The world is meant to have that magic. Change, evolution, is an inevitable part of life. You must understand that those who will develop magic as a result of the spell will be those who have certain . . . understandings. Most of them won't be evil."

"Most."

"Every gift has its price."

He glanced away. "Aye, the Gods give nothing for free, do they?" Bitterness traced his voice.

"There's more."

"Of course."

Branna turned from him and wrapped her arms over her chest as if in protection. "Besides the odds against us even finding *Draiochta Cothrom*, and getting it away from Magnus, we would need many trained sorceresses to work the spell. Despite these challenges, I know it will come to pass."

"How do you know?"

"I have dreamt of this since I was a child, since before the Terror . . . before Magnus ever even took power. In my dream there is a circle of sorceresses and in the center of the circle a high priestess and priest. They represent the Tirian Goddess and the Numian God of the Overworld, Solan—both part of the One. They represent the Balance. Together, they create the conduit that will allow the equalization to take place. I am the priestess, and I knew I had to find the priest." She turned toward him and held his gaze. "And I have found him."

He shook his head. "I am no priest."

"You may not be formally a priest now, no. There are no priests in Numia anymore. But you were an initiate of Solan, a young priest of the first caste?" She made it a question.

He looked up. "Yes."

"And you are the one with the key. Those two things alone are enough to make me think you are probably he, but there is something else. I'm now completely sure you are the priest from my dream, but I . . . I've only just learned of it."

Branna turned and looked at the entrance of the temple. Light streamed in through the opening. Dawn had finally arrived.

She closed her eyes, savoring the moment. She'd waited so long to find the priest.

"Branna, what is it?" asked Lucan.

Footsteps sounded outside the temple, and Branna opened her eyes. A figure stood in the doorway, backlit by morning light. Morgan stepped into the firelit chamber. She saw him take note of her, wrapped in Lucan's cloak, and of her gown laid out near the fire. Morgan raised an eyebrow. "Am I interrupting something?"

"Yes," replied Lucan. "What is it?"

"I've seen signs of Valorian in the area, my lord. I believe we should ride."

Lucan hesitated. He closed his eyes with an expression of fatigue on his face. "Aye," he said with a sigh. "We're coming." He took up her gown and walked toward the door.

Her hand went to her throat, searching for the raven pendant. She gasped.

Lucan turned. "What is it?"

"My pendant, it's gone! The woman, Nia, she ripped it from my neck in Kastum. She must still have it."

"What does that mean?" asked Morgan.

"It means she has an object of mine, a personal link. She can make contact with me mentally."

"Can she hurt you?" Lucan asked, concern clear in his voice.

She shook her head. "No . . . no . . . I don't think so." Then she remembered the mental screaming and the sorceress's twisted magic and knew she'd just lied.

"I WANT THE GIRL." HE SAID IT QUIETLY, BUT MAGNUS made sure his eyes fair sparkled with threat. "I want her either dead or here at Ta'Ror. I would prefer the latter, but I'll take the former. Should she be captured, don't allow her to be harmed, but if she gives you too much trouble, kill the chit. I can get more."

Armillon leaned forward in his chair, refusing to be intimidated. "Magnus, the girl is with the rebels. If we don't know where they are, we don't know where she is." He threw a hand in the air in a gesture of helplessness. "They disappear, my lord—like ghosts. They hardly ever even leave their dead behind. Tracking them is like a nightmare. Their tracks always—"

Magnus reached out in a quick, hard motion and captured Armillon by the collar of his military tunic. Slowly, he stood, pulling the man toward him until Magnus was sure Armillon could smell his breath. "I am very tired of excuses, Armillon. I made you the commander of the Northern Valorian because I thought you were capable of doing a good job."

"Y . . . yes."

"We don't simply let people go here in the Numian Empire. We don't simply let commanders of the Valorian Guard walk away and find a replacement for them. You do know that, don't you? They either perform adequately, or we send them to Vallon where they might endeavor to improve themselves for their next life."

"I understand, my lord."

Magnus held him there for a moment longer, just to drive his point home. Then he pushed him backward, causing Armillon to stumble over the chair he'd been sitting in. He righted himself and tried to regain some of his lost dignity by straightening his tunic.

"We'll find her, my lord. We'll find her and either bring her here or kill her," Armillon asserted.

"And find my nephew and the rebels while you're at it!" roared Magnus in a sudden fit of rage. "Go!"

Armillon turned and hurried out the door.

Magnus put his fingers to his temple. It was a bad day in a bad week. Every moment had been bad since the surprise attack at Kastum.

From the back of the chamber, the soft sound of Crispus's chuckling met his ears. "Soon the rebels will mean naught anyway, Magnus. Even now we're making the final plans to take Ileria once and for all. Nothing will be able to touch you or the Numian Empire after that, my lord."

Magnus considered Crispus's words. He was right. Magnus's headache began to ease. They had to concentrate on Ileria.

He turned and looked at Crispus. "But I still must find my nephew and do what should have been done fourteen years ago. He even fights openly with the Dragon Blade. I saw it in Kastum." Magnus ground the heel of his hand into his eye. The disappearance of the sword was no longer a mystery. Someone had smuggled it out of Ta'Ror.

"We'll find him, my lord. Knowing who he is gives us an advantage. Once we find him . . . I will take care of extracting any information from him myself," said Crispus.

Magnus shivered in spite of himself. Crispus was a twisted soul. He always had been. Before Gallus had banned him from the palace grounds, he'd done things to animals that made even Magnus's skin crawl. "Aye, he's yours."

There was a knock at the door. It opened and Nia stepped through. She curtsied minutely. "Emperor Magnus. Lord Crispus," she said, her eyes cast downward. "You sent for me?" Her voice quavered.

"Yes." He took several steps toward her, the sound of his boots on the marble floor echoed through the room. "You did not do me well in Kastum, did you, Nia?"

"My lord, I did as I was asked."

"Ah, yes . . . you did until you saw that Tirian woman. Who was she that she held such sway over you? You froze like a doe confronted with a hunter's bow."

"My . . . my lord, I don't know who she was."

Magnus raised an eyebrow. "I think you're lying to me, Nia." Magnus walked toward her slowly. "I am surprised by this behavior. First you stop casting the shield for me in Kastum, and now you lie to me?"

He stopped very near her. She would not look at him. Usually, no one else would meet his eyes except Nia. It piqued his anger very much that she would not do so now. He reached out and grabbed her chin, forcing her eyes up. Still, she would not meet his gaze. He released her chin. "Show me your beautiful eyes, Nia," he commanded softly.

Slowly, she moved her gaze equal to his. "Ahh . . . that's better." He found he could not stop himself. He dipped his head and kissed her. She stiffened until she was so brittle it was as though she'd crack if he applied too much pressure. Every fiber of her being protested his lips on hers.

Frustrated, he released her and backed away, pointing a finger. "This won't go unpunished!" he said, his voice shaking. He didn't know if he wanted to punish her for her actions in Kastum, or because she wanted no part of him romantically.

He turned away from her. "Leave," he ordered. He closed his eyes and didn't open them until he heard the door close behind her.

K ERN WAS A FAIR DISTANCE AWAY FROM THE TEMPLE OF Solan. Traveling cautiously all day and into the night, they rode through the forests to bypass towns and villages. They didn't wish to attract the attention of any Valorian that might be roaming the countryside after the events in Kastum. Lucan was sure they were on high alert.

The journey had been a quiet one. For his part, he thought much of his loss. It seemed unreal to him, even after having lowered Ren into the dark womb of the earth with his own hands. It seemed any minute now the boy would come riding around a clump of trees with some newly gleaned information, his eyes lighted with possibilities. It was difficult for Lucan to come to the realization that Ren would never again fight at his side. Lucan would never watch him grow into the fine man he knew he would've been.

The reins cut into his fingers in his tight grip. Ren was gone like so many others. He wondered why he hadn't grown numb to death over time. But each new loss was as painful as the last.

Then there was everything Branna had told him in the temple about *Draiochta Cothrom*. As an initiate of Solan, he'd learned a little about high magic. He'd been taught high magic was akin to focusing your attention beyond apparent reality and then manipulating that which remained unfocused. It made Lucan's head hurt merely thinking about it. For his part, his blade was the only magic of which he'd ever had need.

Branna rode at his side, wearing an extra shirt and a pair of trews he'd had in his saddlebags that were way too large for her. He imagined he could feel the warmth of her body even from a distance. She'd been disturbingly quiet. Now she tipped her head to the night sky. The clouds had cleared and the stars shone bright. She appeared to be deep in thought. Perhaps she was upset over what had happened at the temple.

Kissing her, touching her, had complicated things. Not that Branna was any kind of innocent. The women of Tir na Ban had no requirement to keep themselves chaste. Quite the contrary, actually. The woman held authority there because it was they who had the ultimate power of procreation. Their system worked on maternal lineage, which was much easier to determine than paternal lineage.

He was bothered by the thought of Branna bedding a man other than himself. She had undoubtedly done so, however. Especially since Tir na Ban's population had been so decimated by the Terror. She would have tried to get herself with child long before now. But the thought of her wrapping her long, slender legs around another man, her mouth finding his, her breasts freed to be touched, kissed by another man's mouth, made him half-crazed. Lucan broke off the thought, dragging a hand back through his hair in deep frustration.

He would much rather envision himself covering her body, taking her nipples between his lips, sheathing himself in her silken folds.

It was probably better that she'd pulled away from him when she had. He wouldn't have stopped at anything less than laying her down on the temple floor and doing everything to her that he'd imagined since he'd met her.

Lucan watched her close her eyes. The silver wash of moonlight limned her face like the statue of the Goddess of Love in the courtyard at Callipolis. Her long, dark lashes fluttered against her cheeks as she sighed.

Every muscle in Lucan's body tensed. He had to stop himself from reaching over, catching up her horse's reins, and pulling her near him for a kiss.

Aye, it had complicated things. Lucan looked up at the stars and smiled. But if he had it do over again, he would.

T HEY ARRIVED AT KERN AT DAYBREAK, NEAR FALLING over with exhaustion. This time Lucan showed Branna how to get into and around in the tunnels of Kern. There were subtle markings on the stone walls she hadn't noticed before. Now she and Fiall would have the freedom to move within and without Kern, and that gave her mind ease.

She slid off the mare and avoided meeting Lucan's gaze. He probably felt confused after what had happened at the temple. She'd wanted his hands on her . . . Goddess knew that! She'd wanted his mouth covering hers, his breath mixing with hers. She shivered. Having him touch her had been so much better than any of her imaginings, but the vision had changed everything, complicated everything. The revelation the vision had brought required thought, and until she had time to work out everything in her mind—make things clear again—she couldn't talk with Lucan about it.

Branna quickly moved through the common room toward her chamber, keeping her eyes open for Fiall.

Fiall.

He would be angry with her, she knew. Almost as soon as she thought his name, he was there, coming up on her left side.

"Branna, I am glad to see you are back and unharmed." His body posture and voice were stiff. He fell into step beside her as she turned down the corridor toward her chamber.

Branna stopped and turned to him. "Fiall, I'm sorry I didn't tell you I was leaving. I feared you would try to prevent me from going."

"I am your protector. It is my job to look out for your well-being. I care more about you than I care about Magnus being displaced."

"I care so very much about you also, Fiall. You are like family to me. That is why I regret—"

"You blocked me mentally," he interrupted her. He'd probably sensed she meant to breach the subject of his attraction for her. Obviously, he didn't wish to speak of it.

She bowed her head. "Forgive me."

"I'm just glad to see you back safe. You will have to tell me everything that happened."

She touched his cheek, covering his scar with her palm. Fiall placed his hand over hers. She sighed and closed her eyes. "So much has happened." The sentence was said with deep feeling. She could not tell him everything. The new relationship she had with Fiall would require her to keep things related to her heart a secret.

CHAPTER TWENTY

BRANNA TOOK THE CUP ARTURO OFFERED HER. MUSIcians played in one corner of the common room. The lively sounds of flute, drum, and lute intertwined and echoed off the walls. Smoked meats, cheeses, sweet fruit, and ale were set out on a table. People talked, laughed, and danced joyously to the music in the center of the room, in celebration of their success in Kastum.

True, they had not taken the city, but the battle had been a good one for the Opposition just the same. It was the first time they'd taken a solid and impressive stance against the Valorian forces. The participants had been back for several days now, and for several days, they'd celebrated.

Branna was bathed and well rested again. She'd spent a lot of time healing the wounded from Kastum and had not seen much of Lucan since they'd been back. Obligations seemed to keep him busy. At least, she hoped it was duty that kept him away and not what had passed between them at the Temple of Solan.

She watched him lean against a wall on the opposite side of the room. In his hand he also held a cup. Morgan stood at his side.

"Your man, Fiall, paced the stronghold like a caged cliff cat while you were gone," said Arturo. "I had to show him how to get in and out of Kern before he drove us all insane." He chuckled.

"Thank you, Arturo." Memories of the prescient comments the old man had made the first time she'd met him came to mind. "I wanted to ask you—"

"About Lucan and Fiall?"

"Yes." She tipped her head in a quizzical gesture. "It is rare to meet a far-blooded male who has such strong abilities."

"Ah, well, love is easy to pick up on." He shrugged his shoulders. "It's a beautiful thing, brings much pleasure, but always does it bring pain as well."

She was coming to know that all too well. "Arturo, what do you know of spirit mates?"

"Ah . . . now there's a highly romantic notion . . . spirit mates. Hmm . . . well, it's rare that a person should find theirs. This I know. But"—his eyes twinkled—"I also know it happens."

Branna bit her lip.

"I need no prescience to see that the notion of spirit mates does give you unease, but I cannot see why. It's a blessing to have found a spirit mate while you are incarnate."

Normally, it was. And that vision she'd had proved that she and Lucan were indeed spirit mates, cast from the One at the same time and bonded throughout all their lives. She'd done much thinking about that vision, about what it would mean for them if they worked the ritual of *Draiochta Cothrom*. It would go easier for both of them if they were merely consorts—spirit mates was something altogether different.

"Aye, but not if you know you might lose them soon after finding them," she answered softly.

The mage went silent for several long moments before finally speaking. "I see a circle. I see death and salvation at the same time. That is what you fear. You fear to lose Lucan, or yourself, to the Ritual of the Balance."

She looked at him with amazement shining in her eyes. For certain, the man's far-sight was strong.

"Lady Raven, don't waste your time. You must make the most of what you have this day, regardless of what may happen tomorrow. *Cinnunt* will happen regardless. Believe me, I am one who has learned much about the value of time. Nothing is eternal but the earth, sky, and seasons."

A tear welled up, breached the rim of her eye, and fell down her cheek. She dashed it away.

"Aye, 'tis a frightening thing, isn't it? Facing fears of loss can be overwhelming." His gaze shifted, and she could feel someone coming up behind them. "Ah . . . but we've company. One more thing. Keep your eyes and emotions open to those who are closest to you. Sometimes those we think we know best, we don't know at all." With that remark delivered, Arturo turned and walked away.

She knew it was Fiall before he placed his hand on her shoulder. He bade her sit beside him on a nearby step. She sat and smoothed her skirts over her lap.

When she looked to Lucan again, he watched her with his blue-gray eyes. He tipped his cup to her and drank. She could see his shoulders were heavy with weariness, and sorrow emanated from him. She needed no magic to feel it. He did not celebrate. He was here only to show his presence as leader and took no pleasure in the festivities.

Fiall's gaze also rested on Lucan. "It looks as if our fearless leader is having a rough time of it." Satisfaction laced his words.

"Why should you dislike him? He has been very good to you and only wants what you want."

Fiall shifted his gaze to her. Desire flooded his eyes, and she looked away. He reached out and adjusted the strap of her gown. "Aye . . . he only wants what I want," he said almost to himself. She stiffened at his fingers brushing her bare skin.

He leaned close to her, taking her hand in his. "He is arrogant and far too sure of himself. He is merely a Numian. He doesn't even possess magic. There is no reason for him to think so highly of himself."

Branna went silent, not knowing how to respond. Lucan had never struck her so. She knew that Fiall's hatred for Numians was deep-seated. While she'd come to know that all people were different and generalizing whole nationalities was wrong, Fiall had an intense bias. She could not truly blame him. Fiall had that scar across his face to show for his experiences with the Numians. The Valorian soldiers had staked him and drawn the blade from his brow to chin, deliberately marring his Tirian handsomeness. They had left him staked in the sun for the insects to chew on, knowing an animal would be enticed by the scent of his blood and come to dine. She shivered and squeezed Fiall's hand.

"Believe me, Lucan is not as you've described him," she said.

Fiall made a scoffing sound. "Do you know him so well? Or do you say that because he found the key to *Draiochta Cothrom*? Because he is the priest in your dreams?"

"Aye, those things . . . and other things. I have seen a part of him you have not."

"Ahh . . . yes. The priest in your dreams is to be your consort as well. I'm sure you have seen parts of him I have not."

She tensed. She couldn't dismiss Fiall's comments as teasing. There was jealousy, possessiveness, in his tone. She hadn't told Fiall about her vision, or what had happened at the Temple of Solan. Now she was glad she hadn't. "I have the right to take who I will to my bed, Fiall," she said icily. She tried to stand, but he grabbed her wrist and held her down.

"Aye, barring a love bond, you have that right," he said in a low, angry voice.

"I have no love bond," she shot back. That was untrue. She did have a love bond. It just wasn't with Fiall. But he didn't need to know that. It would only hurt him. He was already jealous of Lucan, whom he perceived as a threat. Fiall must have sensed something between herself and Lucan from the first moment he'd laid eyes on the rebel. That was why he'd drawn steel against Lucan in the beginning, even knowing she'd not been in danger.

She had no wish to hurt the very best friend she had. At the same time, she would not entertain his resentful feelings about Lucan.

His grip on her wrist tightened, and Branna wondered if she would need protection from her protector. "No, you've no love at all . . . do you?" His tone was stinging. She flinched as though he'd hit her.

She straightened her spine and summoned every bit of high priestess she had within her. She would not let him see how much blood he'd drawn with his remark. "Let me free," she ordered.

Fiall let go of her wrist, and Branna shot up and walked away from him without a backward glance.

*　*　*

Lucan could not take his eyes from Branna. She wore a white gown, fastened at the shoulders with brass clips. It bared her smooth, kissable collarbones. She'd left her hair gloriously free. It was a fall of fathomless midnight against the paleness of her skin. He knew now she wasn't the perfection of beauty he'd first thought her. He knew her left ear was lower than her right and about the mole on the side of her throat and how her two front teeth were set slightly crooked. He knew of the scar on her shoulder and the one behind her ear. How he wanted to kiss the mole and those scars, trace the crookedness of her two front teeth with his tongue.

He'd avoided her since returning from the Temple of Solan, thinking to give her some room to breathe. Now she sat across the room from him, her hand entwined with Fiall's. They pressed their heads close together, talking low about something they seemed to think important.

Lucan turned his head away.

Funny how he should be feeling envious of Fiall. He knew Fiall was like a brother to her, and therefore, he shouldn't feel competitive with him. But the easy familiarity of their conversation made Lucan want to be in his place. He wanted to be the one adjusting the strap of her gown and sharing intimate conversation.

Never had he wanted any such companionship with a woman before. He'd always been more than happy to leave dealings with females in the bedchamber. But Branna made him want more. Gone were any fears he'd harbored about allowing distractions into his life. Having her in his arms at the Temple of Solan had driven them all away. He no longer cared.

He would have her for himself.

Lucan looked down into his cup. Morgan had filled it with fire-juice. In one swallow it was gone, leaving Morgan to raise an eyebrow.

"Lucan, be not so sorrowful. The boy is in Vallon now. He is in comfort and awaiting his next life. We should be celebrating his passage, not mourning it," Morgan said, misinterpreting the reason for Lucan's unease.

"His death won't be in vain," Lucan replied. "Even now the messengers are in Ileria. I think the Ilerians will finally accept our proposal of an alliance. If they send troops, we may be able to attack Ta'Ror with enough manpower to topple Magnus."

Morgan's lips curved into a bitter smile. "Now they will have no choice."

"Yes, if they don't join with us, Ileria will fall for certain this time. Magnus cannot be allowed any more far-blood magic."

Lucan looked again at Branna. Her eyes flashed with anger, and she ripped her hand . . . no . . . wrist . . . from her protector's grasp. Fiall dared restrain his Raven by holding her wrist? Something was truly wrong, and anger flared in Lucan against Fiall for treating her thus. She stood and bolted down a corridor.

Lucan handed his cup to Morgan and mumbled that he had to go attend to something.

B RANNA FLED DOWN ONE OF THE CORRIDORS OFF THE common room because it offered the fastest escape route. She didn't know where it would lead. Running her hand along the hallway's rough-hewn walls, she simply walked blindly, engrossed in her thoughts.

She reached the end of the corridor and found herself in front of the small passageway that led to the crystal room and underground lake. There she would be alone and have quiet.

She slipped into the passageway.

The roaring sound of the waterfall met her ears. Only a few

celestial-fire lanterns lit the room. In the dim light she could barely make out the large lake and the waterfall running down the rocks on the far end.

A noise sounded behind her and she whirled, afraid Fiall had followed her. She searched in the half light to determine who it was. By the man's form and the way he moved . . . aye, she knew him by the way he moved better than she'd ever known anyone . . . she could tell it was Lucan right away.

"Are you well?" came his low, deep voice. His face was shadowed.

For some reason, the concern that laced his voice nearly broke her apart. She squeezed her eyes shut, forcing the tears that welled over and onto her cheeks. How could she find this man only to lose him again? She tried to collect herself before speaking.

"Yes . . . I'm fine," she said in the steadiest voice she could manage.

"Because if you need to be kissed, I can do that. If kissing is what you need, I'm your man."

She could hear the smile in his voice, though she couldn't see it on his face. She laughed and sobbed at the same time. Fine, she would follow Arturo's advice and simply give in. "Aye, I could use a kiss," she said in a voice made husky by her tears.

Before she'd even finished her sentence, he strode toward her. He caught her around the waist and brought his face close to hers. His breath was mint scented, and it stirred the fine hairs around the edge of her face. He smelled as he always did, of spicewood soap and leather, although this time it also seemed she could smell his desire.

One teardrop meandered its way down her cheek, and Lucan kissed it away. Then he tipped her chin up and placed his mouth against hers. She could taste the salty tang of her teardrop as he parted her lips and brushed his tongue against hers in a long, slow stroke.

Morrenna's stars . . . thank the Goddess for kisses.

He rubbed and massaged her back and shoulders, and all the tension she'd felt disappeared . . . as well as any hope of sensible thought or control. She sighed into his mouth, and her hands found his strong upper arms, making their way to his shoulders. Although she'd had no direct experience with a man, she'd heard women in Tir na Ban discuss the acts of love. She knew where to put her hands, and mouth, to bring a man pleasure.

And she so desired to give Lucan pleasure.

She let her hands go where they would, running them over his back and down his sides and then lower, brushing briefly against his member from the outside of his trews, then returning to more thoroughly rub the length of it. He broke the kiss, uttering a fervent oath. "I won't be able to hold back if we go much further with this, Branna."

She looked up at him quizzically. He spoke as though holding back had anything at all do with them. She knew her lips were red and swollen from his kisses. Her eyelids were heavy, and she felt drugged. "No holding back, Lucan."

He let out a pent-up breath and picked her up in one fluid motion. He carried her to a large rock that flanked the lake and set her down. She parted her legs and he stood between them. She worked the laces of his jerkin free and then pulled it up over his head. Her fingers went to the buttons of his shirt next. When they were undone, she slid it over his head to expose the hard, smooth expanse of his muscled chest. Still, there were marks on him from the battle at Kastum, as well as old scars. She ran her hands across them, feeling them coarse and ridged under her fingertips, reveling in his warmth and strength. Goddess, but she'd dreamed of doing this.

He undid the shoulder clasps of her dress. The front of her gown slipped down over her breasts, leaving her naked to the waist. His first touch was the softest caress. Gently, he teased her skin. Pleasure flooded her lower body and tightened her nipples. He cupped the weight of her breasts in his hands, rubbing his thumbs back and forth over their rosy tips.

Branna drew her hands down the length of his chest, over the rippled muscle of his abdomen, and brought them to the lacings on his trews. She undid them and let her hand slide under the waistband of his undergarment. She found the evidence of his arousal and stroked the length of it with uncertain fingers. Lucan groaned and caught her hand. He brought it to his mouth and, catching her gaze, kissed her fingers slowly, his tongue stealing out to taste them briefly. "Best not to do that now. I would keep my control as long as possible."

He gave her a look worthy of Malus, the God of the Underworld himself, and pushed her backward a little, bracing his hands on either side of her on the rock. He tipped his head down and brought one of her nipples into his warm mouth, then laved it with his tongue and nipped at it with his teeth. Branna arched her back, willing more of herself against his mouth.

A slow, warm brush of power licked its way over her skin—silk rubbed up the length of her body . . . and Lucan's too, she knew.

He looked up and gasped. "What is that?"

"Magic," she said. "Magic to hold us, to bind us. A sexual spell." The power licked up them again, starting from the base of the spine and surging up out of the tops of their heads.

He shuddered, and Branna knew it was from pleasure. Then he dropped his head back to her breast, his warm tongue running over her until she moaned.

She felt his hand on her calf, working its way under her skirt. Slowly, caressing her leg every inch of the way, his hand traveled upward to the apex between her legs. He worked his way around her undergarment and teased her, caressing every fold and the sensitive bud that topped it all. He eased a finger within her and began to thrust. An almost feral sound of longing found its way from her throat and into the open.

She tipped her head back and closed her eyes. Her body was on fire. It was as simple as that, she thought incoherently. Lucan had set fire to her. Goddess, she was his own now . . . every fiber of her being. He could do anything to her he liked and she would let him.

His gentle thrusting grew deeper, and Branna thought she would surely lose her mind, but then Lucan faltered. "You are virgin?" His voice was rough with desire, but through it was surprise. She managed to nod. Why he thought that important enough to mention, Branna wasn't sure. In Tir na Ban, the penetration of the maidenhead was something to be celebrated.

Another oath escaped his lips. "Too late now," he murmured. Lucan dropped his head and kissed his way up from her breast to her throat. His free hand went to the back of her neck to draw her forward and his mouth covered hers. His tongue plunged deeply into her mouth, exploring every part of it. The rhythmic movement of his finger within her resumed, and Branna felt Lucan's thumb gently brush back and forth across the small, throbbing place that grew more sensitive with his every heated breath that branded her skin, every pass of his hand on her body.

Something was building inside of her. She didn't know what it was, but she didn't want Lucan to stop doing whatever it was that was making it happen. Branna moaned out her pleasure at his hands and poured it back into his mouth. Finally, when she thought she could stand it no more, the ecstasy flowed over its limit and stars burst in her mind. She cried out his name as waves of pleasure washed over her, and he caught each syllable against his mouth.

Branna's eyes fluttered open and met his heated gaze. "I want you within me," she said. Goddess . . . how she did!

The muscles cording his neck tensed. It was clear he restrained himself for her sake but was barely holding on. He rested a hand on either side of her, leaned forward, and kissed her. His tongue plunged into her mouth and, groaning, he pulled away. "I'll take your maidenhead if I come within."

She smiled. Was that what he was worried about? Strange how these Numians valued a simple flap of skin tucked so far within a woman. She glanced down. His trews were unlaced at the top but still pulled up. She could see the beginning jut of his pelvis and the trail of fine black hair that led from his abdomen, traveling below the waistband of his undergarment.

She wanted to see more.

She reached out, caught the edge of his trews, and pulled his hips against her, causing the hard length of him to brush her. "It is yours to take, Lucan. I can think of no other man I'd rather give it to."

A sudden guttural battle cry ripped from the shadowed entrance behind Lucan. A form separated itself from the darkness and flew at him, knocking him back.

CHAPTER TWENTY-ONE

"FIALL!" BRANNA YELLED. REACTIVELY, SHE DREW THE front of her gown up.

The two men rolled on the ground, punching each other. Lucan managed to extricate himself and roll away. Out of breath, he stood with a hand out to stay Fiall. "I . . . I have no wish to fight you. *Solan!* I don't even know why I am fighting you."

Fiall knelt on the ground, also out of breath. "Because you want the only thing I want." He turned his gaze on Branna, and the expression that graced his face in the half-light made her blood run cold. "The only thing I ever wanted. The only thing that means anything to me."

"Fiall," she slid from the rock and went toward him, holding her gown in place. "Why, in all the time we've known each other, have you not told me?"

He stood and held his hands out in a plaintive gesture. "And risk losing you altogether? Your dreams of the priest . . . of him," he indicated Lucan. "They took away any possibility of my winning your affections. It was so hard"—he released a shuddering sigh—"so hard to hide my emotions from you."

"Oh, Fiall—"

"I knew this day would come. The day when you'd find the priest was ever on the horizon, but that never changed the fact that . . . that . . ." Fiall slipped into his native tongue. "I loved you and I love you still."

And would now be the time when she would have tell Fiall the inevitable? Would she have to tell him, in this bitter moment, that she did not feel the same way he did . . . that she'd never felt a flicker of love beyond friendship for him?

No, she wouldn't . . . because he already knew. Branna and Fiall shared a look then of ultimate understanding. He'd always been able to link with her mentally, and now, standing before her, sharing intense emotion, he knew exactly what she was thinking.

He spoke in Tirian, his voice hard and flat. "No . . . you don't have say it, Branna. I already know."

He turned to Lucan. "You thought I was the lucky one, didn't you? Because I shared her intimate thoughts and was close to her in a way you could only dream of. Well, I'm telling you right now that you're the lucky one. You're the one that will have her kisses and have her sweet body moving under you in the night. That's something I'll only ever dream of."

Fiall stalked up to Lucan. "But here's something I won't have to dream of for the rest of my life." His fist caught Lucan just under the eye. Lucan made no move to block him and simply took the punch.

Branna gasped.

Fiall turned on his heel and walked away. Lucan came up from behind, placed his hand on Fiall's shoulder, and whirled him around. Lucan's fist came forward hard and fast. Fiall staggered backward and tripped, ending up sprawled on the ground.

"There's a lot to be said for dreams realized," said Lucan, looking down at the other man.

Fiall sat on the ground for a moment, catching his breath. Then he stood. "Fine, Numian," he spat. "We're even . . . until next time." Holding a hand to his face, he turned and stalked out the entranceway.

Branna stood immobile for several long moments, suddenly bereft. She'd gained a lover and lost a friend in the space of a few minutes. *Morrenna's stars.* She looked at Lucan with what must have been a stunned expression on her face. Where was Fiall going to go?

"Go to him," Lucan said. He touched the tender flesh of his face where Fiall had hit him and winced. "Solan knows I don't like the man, but he needs you now."

Branna took off after Fiall, securing the clasps of her dress at her shoulders as she went. She caught up with him in the common room. He'd just entered the corridor that would lead him outside . . . and out of her life forever, Branna worried.

"Fiall, wait," she cried. She saw his steps falter, pick up speed, and then finally cease as though he didn't know whether to stop or keep walking. He didn't turn around, and his shoulders were hunched forward.

She came up on his left and took him by the upper arm. "Where are you going?" A lurid bruise was already beginning to bloom around his eye. Blood trickled from a cut in his eyebrow.

"Just away for a little while. I need to be free of these walls. I need to do something." He glanced away and pulled his mouth in a tight line.

The look on his face was strange . . . detached. "Do what?" As unobtrusively as she could, she tried to probe his mind, but he'd thrown up powerful blocks against her.

He turned toward her faster than she could believe and pressed her up against the wall of the corridor behind them, his strong hands pinning her shoulders. His mouth hovered near hers, and Branna caught her breath, afraid he'd kiss her. He smiled and it was cold. "What does it matter to you what I do, my lady Raven? You don't care about me."

He lingered there for a moment, seeming to enjoy her discomfort. Then he pushed away and turned his back.

Branna took a deep breath in an effort to calm herself. When she could speak, she said, "You know that's not true, Fiall. I want to make sure you'll not be hurt when you leave here, that's all."

He half turned toward her, fisting his hands. "I'm going to do something that needs doing."

"Will you return?"

"Yes, Branna. I just need some time."

She thought it a good idea, perhaps. She too needed time to adjust to the strange turn of events. "Do you promise you'll be back?"

He smiled slightly, and the old Fiall seem to flicker there for a moment. It made her heart thunder in her ears. "I promise on the Goddess's very breath . . . I'll be back."

She stepped forward and grasped his arm. "I do care very much for you, Fiall. You know that, don't you?"

The glimpse of the old Fiall vanished at her comment, making her regret saying it. His cold mask slipped back into place, and his mouth twisted in a bitter smile. "But not as much as I care for you . . . never that much," he whispered. "Now let me go."

Branna released his arm, backed away, and let him walk into the darkness of the corridor.

* * *

LUCAN TOUCHED THE SKIN BENEATH HIS EYE AND GRI-
maced. He only hoped Fiall was in as much discomfort right
now. He laced up his trews, picked up his shirt, and then searched
in the half-light for his jerkin.

Solan. It had been a horrifying end to a sweet experience. One
that had only promised to become sweeter. Having Branna beneath
him, reacting to every brush of his hands, tongue, and teeth had
been so much better than any of his many fantasies. His groin
tightened at the memory, in spite of the pain of his face.

Solan!

He located his jerkin and angrily scooped it up. Then he stalked
to the common room. He had to find Morgan. Lucan wasn't sure
what Fiall would do at this point. He didn't think the Tirian capable of any true harm, but love unrequited could cause a man to do
things he normally would not. He understood that Fiall would be
leaving Kern. His pride would not allow him to linger. The Tirian
warrior needed to be followed and watched.

Celebrating people still danced, laughed, and sang in the common room. The joyous sounds were in keen contrast to his temper.
His face must have shown it because the crowd parted for him and
concerned murmurings formed his wake. He spotted Morgan talking to Arturo.

Morgan's light blue eyes watched him approach, his gaze traveling up from the jerkin and shirt he held in his hand, to his bare
chest, to his face with the blossoming bruise and already swollen
eye. "What's the matter, Lucan? Did you try for a woman that didn't
want your attentions?" He grinned.

Lucan nearly growled. "Not even close, Morgan. You wouldn't
believe me if I told you. The Tirian warrior, Fiall, has just left Kern."

Arturo raised an eyebrow as if in comprehension.

"I want at least two scouts on his tail, watching everything he does. If he attempts to hurt someone or himself, tell the scouts to restrain him," Lucan continued.

"Right," said Morgan. He hurried away.

Lucan turned to Arturo. "What can you see, old friend?"

Arturo looked past Lucan, letting his eyes go out of focus. "I see a circle and I see balance. I see danger and bloodshed. I see . . . love found and then lost." He shook his head. "But all else is dark, Lucan. I cannot see anything more. I can tell you one thing, even though it might not give you ease. Whatever happens . . . it is meant to be." Arturo's eyes came back into focus.

Lucan remembered his own vision. No, it had not given him ease.

N IA WALKED DOWN THE CORRIDOR OF THE NORTHERN wing of the palace, worrying the moonstone crystal she'd accidentally purloined between her fingers. There was much afoot this night with the Lady Raven. She could feel the younger woman's unease and restlessness through the piece of jewelry.

But then she was not the only Tirian sorceress who suffered unease.

Magnus had always had a special liking for her, although he'd always shown restraint. But since the Opposition had grown bolder, so had Magnus. It was as though he wished to wield power over her because he could not control the rebels. Since his encounter with his nephew in Kastum, things had become unbearable. It had all started with a kiss she hadn't returned. She'd suffered his clumsy gropes on more than one occasion since.

Nia stiffened her spine. She could not allow it. He'd taken her family, her country, her freedom—and, yes, for a long time even her mind, but she would not allow him her body. She was a Tirian. She decided to whom she would give herself. No man would manipulate or force himself into her bed.

One of Magnus's problems had always been his lack of understanding of Tir na Ban's culture and pride . . . and the strength of its women.

There'd been a time when she would have succumbed to Magnus's pressure. She'd been so beaten down, so manipulated, that she'd given up almost all her power to him. Seeing the Lady Raven and the moonstone crystal pendant she'd worn had changed that. The Lady Raven had awoken her as if from a dream—or a nightmare—and she'd done much thinking of the threats Magnus had hung over their heads all these years to force their aid.

Nia now remembered that she held power, strength, and a desire for freedom, as did the other captured sorceresses. With help from the Opposition and the Lady Raven, they might be able to wield that power over Magnus.

Now time was growing short. Nia knew Magnus was launching a large offensive against Tir na Ban's cousin country, Ileria. If Ileria fell, Magnus would enslave their mages and sorceresses, as he had Tir na Ban's. Nia shivered.

She turned a corner and saw the door she sought, flanked by two Valorian soldiers holding long Numian war staffs.

"Allow me within," she commanded. All the Valorian knew her on sight. She was Magnus's pet sorceress and had his ear. One unkind word from her lips spelled death for them.

"Yes, my lady." They backed away from the door.

She went within the chamber and saw it lying on a half pillar in the center of the room . . . *Draiochta Cothrom.* It lay in a heavy glass case. Four celestial-fire torches lit the room. No rich furniture, gilt-framed paintings, or delicate vases adorned this chamber. There was only the book.

Two more guards flanked the pillar. They eyed her uneasily.

"Unlock the case," she ordered.

They did not move. They only stared straight ahead, gripping their war staffs.

Nia sighed as though greatly put out. "I am here at Magnus's behest. He wishes me to verify something about the book," she lied.

The guards did not move for several moments. Finally, one of them produced a key, unlocked the case, and flipped the lid open.

She stood in front of the book. It was a large tome, bound in thick brown leather, and was deceptively plain looking despite its size. The only markings it bore, besides the eight-pointed star-shaped keyhole on its cover, were ancient runes carved into its spine. It was not possible to open by any means, magical or otherwise, without the key. The key was secreted away in someplace she had yet to discover.

"Leave me," she commanded.

"My lady," said one the guards, "this is highly irregular."

Now she would have to bluff. She turned away from the book and toward the soldier. She narrowed her eyes. "Shall I tell Emperor Magnus you kept me from performing my duty?"

The guard flinched but did not move.

She lifted a brow. "Or shall I send for Lord Crispus . . . ?"

"We'll leave you now, my lady," said the guard. They quickly left the room.

She let a small smile play with her lips and turned back to the book. It was not possible to destroy it. If it were, Magnus would've already done so.

From her sleeve, she produced a tinderbox. Was this the real *Draiochta Cothrom* or a clever decoy? She struck the small wooden stick against the stone pillar and it flamed up. She placed the flame under the edge of the book. The leather binding smoked and then caught fire.

She extinguished it with her sleeve and fell to her knees before the book, closing her eyes and praying to the Goddess for the first time in many years.

It was a fake. That meant the real book was somewhere else—and Nia suspected where. She buried her face in her hands. It seemed Magnus might get what he wanted from her after all.

CHAPTER TWENTY-TWO

BRANNA TOSSED AND TURNED IN A FITFUL HALF SLEEP.
All night, she'd been plagued by nightmares. Sweat soaked her
brow, and her head pounded with a rhythmic vibration, reminding
her of a heartbeat. It also reminded her of the signal that had filled
her mind in Kastum, though this one was not painful. She kicked
the blankets away from her and twisted on the bed.

*Lady Raven . . . Branna . . . daughter of Cattia . . . granddaughter
of Sorcha . . . eternal daughter of the Goddess, Maiden, Mother, Crone,
Deva . . . I call to you . . .*

Branna sat straight up. Had that been a voice? It had sounded
like a female calling from a great distance. She glanced around
the room. The fire had died, and a small amount of celestial-fire
burned in a lamp in the corner of the room. It cast a dim light, allowing shadows to slink and twist through the chamber.

She laid down and closed her eyes, trying to relax enough to hear any mental messages, but her mind strayed to Lucan and then to the Ritual of the Balance. Sweet Goddess! No, she could not calm herself. She couldn't tame her tumultuous mind enough to receive anything. Frustrated, Branna bolted from the bed and began to pace the length of her chamber.

Had it been Nia she'd heard calling to her? Was it the abducted Tirian sorceress who caused her so much unease this night? Was it her twisted magic, coupled with the power she now had because of the moonstone pendant she possessed?

Or was it everything that had happened that eve?

It could be either. Branna didn't know.

The fire that still burned within her was the only thing she knew, and the only one who could put out the flames was the man she was afraid to bind to her heart.

She turned on her heel and went to the spring. Kneeling, she cupped some of the water and brought it to her face.

Warm.

The water was as hot as she felt. She needed cool water. Grabbing the celestial-fire lamp, she headed for the door.

"Sweet Solan." The oath she'd heard Lucan use so often slipped from her tongue. The mountain was truly black when all the lamps were extinguished at night. She stepped out into the hallway, her lamplight barely biting into the oppressive darkness. She went down the hallway and into the common room. A barrel of sweet, clean mountain water awaited her there.

The lantern cast long shadows that flickered and moved over the rough-hewn walls and ceilings of the common room. Sentries stood watch at the far end. They all held celestial-fire lanterns of their own and laughed and talked in low voices, paying her no attention. Branna knew another force roamed the exit corridors and still more stood watch outside of Kern, in the trees and between the rocks.

Along the edges of the room, people slept on bedrolls or were simply passed out, having drunk too much ale or Pirian fire-juice during the previous night's celebrations.

She located a barrel of water and took the silver dipper in hand. Even the feel of the cool metal of the dipper was no salve for her fire. She raised water to her mouth and it slid down her throat, cold and refreshing. Releasing the dipper, she splashed water onto her brow and let it trickle down the front of her chemise, chilling heated flesh.

Something moved out of the corner of her eye, and she felt a brush against her arm. Alarmed, she dropped the lantern. It clattered to the ground and extinguished, plunging her into near darkness.

She stood still, one hand on the rim of the barrel, the other groping at her waist for her nonexistent athame. Hot breath branded the back of her neck, teasing the small hairs there. "Fiall?" Her voice broke in sorrow on the name.

She whirled but there was no one—only shadows. Was she going insane? Or was she merely being silly? Branna let her beating heart return to normal. Many phantoms haunted her this eve.

Carefully, Branna picked her way past the sleeping bodies and tables, heading back toward the corridors arching off the other end of the common room. They looked like the gaping maws of beasts to her . . . completely black. There'd be no way for her to find her way back to the chamber without light.

But it wasn't to her own chamber that she truly wished to go anyway.

Bringing her eyes out of focus, looking beyond apparent reality and into the Universal Fabric behind it, she located Lucan within Kern. The connection they shared stretched strong and golden between them.

The corridors she traveled through to get to him were black as black could be, but the connection guided her to his chamber door without falter. She expected it to be locked, but when she pushed, it gave. The remnants of a fire lit the room in a soft glow.

Her brow furrowed. He'd left his door open. That was odd. Perhaps he'd wanted her to come to him. If that was so, why had he not come to her?

All her questions ceased to be important when she saw him lying on his bed. He was nearly spread-eagle across it, the upper half of his body bared to her eyes. Firelight licked and flickered over his form. The blankets covered him from the waist down, and Branna wondered if he wore anything under them. She hoped not. One arm was thrown wide, and the other was tucked under his pillow.

She could see his shirt and jerkin balled up and discarded in the corner of the room. The clothing looked to have been thrown there in intense irritation.

She gently closed the door behind her . . . and slid the lock into place. She'd a mind to finish what they'd started by the lake. Nothing would disturb them this time.

She tread across the room toward his bed and looked down at him. The firelight illuminated one dark and swollen eye. His tousled hair spread like shadowed onyx over the white pillow. Tendrils lay across his cheek. She reached out to smooth the silky hair back but drew her hand away with a quiet gasp as she realized what he wore on the chain around his neck.

The key to *Draiochta Cothrom*.

She could not stay her hand for long. She reached out and touched it in horror and fascination.

Lucan had her wrist in a trice. He tumbled her over onto the bed and pinned her down. His long knife, which Branna belatedly realized must have been under his pillow, went to her throat. She swallowed hard.

CHAPTER TWENTY-THREE

L UCAN FELT THE BRUSH AT HIS CHEST WHILE CAUGHT IN the middle of a dream of a black-haired, cat-eyed beauty. It was with pure instinct that he reacted by drawing steel against whoever had touched him. It was with pure relief, mixed with an equal measure of regret, that he found the slim body beneath his to be Branna's, the very one he'd been dreaming about. He should have known. The smell of skyflower was redolent.

He moved the long knife from her throat—and never, never, did he wish to see such an image again—and placed it on the bedside table. He did not release his sweet intruder, however.

Using a gentle finger, he traced the line of her cheek. "Branna," he said softly. He put everything he felt for her into her name.

Her eyes fluttered closed against his touch and she sighed. Long, dark lashes swept down against vanilla-silk skin. "Forgive me," he murmured. She gave a slight nod of her head and a sigh.

He'd hoped she would come to him this night and had left his door unlocked. He'd almost gone to her, but he didn't know how strongly she felt for the loss of Fiall. She needed to come to him of her own free will. He did not wish to press her.

Now he felt the need to press her in almost every way, especially against the bed with his hips. Already he was tightening, rising for her. All it took was for him to look at her, remember how she'd responded to his touch by the lake.

Solan . . . already his body was taut with desire for her. And if they were to continue with what they'd started, if she'd meant what she'd said about wanting him within her . . . he would need every ounce of his control, for she was a maiden.

A maiden.

It still surprised him, and he'd had hours for it to sink in. Branna was far past the age any Tirian woman should be a virgin. But the way she'd been with him by the lake, open to giving pleasure and receiving it without shame . . . aye, that was all Tirian.

Her eyes fluttered open, and he caught his breath. She reached out and ran a finger, featherlight, down the length of the bruising on his face. He caught her gaze and silently gave his permission for her healing touch. She covered his eye with her hand and the heat and magical shimmering began. When she removed her hand, the soreness went with it.

"Why should you haunt me so? You are in my waking thoughts and in my dreams. You are in my every breath and are a part of me. I have felt it on some level from the first time I laid eyes on you," he whispered.

"We are joined, you and I. More than just simple lust is this," she said, tracing the line of his jaw with her index finger, then fingering the braid at his temple.

As much as he didn't want to admit it, she was right. She

thrummed in him like some mystical vibration, clear to his core. "Yes," he said, drawing his finger down past her collarbones, over the swell of her breast to her nipple. He teased it until she caught her breath.

"We have been traveling together for a long time, you and I," she said in voice fast growing heavy with desire. "Through our lifetimes and after them, over and over. You and I are like a circle. There is no end and no beginning, only flow of experience, around and around."

She spoke of spirit mates. A bond that held them through life . . . and death as well. Lucan did not doubt it was true for himself and Branna. He'd never felt this kind of emotion for anyone else.

She reached up and caught the key that dangled from his neck. Unexplained pain flashed in her eyes. She drew it over his head, twisted to the side, and put it on the table flanking the bed. "We don't need that between us tonight."

He lowered his mouth to hers and tasted her lips, then parted them and brushed his tongue against hers. Then her hands were on his shoulders, pushing him up. He let her, curious to see what she would do. She pushed him to his back and straddled him, sitting over his groin, the bottom edge of her chemise spread out around her. Only the blanket separated them, and she must have felt how ready he was for her.

Her nipples were excited and pressed through the white fabric of her chemise. He reached up and brushed his fingers over them, back and forth. She arched her back, filling his hands with her breasts. He rose up, intending to push her back onto the bed beneath him, but she put a hand to his chest and pressed him down.

She raised an eyebrow. "I would have my way with you. You won't deny me the touch of you this time."

Oh . . . aye . . . control was going to be hard-won this eve. But how could he refuse her when she looked down at him with those beautiful Tirian eyes and her hair shadowing her cheek. She bent her head to his. Her hair brushed against his chest as she took his mouth in a sweet kiss, then parted his lips and went deeper. Her tongue flirted and rubbed against his. She nipped at his lower lip as she broke the kiss and moved to lay a road of kisses down his sternum and past his abdomen.

She moved the blanket from him, and he heard her breath catch. Aye, he slept naked. He hoped he hadn't shocked her. From the heated look she gave him, he thought she was more pleased with the discovery than she was chagrined.

Her long fingers found the length of him and stroked. His hands reached out, searching for smooth skin under her chemise, but her hands caught his and pressed them back onto the bed before returning to their wicked teasing. The first warm flow of magic brushed over his skin, intensifying with their arousal.

Lucan closed his eyes as she covered his body with hers. Her chemise had ridden up, and the soft skin of her inner thighs brushed against his legs as she moved over him. He had to stop himself from throwing her onto the bed, parting those thighs, and sheathing himself within her to the hilt.

He gasped as her warm mouth closed around his rigid length. It ripped a ragged groan from his throat. *Solan* . . . she bound him to her with sex magic, sure as anything. As surely as he had possessed her by the lake, she possessed him now. His fingers curled into the blankets on the bed as her mouth and tongue wove a spell of dark enchantment over him. Her breasts brushed against his thighs, and he could feel her hardened nipples through the fabric of her chemise. Subtle magic flowed over them in a steady stream now, brushing along their bodies like silken butterfly wings.

He could stand it no more and gently pushed her back into

a kneeling position on the bed. That gentleness cost him. All he wanted was to sink himself inside her.

He knelt in front of her. Slowly . . . very slowly, he ran his hands up the length of her thighs, past her nest of dark curls and up her hips, concentrating on every inch of her skin, pushing her chemise farther up her body. His thumbs passed over her belly button and barely grazed her dark nipples. She raised her arms, and he pushed the chemise up and over the top of her head, then let it flutter like an ethereal mist to the floor beside the bed. It had no place between himself and her.

Solan help him.

He let his eyes drink their fill of her as she knelt in front of him. She was exquisite.

He moved his hands to the small of her back and pulled her close, pressing her soft nakedness to him. Then he pushed her down onto the bed. She positioned herself under him with a contented sigh.

He laid next to her and braced himself on an elbow, leaving one hand free. He ran that hand down her body, catching at her breasts. He teased one nipple until she made low sounds, and then traced lower. She parted her legs slightly, almost shyly, allowing him access to her sweetness. He ran his fingers over her, exploring every silken fold and teasing the small bud of her pleasure with his thumb until she writhed under his ministrations and moaned. He slipped a finger within her and stroked. She made a small sound of pleasure in her throat and parted her legs wider. "Lucan, please," she breathed.

It was all he could take.

He shifted over her and placed his hands under her hips, lifting her against him. He pressed himself against her heat and pushed inside . . . not too far, only to her maidenhead, though the bounds of his restraint were quickly reaching their limits.

She moaned, and he could feel his control starting to snap. He needed to be fully inside her . . . now. "'Twill hurt," he managed to get out, "but only for a moment."

She nodded, and it was enough for him. He thrust and her maidenhead gave. Her back arched, and her fingernails dug into his upper arms for a moment and then relaxed. He remained inside of her, motionless, making sure she was all right. *Solan* . . . she was a tight, silky sheath. She opened her eyes, caught his gaze . . . and smiled.

Aye. She was more than all right; she was damned near perfect.

He drew himself out of her, then pushed back in. He established a pattern that she quickly understood. Her hips met his every thrust, and with every thrust the magic grew in intensity, building like their climax. It shimmered gold and white, swirling around the bed.

She closed her eyes, and her fingers clutched the blankets on either side of her. Lucan pulled up, bracing his legs so he could still thrust within her but at the same time let his hands range over her stomach and breasts. He found the place farther down where he knew she would like to be touched and caressed her there. Sweet sounding moans escaped her lips, and it did not take long for her to climax. He felt the racking spasms that shook her body over every single inch of him. He answered in kind. A groan found its way from his throat, and he spilled himself into her, pinning her to the bed with his hips.

Out of the corner of his awareness, Lucan noticed the magic reach a crystalline crescendo around them. It exploded, making a gentle tinkling sound. The gold and white expanded outward in a burst, then fell like glittering snow, evaporating before it hit the floor.

After a moment, happy beyond belief and sated, he rolled to the side, letting his legs tangle with hers. He drew her near, smoothed her hair away from her forehead, and planted small kisses on her neck. She brought her arm over his side and kissed him lingeringly.

"Will it be so, uh, colorful every time we make love?" he murmured against her mouth.

She shook her head and smiled. "The spell was designed to bind us soul-to-soul for the ritual. There will be no spell the next time we make love."

His arms tightened around her. "And there are going to be many next times, my lady."

Her smile faltered. "I hope so." She tucked herself against him and closed her eyes. Eventually, her breathing evened out and he knew she slept.

I N THE MORNING WHEN BRANNA AWOKE, SHE FOUND herself pressed up against Lucan. Still, he slept, his chest rising and falling in a regular rhythm. She lay against him and purposefully matched her breathing to his.

When Lucan finally awoke, he pulled her to him without a word, his eyes heavily lidded and filled with a hunger she was more than happy to satisfy.

They stayed abed for much of the morning. In fact, they stayed cloistered in Lucan's chamber for the entire day. Lucan stole out of the chamber once and brought back sugared bannocks and fruit. He fed the food to her and she to him. But that led to the tasting of fingers and other parts of the body, and they ended up back in bed again, making love until late morning.

When he bade her to join him to bathe, again an attempt to ready themselves for the world outside his room, still they could not manage it. The soft, warm water around their bodies would have them linger, in the water . . . and then in the bed again. By early evening they'd given up their efforts to have anything resembling a normal day.

Branna was in his bed still . . . and still not dressed at evening time. She tucked the blanket around herself and watched Lucan work at kindling a fire. He wore a pair of unlaced leather trews without any undergarment beneath simply because every time he shrugged them on, she pulled them back off again. She smiled at the thought as she watched Lucan throw wood onto the fire.

She glanced at the key to *Draiochta Cothrom* that lay on the table. Sweet Goddess! How cruel could *cinnunt* be?

"What did you mean last night when you said you didn't want the key between us?"

She looked up and saw his intense gaze upon her. She'd been staring at that damned key, and her expression probably hadn't been anything he'd find comforting. Goddess! She had no answer for him.

"I ask because Arturo said something to me last night about the ritual," he continued.

She started a lie but couldn't push it past her lips. No, she could not lie to him. She broke his gaze and fingered the edge of the blanket. "The ritual never leaves both the priest and priestess standing in the center of the circle."

"What do you mean?"

"The Ritual of the Balance will take one of our lives as payment for the altering of the Universal Fabric. Such a huge change in the reality of Terrestra is not for free." She looked up and found his gaze. "Always, there are costs."

Lucan pushed a hand through his hair. "Aye . . . but the cost is too high."

"No. It is not too high for the salvation of Tir na Ban, nor too high to save Ileria . . . not to mention Pira, Bah'ra, and Numia itself. The Ritual of the Balance is the only thing that can stop Magnus's tyranny."

"It's too high if the ritual takes you, Branna." His voice was rough.

She looked away from him. That was the problem; neither wanted to lose the other.

"How do you know the ritual will kill one of us? The ritual has never been performed, has it?" he asked.

She looked up at him. "No. But it is writ in runes on the spine of the book, as a warning to all who would perform it."

A haunted look flooded his eyes.

"Lucan, what is it?"

His eyes went out of focus, almost as if he was having a vision. She knew he had a touch of the mage within him. Now it seemed to be manifesting.

His gaze steadied and found hers. "I won't lose you to the Balance."

She slipped out from beneath the blankets and crossed the distance between them. Winding her arms around his neck, she willed his mouth down to hers for a kiss. "Nor I, you."

"Then we don't have anything to worry about, do we?" His lips curved into a smile before they took hers.

CHAPTER TWENTY-FOUR

Dawn had broken. Branna knew it only because she was attuned to the passage of the Sister moons around the planet. There was no other way for her to know, since no daylight ever reached within the mountain. She had to find sunlight upon her skin this day.

Lucan still slept beside her. She brushed his brow with her lips before rising to locate her chemise. It was still early enough for her to find her own chamber and a gown, before too many were up to see her leave their lord's chamber barefoot and in her sleepwear. Anyway, it was better she left him before he woke, else they risked a repeat of yesterday—though that wouldn't be so bad. Not bad at all . . .

Branna hesitated, looking toward the bed. The expanse of Lucan's chest was bared, and his hair was tousled. She wanted to tousle it further. Maybe she'd just get a change of clothes and then sneak back into bed beside him.

She shook her head. No, it was time for Lucan to return to the running of Kern. It was time for her to begin thinking about ways of getting the *Draiochta Cothrom*. There were people depending upon them—six nations, in fact. She knew, despite all, *cinnunt* would not be denied, no matter how much she wanted to hide from it in Lucan's bedchamber.

Time grew short. Branna felt the urgency running through her veins.

She stepped out into the corridor and eased the door shut behind her.

"Sal'vi, Lady Raven."

She gasped in surprise and turned to find Morgan looking at her. "Morgan. Do you always slink around behind people, watch their every move, and then scare them half to death?"

"Well, actually, most of those things I do for the Opposition. Except the scaring part, of course." He pulled his well-formed lips into a grin, and his blue eyes glittered with mirth.

"Hmm . . . of course."

"I was looking for his lordship." He paused and cleared his throat. "He's been missing now for over a day. Have you seen him?"

Of course he knew she'd seen him—every glorious inch of him from head to toe. "He sleeps now." Obviously there was no need for subterfuge.

"Ah. Well, I'll come back later." He began to walk down the corridor. "Oh, my lady." He half turned toward her. "Fiall has returned. He came back in at dawn this morning, according the sentries. He awaits you in your chamber."

Fiall was back.

Branna ran to her chamber, completely forgetting about her state of dishabille until she stood in front of the chamber door. Here she was, coming from Lucan's room barefoot and in her chemise, with her hair loose and tangled by his hand. Goddess!

She placed her hand on the door and pushed. It swung open, revealing Fiall sitting in one of the chairs that flanked the hearth. He'd started a fire and it lit the room, casting long shadows. He raised his bowed head and stared at her coolly.

Same cool façade . . . same mask . . . not the Fiall she knew . . . not by a quarter length . . .

Fiall raked his eyes down her, taking in every little detail. She noted his eye right away. It was swollen and colored black-and-blue. Blood crusted the skin of his brow. She felt slightly satisfied about that. She wouldn't offer to heal it for him until he'd apologized for acting so possessive and jealous when he had no claim.

She stepped into the room without a word and found a loose-fitting gown of pale green, which she slipped over her chemise, and a pair of slippers for her bare feet. She even found her belt, which still had her athame attached to it, and wound it around her waist. Only then did she go to Fiall, her fingers untangling her hair and working the length into a knot at the nape of her neck. Fiall watched it all with a sullen expression on his face.

"Are you successfully armored against me now, Branna?" he asked softly in Tirian.

She paused, releasing the half-done knot, and letting her hair fall down around her shoulders. Kneeling before him, she placed her hands over his. "Nothing could armor me against you, Fiall. You wound me to the very quick with your pain. I love you, as a sister loves her brother, as my best friend. I would not see you injured at any cost."

His brow rose and his lips twisted into a bitter smile.

"You must understand that I have waited for Lucan all my life."
Fiall seemed unmoved.

"And that not only is he my consort, Fiall, he is my spirit mate."
Something in his eyes flickered at that, but he remained silent.
He leaned forward and placed a hand a short distance from her
abdomen. A strange expression dawned on his face.

"What is it?" she asked.

He withdrew his hand. His face and eyes were now carefully
masked. "You've made love with him . . . repeatedly."

She forced herself up and walked away from him. Then, pro-
pelled by sudden anger, she spun around, the long mass of her hair
swirling about her. "I won't allow you influence over the choice of
partner I make."

"Calm yourself," Fiall said. "I came to make amends."

She relaxed. Oh, she hoped it was true. Then she remembered
sensing him near her the other night when she'd gone for water and
tensed. She'd been sure it was Fiall who stood behind her. Again,
she tried a mental probe on him, and again she was blocked.

"When did you come back to Kern?" she asked.

"This morning."

"And not anytime before then?"

His eyes darkened. "No."

She wanted to draw him out further and opened her mouth to
do so, but Fiall cut her off. "Branna, I would make amends, but I
don't want to say what I have to say between these walls. These are
his walls. Would you like to take a ride with me? Get out from behind them for a bit? They are oppressive to a Tirian, are they not?"

Yes, they were. And she'd wanted to find some sunshine today
anyway. Still . . . foreboding touched her deep within. Something
inside her was telling her not to leave Kern with him.

But this was Fiall. This was the same boy she'd grown up with, the boy she'd played the childhood game of Baccaphan with. The boy she'd tended and healed when he'd had brushes with the Valorian. The one she'd watch grow into a man, as he'd watched her grow to womanhood. Maybe taking some time alone with him would bring him back to her. Maybe she and Fiall could find their old way of being. She'd take the risk for that possibility.

"Yes. I'd like that."

L UCAN WALKED TOWARD THE COMMON ROOM. HE HOPED to find Branna and drag her back to his chamber for a while. When he'd awoken to find her gone, the sense of loss he'd felt had been acute. He'd put his face to the pillow she'd used and inhaled, trying to find some clinging scent of skyflower . . . just to let him know it hadn't all been a dream.

From a practical point of view, it had probably been better that she'd left him. If she'd stayed they might very well have whiled away yet another day at each other's hands. While Morgan was excellent at running Kern, he could not do it alone forever.

He'd just breached the entrance of the common room when Morgan came up to him. "My lord, the Tirian warrior has returned."

Morgan looked awfully worried over such an unimpressive, and disappointing, piece of news. "Yes . . . and?" Lucan replied. Abruptly, his skin tingled with warning. "*Solan*, what's wrong?"

"The Tirian returned without any sign of the two scouts I sent after him. A moment ago I had word that the scouts have been found dead not far from Kern."

"You think Fiall killed them?"

"Aye, my lord, their throats were cut with a Tirian long knife."

Lucan knew that the Tirian blade was serrated and made a

markedly different wound from a Numian long knife. His hands fisted. "Is Fiall here now?"

"No, my lord. The news grows worse. He was spotted leaving Kern . . . with the Lady Raven."

Lucan felt the blood leave his face in a rush and was fully aware of the naked fear that stood on his features.

Morgan saw it too. "I'll saddle the horses. You, find your blade," he ordered Lucan. Then more gently he said, "We'll retrieve her, my lord."

"Aye, we'll, and if Fiall has hurt even one hair on her head he'll pay dearly not only in this life but his next hundred," Lucan managed to grind out.

F IALL HADN'T MET HER EYES ONCE SINCE THEY'D LEFT her chamber, and had said very little. He rode beside her, his spine stiff. Branna sought the athame on her belt merely for reassurance. She'd begun to realize that leaving Kern with Fiall was not the best choice she could have made. She'd ignored all her extrasensory feelings because it was Fiall. She had gone against her inner voice because she thought Fiall would never mean her harm, but she was not so sure anymore.

She touched her athame again, her eyes roving to the long knife sheathed at Fiall's side and the sword and scabbard attached beside his saddlebag. Her athame was nothing against his weapons.

They'd long since ridden past the sentries of Kern, and Branna knew they were in territory where no protective Opposition eyes peered down at them from the trees or from between the rocks. When she didn't know this stranger who only looked like her friend Fiall, it was a dangerous place.

Branna reined up her mare. Fiall turned his horse and regarded her coolly. "Fiall, it's time I go back. I thought perhaps once we were far enough from Kern you would speak with me, but it looks as though you don't wish to discuss what lies between us. I'll leave you now." Her words came slowly, sadly.

Fiall's mouth twisted into a bitter smile. "Branna, Raven, you're slipping."

"What do you mean?"

"Where is your far-sight? Did you push it away because you trusted me?"

Realization tightened a strong, cold fist in her stomach. She stared at him for several long moments. "Was I wrong to trust you . . . my protector?"

Shame flickered briefly in his eyes and was supplanted by pain tinged with . . . hatred. Aye, hatred. Branna could not believe it.

Fiall urged his horse several steps toward her. She backed hers up the same distance. "Aye, you were wrong . . . on so many levels," he said, his voice low and rough.

He spurred his mount forward in an attempt to take the reins. She sucked in a surprised breath and guided her horse to the left, then around back toward Kern.

"Ai'yah!" She dug her heels in hard, and with a violent jolt, the horse took off at a flat-out run. Finding her athame at her waist, she drew it. It was no match against a Tirian long knife or sword. All Fiall had to do was draw either and she was helpless—completely vulnerable on top of her fleeing horse.

He didn't draw his sword. Instead, he came up neatly on her side, grabbed her around the waist, and pulled her onto his mount. She brought her athame down into his thigh, sinking deep into the flesh. She felt warm blood spurt, and Fiall cried out. With every intention of stabbing him again, she drew it back up, but he grabbed her wrist. He wrenched the blade from her fingers and threw it to the ground. Along with her athame went her hope.

She struggled against him, trying to find a place to kick or bite. He drew his long knife. The wicked, silvered edge of it found her throat. Branna went still.

"Don't move," he said, his mouth close to her ear. "Don't struggle. I wouldn't want the blade to slip."

She thought he didn't sound certain of that.

They rode a long way at a fast pace until they finally entered a copse of trees and slowed down. Branna could see a large clearing beyond the copse and movement within it. The men and horses that roamed there looked . . . Goddess . . . like Valorian. Her blood went cold.

Fiall finally spoke as they neared the edge of it. "I gave you up, but not your precious Lucan . . . not the Opposition. The Opposition needs to fight Magnus." His voice lowered dangerously. "Lucan, I'll take care of myself."

"Fiall, what are you doing?" Her voice broke. She sent the intense sorrow she felt radiating out from her to him, knowing she touched him with it. Fiall was a better empath than she. He felt her emotion.

"You used to say you'd let no harm come to me, remember? Where is the man who said those things?" she asked.

His voice cracked with pain. "He's gone, Branna . . . gone."

In that instant, she knew she had a chance of bringing him back to his senses. "By doing this, you preclude all chance of the Ritual of the Balance taking place."

"That's why I'm doing this. Magnus won't kill you, as the ritual might."

"No, he'll keep me caged and manipulate me into using every bit of my magic for his own ends. It's worse than death."

Fiall sagged against her in weariness. "But I'll know you'll be alive," he said softly, then in a harsher tone, "Feel fortunate, for I won't suffer Lucan to live."

Anger and a deep sense of protectiveness welled in her. She knew Lucan was capable of defending himself, but the prospect that Fiall might succeed in his goal spurred her to intense terror. She felt the emotion she had for Lucan . . . her love and protectiveness . . . lash out and draw blood from her abductor.

"You leave him alone. I swear if you hurt him, I'll make sure you pay for it." It was an empty threat if she was to be kept at Ta'Ror for the rest of her days. She knew that and so did Fiall. All the same, it was perhaps the wrong thing to say.

Fiall's body grew tense against her back. The long knife nicked her throat, and she felt hot blood trickle down her skin. "We'll see about that."

The horse stepped through the tree line and into the clearing. A man Branna recognized as Commander Armillon rode up to them. She began to struggle, and Fiall stilled her with the touch of his long knife.

"Aye, that's the witch," said Armillon. He reached out and grabbed her chin. "You dared try ensnaring me, did you? Well, just look at who's caught now."

Fiall moved his long knife to the man's wrist. "Remove your hand. You gave your word she wouldn't be hurt."

Anger flared in Armillon's eyes. "Aye, she won't be hurt, but it's not because you will her uninjured. It's because Emperor Navius Magnus doesn't want her mishandled."

"It's enough," answered Fiall. There was a note of stinging defeat in his voice. He removed the blade as Armillon took his hand from Branna.

"And the man, Navius Lucan?"

"I told you. I cannot give him to you. I don't know the location of either Magnus's nephew or the Opposition," he lied. "I only knew where to find the woman you sought."

Armillon reached out. "Give her to me."

Fiall's arms tightened around her protectively for a moment. For a fleeting second, she thought he'd turn his horse and race away with her, but his grip relaxed and he moved his long knife away. "She's yours," he said sullenly.

She closed her eyes as Armillon's hands closed around her waist and she was traded from one abductor to another.

Armillon produced a rope and wound it around her wrists. She gazed at Fiall. His expression showed a jumble of emotion. Regret was there, she saw it clearly.

He knew well the magnitude of his betrayal.

L UCAN AND HIS MEN FOUND HER MARE IN A MEADOW many quarter lengths from Kern, placidly pulling up grass from the ground. Not far from the mare, Morgan found her athame, the blade stuck into the earth as if thrown there. When Lucan pulled it out, there was fresh blood on it, mixing with the dirt.

He only hoped the blood was Fiall's and not Branna's.

Around the area where the athame was found, the horse tracks showed signs of confusion and struggle. Then the two trails separated. One led to Branna's mare, the other away from the mountains, leading to the south—roughly the direction to Ta'Ror.

Lucan and Morgan, along with a brace of Opposition, rode full bore to the south. Lucan didn't think past the trail that lay in front of him. If he let his mind wander it went to the two Opposition scouts the Tirian warrior had cut down, then to an image of

Branna killed the same way—the serrated edge of a long knife ripping her flesh, spilling her blood.

His hands tightened on the reins. He didn't have the luxury of sorrow and fear now. He had to turn all his attention to the task at hand—finding her.

Lucan's horse slowed at the edge of a thick copse. Here the trail ran cold, into bramble and deadfall. His heart sank. Carefully, leading the way, he urged his horse into the trees. Perhaps they'd find some sign of their passage within. It was not long before he heard sounds from the clearing on the opposite side of the copse.

Valorian.

Lucan raised a hand, silencing the men behind him, then moved to the darkened edge of the tree line. Commander Armillon sat mounted and facing Fiall, who had Branna on the back of his horse. Fiall held a long knife to her throat. Rage shot through Lucan, but he quelled it. Now was the time to have a cool head.

Lucan took inventory. There were about twenty Valorian to his eleven rebels. That would make the fight about two to one—one rebel for two Valorian. But there were Valorian archers too, and they were nothing to be trifled with. No Opposition archers had come with them to even the odds.

Solan! He'd not been expecting to battle Valorian this day.

"My lord." Morgan came up next to him. "Should we take them by surprise?"

"They've archers with them."

"Aye, they've archers. They also have Branna."

Lucan watched Armillon wrap his hands around her waist and pull her onto his mount. He wasted no time binding her wrists with rope.

"Aye, we'll take them by surprise," Lucan said roughly. "Tell the men to form a perimeter. We'll surround them and give ourselves a better chance. Tell them to go for the archers first, while they're off guard and not yet ready to let arrows fly."

"Yes, my lord." Morgan moved to position them.

When they attacked, Lucan went straight for Armillon and Fiall with his sword drawn. Fiall had the sense to back away, but the commander didn't move. He merely wrapped his arm around Branna's waist.

"Ah . . . so, it's the nephew himself who comes for the witch," Armillon drawled out. "It's my lucky day. I get two for the price of one."

Branna started to struggle.

Lucan had no chance to reply. Fiall drew his sword and came at him, a battle cry issuing from his lips. Steel met steel, and the force of it reverberated down Lucan's arm. They maneuvered their horses in a deadly dance, their swords singing through the air. Lucan caught Fiall deep in the upper part of his sword arm. Fiall hissed in pain and dropped his blade. It stuck in the earth, thrumming.

Fiall did not find Lucan's eyes when he raised his gaze from his lost sword. He looked past him, into the clearing beyond.

Lucan reined his horse around. Out of the surrounding trees, a whole force of Valorian, above and beyond the number Lucan had counted from the copse, stepped into view.

The line of Valorian was replete with archers.

At the same time, Branna freed herself from Armillon and landed on the soft grass. True accomplishments, considering her hands were bound. She picked herself up and ran for the edge of the copse.

Lucan knew what would happen before it did. Cold terror rose up from his stomach, and when it reached his mouth it was a hoarse-sounding yell. An arrow loosed itself from an archer's bow and made contact with the front of her shoulder. It felled her back onto the grass, where she lay unmoving.

"No! You fools!" Armillon shouted at the archers. "She was not to be harmed. Magnus will give you to Crispus for this."

His voice reached Lucan from someplace far away. He remained motionless, staring at her crumpled form. Blood soaked through the front of her gown. From behind him came another faraway sound, growing louder. It was part battle cry and part sorrowful keen. Lucan turned his horse toward the sound just in time to see Fiall's long knife flashing in the sun. It made contact with Lucan's flesh, biting through skin, muscle, and into bone. Lucan toppled from his horse and hit the ground.

Armillon laughed. "Aye, that's what happens when you let your battle sense be blinded by love. You become distracted and then you die."

The last thing he saw before the world went black was Morgan and the remaining Opposition retreating back into the copse with the Valorian pursuing.

CHAPTER TWENTY-FIVE

Branna OPENED HER EYES. THE NIGHT SKY, BEREFT of moons, stretched above her. Only starshine lighted the world. She moved and pain seared through her, plunging her into darkness again.

When she woke next it was day. The leaves of the trees above her moved in the wind and dappled the morning light coming through them. She knew better than to make any abrupt movements this time. Something wet soaked her shoulder. Gingerly, she moved the arm that did not pain her and touched her shoulder. Her fingers came away stained dark with her own blood.

A man knelt beside her. He was young, maybe just a bit older than Ren had been, with very light brown hair and brown eyes. A Valorian uniform garbed him, a dark blue military tunic over a shirt of lighter blue. Over both garments, he wore a jerkin of hardened leather bearing the emblem of the Dragon Throne.

The soldier caught her hand and wiped the blood from her fingers with a bit of wet cloth. "You're awake," he said, as though she needed that fact pointed out to her. "While you had no consciousness, we broke off the tip of it. Once we're at Ta'Ror we'll draw the rest of it from your shoulder."

The tip of what? Then she remembered piercing agony as something ripped through the sinew and muscle of her shoulder, meeting bone. It must have been an arrow that had hit her.

"We're almost at Ta'Ror, my lady Tirian."

He meant the title as a mark of respect, but the country of her origin falling from the Valorian's lips caused a cold wind to blow through her.

"Never fear," the man continued.

Never fear . . .

She thought of Lucan and only then did she fear. She reached out with her good hand and caught the man by the top of his jerkin, battling a wave of nausea from the motion. "There was a man . . . the nephew of your lord Magnus. His name is Lucan," her voice broke on his name. "What happened to him?" Sweet Goddess. She was afraid of the man's answer.

The man's eyes hardened. "The man who turned you in to Commander Armillon cut him down with his long knife, my lady Tirian."

Her grip eased on his tunic in a failing of strength and she let her hand fall. Bitter tears welled. She closed her eyes and the tears flowed over their barriers, down her temples and to the ground.

"He lives," he said quickly. "I don't know for how long, but he lives still."

She opened her eyes and searched his face for validation that his words were true.

"There," he said, pointing to the edge of their crude encampment.

She battled to stay aware as she tilted her head up enough to see him. He lay on a litter, like the one she rested on. His face was ashen and dried blood caked his right side. She could not tell where his wound was, or how deep it went. His hair was not glossy black silk anymore. It had lost its sheen. His wrists and ankles were shackled.

She located the rise and fall of his chest. He lived. It would have to be enough. She relaxed against the litter.

"I said we'd pull the arrow when we got to Ta'Ror . . . but do you have healing magic? Could you heal yourself now, if we removed it?" the man asked.

She shook her head. "I would need another trained sorceress or mage to help me." Even healing Lucan was impossible now. He was not able to give her his permission and aid. The words she'd spoken to him in Kastum came back to haunt her . . . Magical healing doesn't work with very grievous or mortal wounds. Branna wondered if Lucan's injury was one of these. She would have to take a closer look at him to ascertain that. Silently, she cursed the Goddess and all her rules.

"I might be able to heal the man, Lucan, if he becomes sensible." She searched out the man's gaze and held it. "Will you please tell me if he regains consciousness?"

"Aye, my lady, but they don't want him too healed. That rebel was always wicked skillful with a blade and quick-minded. They've been searching for him for a long time now. They like him the way he is right now, nice and harmless. Lord Crispus just wants him sensible enough to tell him the whereabouts of the Opposition's stronghold when he tortures him."

Torture.

The Goddess had surely forsaken them.

* * *

MAGNUS WATCHED FROM THE WALKWAY ATOP THE palace wall. A messenger had been sent ahead, letting him know that Armillon had captured both the Tirian witch and his nephew. He smiled as the portcullis rose and the first of the Valorian force marched into the courtyard.

Yesterday, he'd received word that Ilerian troops had crossed the Numian border, probably headed to join with the Opposition. They were fools to leave their borders so unprotected.

He'd sent half his troops to Ileria that morning. The other half remained to defend Ta'Ror. He'd scraped up and coerced every ablebodied man in Numia and its provinces to fight. There would be no way Ileria would retain its sovereignty now. The sheer manpower Numia boasted ensured victory, and now that they had the Opposition's leader, the rebels would be easier to defeat.

Aye, it had been a fine day. His smile widened. And a fine night as well.

The previous evening, Nia had finally given up her fight against him. She'd come to him and heated his blood with her long-lidded Tirian eyes and aroused his body with her lips and hands. Boldly, she had led him back to his chamber to finish him off.

He'd make her his queen if he could . . . and maybe, just maybe, he would. Magnus needed heirs, but one reason he'd never taken a wife was because he'd always harbored hope that Nia might one day rouse to his charms. Aye, he was capable of love. Though, he'd never admit to it.

She lay underneath the blankets of his bed still, soft and warm and awaiting his return. And return he would . . . and soon. He wanted to get a good look at the new sorceress first, and again see the man who'd been his faceless, nameless nemesis all these years— his own nephew.

Magnus would keep him alive only for as long as it took to get every bit of information about the Opposition out of him. With Lord Crispus directing his torture, that wouldn't take long at all. The strongest wills were reduced to dust at his skilled hands. If Crispus didn't manage to kill him, Magnus would do it himself, just to make sure it got done this time.

The litters carrying the two prisoners came through the gateway, and Magnus walked down the stairs and into the courtyard.

She had a right fair face, the stray Tirian witch. As he neared, she roused, as though she felt his gaze upon her, and looked up at him with cool, clear green eyes. There was intelligence in those eyes and much enmity, but no fear . . . not a drop. He made a mental note to change that.

His gaze flicked from her soiled slippers, up her ripped green gown, which was made of some coarse material, to the wound in her shoulder, and finally to the arrogant tilt of her chin. A thick, silky fall of straight black hair framed her fearless eyes. Aye, she'd need much twisting, this one. He wondered if she was worth the effort.

He kicked the side of her litter, causing her to grimace in pain. "Take her to a chamber in the sorceresses wing and lock her in. And for Solan's sake, blindfold her. She's a Tirian far-blooded witch, you dolts. You leave her eyes unmasked and she's capable of magic."

"Yes, my lord," said a young Valorian who appeared to have the task of taking care of the chit. He found a cloth and used it to cover those disturbing eyes.

Magnus turned to the litter on which his nephew lay. The sapling Magnus had once known had grown into an oak, but for certain, he was a dying oak. A deep gash bit into his side, and he'd lost a lot of blood; the tribesman's braid at his left temple was coated in it. Magnus had half a mind to simply let him die, but they needed his knowledge. Magnus narrowed his eyes. He hadn't noticed it in

Kastum, but Lucan looked much like his father, Gallus. Memories flooded his mind and he looked away.

"Take him to the prison, but send him the palace physician." With his order given, he turned on his heel and headed back into the palace and his bedroom, where the lovely Lady Nia awaited him.

THEY LAID HER ON SOMETHING SOFT, PROBABLY A BED. Branna couldn't tell for certain because of the blindfold. Servants bustled around the room, taking orders from a man named Lord Crispus. His strong, no-nonsense hands poked and prodded her shoulder until she wanted to scream, but she wouldn't give them the satisfaction of her suffering.

Someone placed something at her mouth. It felt like a piece of leather. "Bite down, girl," Lord Crispus said in his low, rasping voice. "Before you have a healing, that arrow has to come out."

Branna bit.

Many hands held her down at her legs and at her good shoulder. Someone grasped the end of the broken arrow and ripped it out. The barbed tip tore through fresh muscle and tendon. Her back arched and she pushed the leather from her mouth with her tongue and gave a full-throated scream. For all her shame, she couldn't help it. Before dark oblivion found her once more and dragged her down into its depths, she thought of Lucan.

BRANNA AWOKE WHEN SHE FELT SOMEONE SIT DOWN ON the bed beside her. She tried to raise a hand to remove her blindfold but quickly realized they'd bound her wrists and ankles, and then tethered her hands and feet together with a length of rope. She could not bring her hands up past her stomach.

The blindfold was yanked away from her eyes. She blinked and squinted in the bright light, letting her pupils adjust.

Magnus sat next to her on the bed. She knew hatred blazed on her face as she gazed back at him. A shock of icy white hair fell past broad shoulders. His light blue eyes were as cold as a sword's blade and just as piercing. There was no resemblance to Lucan, inside or out. Dismissively, she looked away. She noted that her shoulder had been bandaged. Blood soaked through the white material that wrapped it. Glancing around the room, she saw it was furnished in dark woods, expensive-looking tapestries, and cold white marble.

"That's amazing," he said.

She looked back at him, channeling all her hatred into her gaze.

"Truly amazing. You don't fear me at all, do you, girl?"

She said nothing.

He brought his face close to hers. "Well . . . you better start learning, chit, because you've reason to fear me," he whispered. His breath smelled like sweet wine.

Magnus put his mouth close to her ear, and she turned her face to the side. His voice was a soft caress. "I've got Lucan imprisoned. Even now the torturer sits with him, weighing out how he'll break him. Maybe I'll send you down there too. Crispus is very, very good at what he does. He knows about herbs and how to use them to keep a man conscious while he . . . works on him. He will dismember Lucan, slowly . . . piece by piece."

She shuddered violently and turned her face to his. "If you harm him, I'll make sure . . ." She paused. Everything was an empty threat, but she did possess one power. "I'll make sure your sorceresses revolt against you. I am the Tirian Raven and will wield that power over them."

His reply was swift. "Only if we let you live, chit." Then an expression of evaluation and calculation dawned on his face. "The Tirian Raven," he said thoughtfully.

Magnus turned and addressed the woman Branna recognized as Nia. She'd not known she was in the room. "Nia, is that why you froze in Kastum and withdrew your aid from me? Because she is your Raven?"

Nia smiled, though Branna noticed it did not reach her solid brown eyes. They were on Branna with a strangely intense gaze. Branna wondered for a moment if the other woman remained entirely sane. "My lord, after fourteen years here, the Tirian Raven means nothing to me. I speak for all the sorceresses."

Magnus turned back around. "Ah, you see, you hold nothing over me. But I now have leverage over you." He leaned forward. "You've just betrayed yourself, chit. You care about my nephew, don't you?"

She knew regret flickered over her features, laying bare the truth of what he said. She'd given herself away unthinkingly.

"What's more, you've lain with him. I can tell. The mark of him is all over you." He flicked at her hair. "From your head to your feet. Now the only question is, were you just a tumble to him, or were you more? Do you hold value to him as he holds value to you?"

Branna closed her eyes in misery.

"Hmm . . . I need to deliver a message," he said to himself, going out the door and leaving her alone with Nia.

The Tirian sorceress walked to her bedside. She removed the bloody bandages and placed one of her hands over Branna's wound on the front of her shoulder and the other on the back. They locked gazes in a moment of silent agreement, and Nia's hands became warm. After the sorceress was finished, Branna rotated her shoulder, testing it out.

"My lady Raven, we haven't much time," Nia said.

Branna looked at her blankly.

"Ileria has left its borders unguarded in an attempt to join its forces with the Numian Opposition. Magnus has discovered this and has launched an immense attack against Ileria sooner than was planned."

Goddess. The Ritual of the Balance had to be performed . . . and soon. Their time was up. Branna closed her eyes in defeat.

"I know you have no reason to trust me after the way I behaved in Kastum, but truly, my lady, I'm ready to aid you now," said Nia.

The woman was right. Branna had no reason to trust Magnus's sorceress. But neither did she have a choice. She opened her eyes. "It was you who tried to contact me mentally three nights past."

"Yes, I was afraid you'd not heard me. My mental messaging ability leaves something to be desired sometimes." The woman paused before speaking again. "Living here, in Numia, under Magnus"—she bowed her head—"has twisted my magic. It has changed it into a strange and terrible thing. I cannot kill, but I can do vicious things with it. It's only a question of time before my fear sends me all the way to darkness."

An undercurrent of shame came from Nia, pulling at Branna until she nearly drowned in it. She wanted to reach out and touch her, calm her, but her hands were bound.

Nia raised her eyes to Branna's. "I've got the *Draiochta Cothrom.*"

If she had the book and could convince the other sorceresses to help them, all they needed was Lucan . . . a healthy, warm, and alive Lucan. Tears welled in her eyes.

"But we need the key," said Nia. "I discovered where Magnus keeps it—under heavy guard in the politician's wing. But the sorceresses are not allowed there."

"We have a duplicate of the key." Branna dropped her gaze. "At least, we may still have it." She closed her eyes and let tears roll silently down her cheeks. Goddess . . . her mind was a mess.

Nia used the edge of her sleeve to wipe away her tears. Branna's eyes flew open at her touch. "There is a man in the palace, Magnus's nephew, Lucan," said Branna. "He's in much danger and has suffered grievous wounds. I don't know if he'll live through the night. Could you locate him?"

"Yes, I know where he is even now, my lady." She gave a sigh of relief. Perhaps the Goddess hadn't forsaken them after all.

S OFT HANDS MOVED OVER LUCAN'S BLOODY SIDE. Warmth emanated from them into his wound, taking the pain of it from him. A sweet mouth claimed his. He opened his eyes and saw green ones. Black hair brushed his shoulder. She broke the kiss and moved, sending the scent of skyflower into the air.

Branna . . .

He reached out to take her into his arms, but she slipped away. She floated in front of him, swathed in ethereal white. No blood stained her pristine skin. No arrow defiled the perfect round sweetness of her shoulder.

Branna . . .

"You must awaken," she said to him.

"No." If he awoke, she'd be gone. Better to stay here, where she was.

"You must awaken." This time her voice was plaintive. "Awaken and I'll find you in waking reality."

She disappeared and he was alone . . . deep in the cold Agarian River. The current whisked him away from Ta'Ror, away from Branna. He thought of all he'd lost in his life . . . his father and mother, his brothers, his sister . . . Ren . . .

No! He would not lose yet another whom he loved! He would not lose Branna.

He pushed his beaten body up, pain searing him from the inside and out, up through the drowning water. He struggled through the strong current, just as he battled up through the many levels of consciousness that he'd slipped beneath. He broke the surface of the water at the same time he breached the top layer of his awareness.

Lucan came awake not in any gentle way, but violently. He groaned in deep pain. He could not locate the exact center of his agony. It covered over him, licking and biting at his muscles, sucking his life force away. His right side felt sticky with his own blood.

He noticed right away that his hands and feet were shackled. He cast a desperate glance around him, and then let his head fall back and his eyes close. *Blood of Solan.* He couldn't breathe. Every breath he drew was fire burning through him. He swallowed hard.

And worse . . . he was back in the prison at the palace of Ta'Ror.

Someone placed a hand to the back of his neck and urged his head up. He opened his eyes. A bowl of foul-smelling liquid pressed against his lips. He tried to swallow the bitter-tasting fluid but couldn't. Some of it dribbled out the corners of his mouth.

"Easy, now, easy."

Lucan looked up at the wielder of the bowl. Lord Crispus's cherubic, dimpled visage met his gaze. Lucan spat the bitter brew back in his face, soaking the older man.

Crispus closed his eyes and patiently wiped the liquid from them with the edge of his shirt. He smiled. "Come now, Lucan. Don't you remember me? I served your father."

"Aye, I remember you," Lucan rasped. White-hot rage colored the words.

He nodded at the bowl. "Did you think this was poison?" He clucked his tongue. "I wouldn't do something like that. The brew was to help you to heal . . . so we can bring you to heel." Crispus smiled.

Lucan only winced in reply.

Crispus spoke in a lighthearted, singsong way. "If you tell us what we want to know, it won't hurt so bad. What's more, you tell us what we want to know . . . and it won't hurt so bad for that little black-haired beauty who came in with you." Crispus smacked his lips. "Mmm . . . she's a fine little piece. I might just like a taste of her myself."

Solan. He knew just what to say to incite him to rage. Lucan rose up from the pallet he was on, with every intention of throwing himself on Crispus, but he collapsed right back down, grimacing with pain and almost blacking out.

"Now, now, don't get so excited. You'll hurt yourself." He nodded sagely.

Lucan closed his eyes in defeat. Aye, they'd found his weak spot, but he couldn't tell them what they wanted to know, not for anything in the world . . . not even for Branna.

"Well . . ." Crispus rose. He sighed as though they'd just had a friendly conversation and he was parting with regret. "Since it looks like you'll live after all, I don't think a magical healing is in order. Your wounds will just bring you closer to where I'll need you to be tomorrow." He turned and walked toward the chamber door. "Get some sleep. You'll need your rest for what I've got planned for you." He grinned and then disappeared out the door.

Lucan grimaced. Aye, he was looking forward to it.

NIA CAME IN THE MIDDLE OF THE NIGHT. BRANNA heard the two sentries thump to the floor outside the door as the other sorceress used her twisted magic to make them lose consciousness.

Nia pulled the blindfold from her eyes and cut her bonds.

Branna sat for a moment, rubbing the circulation back into her arms and legs.

"The man you asked me about," said Nia. "He is hurt very badly, but they did not perform a healing on him because they believe him strong enough to live through the night. They hope to use his wounds against him on the morrow when Lord Crispus begins his torture."

Branna's head snapped up. So it was Lord Crispus who planned to break Lucan. If they were successful with their plan this eve, he'd never have the opportunity to try. "Do you know if he's regained consciousness?" She'd contacted Lucan while she'd been sleeping, coaxing him to full waking awareness. He'd been very far gone . . . halfway to Vallon. They were wrong about him being able to live through the night.

"Yes, my lady Raven, he has."

Branna expelled a breath of relief.

Nia stepped forward and pressed something into her palm—her moonstone pendant.

"Thank you, Nia." Branna eagerly returned the piece of jewelry to its place around her throat.

"No . . . thank you. Thank you for waking me and allowing me to awaken the other sorceresses."

"Are they with us?" Branna asked.

The older woman nodded.

Cinnunt was such a strange thing. Branna let out a long, relieved breath. "All right then, let's get him out." She rose from the bed. Her arms and legs were still tingling, but she did not want to waste any more time.

They slipped through the hallways of the palace. Nia led her to a lavishly decorated room lit by tall, standing celestial-fire lamps. Furniture made from dark wood adorned the corners. Thick carpets covered the marble floor and hung on the walls.

"This is one of Magnus's private chambers," Nia whispered to Branna.

Nia guided her to the wall in the back and pressed on it. A secret door swung open, revealing a stairway. They hurried down the long, steep flight of stairs, which was lighted intermittently by celestial-fire lamps. Down and down they went, descending floor after floor into the bowels of the palace, until they were deposited in a long, dank-smelling corridor.

"We're going underground now, my lady. We will come up in the prison," said Nia. The older woman took Branna's hand and squeezed. "We are almost there."

Branna reached out with her mind and touched Lucan. She could feel how dimly his life force flickered. She was not reassured.

CHAPTER TWENTY-SIX

WHEN THEY REACHED THE PRISON, NIA BADE BRANNA stay in the shadows. Nia went behind the two guards that stood watch on Lucan's door. The shimmering around her flared to dark purple light, and the two men slumped to the floor, unconscious.

Goddess . . . Twisted magic. Magic warped by years of fear and manipulation.

Branna shivered, but she did not hesitate. She ran to the fallen sentries and searched them for the key to the prison cell door. When she found it, she slid it home and turned until the lock clicked open. She pushed the heavy door open.

Lucan lay on a long table. They'd done nothing for the wound in his side, and he'd lost a lot of blood. It had soaked through his shirt, jerkin, and trews on the right side, leaving his skin a pasty white. Blood crusted to a dark brown around his wrists and ankles, where the shackles had bit into flesh. Sorrow welled up in her throat, eyes, and chest until she thought she'd choke.

An ominous-looking set of sharp cutting implements lay on the table beside his head. They were laid out neatly . . . lovingly . . . on a long piece of black material. Branna rolled the instruments up in the fabric and threw them with all her might into the far corner of the cell. They clattered when they hit the stone wall.

His eyes weren't open. Branna knelt and touched his forehead and then placed her lips to his unmoving ones.

Cold. Too cold.

With a desperate sob, Branna worked to unlock the shackles at his wrists.

"He's nigh to the brink of Vallon, my lady," said Nia. "I don't know if a healing will do him any good. He might be in the Goddess's hands now."

"She can't have him," she bit off. At least, not yet.

Lucan stirred and opened his eyes. "But . . . you can have me whenever you want me," he said with effort, his lips trying their best to find a smile.

"Lucan," she sobbed out and fell to kissing his lips and cheeks. Then she drew back, wiped the tears from her face, and tried to separate herself from her emotions. They needed to work fast. "Nia, his wound is a dire one, but maybe if we both work together to heal him—"

"We might be able to bring him back somewhat if we work together, but it won't be a full healing," Nia interrupted.

"If we can heal him enough so that he doesn't die and he can make it out of here under his own power, I'll be happy." Happy was an understatement; ecstatic and blissful was more accurate.

Nia came to stand at the table, and Branna carefully pulled his bloody shirt up, peeling the fabric gently away from the wound.

Goddess, it was deep. The angry gash ripped through his ribs on the right side and reached to his hip bone. Branna tried not to let the fear show in her eyes.

Nia and Branna each placed their hands on the wound. Branna looked deep into Lucan's eyes. "Accept and allow this."

He nodded his head once, and then his eyes closed.

The prison cell filled with the sparkling and shimmering light of their combined magic. As Branna looked past to the Universal Fabric, she could see it swirled with dark purple, gold, and white. Branna felt her hands grow extremely hot . . . so hot it seemed her own flesh was on fire. Patiently, she coaxed the pain and infection out, and the injury closed, seeing his skin smooth and unmarred.

Her hands cooled, and she knew Lucan had accepted all the healing he could from them. Whatever was left unhealed was now in the hands of the Deities of the One.

She and Nia removed their hands. Branna looked down at the wound with trepidation. A long, angry scar tracked from the top of his rib cage almost to his waist, but the wound was knitted closed. It was more than she could have hoped for. Lucan would live . . . for the time being.

Branna looked at his face. The unhealthy pallor that had shrouded it was gone, replaced by a ruddy glow that was increasing with every moment. Even the luster of his hair was beginning to return.

Lucan pushed himself up and swung his legs over the side of the table. He stood, wincing a bit and testing out the stability of his legs. He turned toward Nia and tipped his head. "Thank you, my lady."

Then he turned toward Branna and took her by the waist, bringing her against him. He inclined his head and searched her eyes.

"Thank you, my lady," he said in a voice laced with emotion. "You found me while I slept."

"I found you in dreaming reality, and I said I'd find you in waking reality as well." She smiled. "Now that I've found my priest, I'll not let him slip so easily from me."

He started to speak and then closed his mouth. He bent his face to hers and kissed her instead, and that was all he needed to say.

M AGNUS'S AGONIZED BELLOW RENT THE QUIET SOLI-tude of the palace at sleep. He stood over the bed where the Tirian Raven had been restrained, fingering her broken bonds.

Nia hadn't been in her bed when he'd gone to her in the night; neither had any of the other sorceresses. Magnus had gone to the chamber where he'd ordered the stray Tirian witch held, knowing like a knife twisting in his gullet that she'd be gone. The guards who'd been at her door had been asleep on the floor. Now they slept forever, condemned instantly for their lack of care.

His sorceresses had flown their cage. That was a loss. It was a mistake for which they'd pay. Tir na Ban would suffer for it.

Magnus fisted the bits of rope in his hands, and a low keening sound escaped him. Nia was gone. She'd betrayed him.

Crispus cleared his throat. "My lord, what has happened?" he asked.

"She's . . . they're gone." Magnus threw the rope back onto the bed.

"The sorceresses?"

Magnus rounded on him. "Of course the sorceresses. Of whom else did you think I spoke?"

Crispus raised an eyebrow and asked softly, "And what of *Draiochta Cothrom*?"

His question made Magnus's blood run cold. He'd kept the true Book of Magical Balance in a compartment under his bed. There could be no safer place for it. The sentries guarded a decoy. Realization stabbed him in the solar plexus. Was that why Nia had come to his bed?

Solan . . . he'd been such a fool.

"She—she couldn't have known where I kept the real book," stammered Magnus.

Crispus tipped his head to the side. "She's a witch, Magnus."

Magnus pushed Crispus aside and ran to his chambers. His advisor followed. Magnus knelt and pulled the secret compartment out from under the bed, but he knew what he'd find before he opened it.

He slumped down. Nia had never cared for him at all. She'd just used him to get the book. The knowledge ripped through him, leaving intense sorrow and burning rage in its wake. He stood and straightened his shoulders.

"They have the book, but they don't have the key," Magnus said calmly. "The key is kept under heavy guard. Even if she knew where it was, she couldn't have gained access to it."

Crispus's lips curled. "You underestimate them," he snarled. "And you delay. Even now they are probably freeing your nephew and fleeing the palace, and you stand here mooning over that silly chit, Nia."

Magnus closed the distance between himself and Crispus, placed his hands around his throat and squeezed. Cold rage flowed up and out of him. He couldn't stop himself. His control washed away in a flood of emotion, and his advisor had been stupid enough to open the floodgate. Crispus's eyes bulged, and a strangled sound escaped his now blue lips. In vain, he tried to pull Magnus's hands from around his throat.

"You always were a sick, twisted son of Malus," Magnus spat. He released Crispus before all the life ebbed from him. Crispus slumped to the ground at his feet, gasping and coughing.

Then Magnus realized that Crispus was laughing as he gasped and coughed. *Blood of Solan* . . . he'd enjoyed being half choked to death.

Disgusted, he stared down at him. What had he become that he kept such company? He was a monster. A far cry from the fabled majesty and beacon of justice his brother had been. Magnus bowed his head in a momentary twinge of intense regret and self-hatred. He hoped his father and mother couldn't see him from Vallon.

It was no wonder Nia couldn't love him.

"The stray witch is what pushes Lucan to the edge, my lord," gasped Crispus. "I will find the chit and draw Lucan out using her."

Magnus stepped past him and into the corridor. He needed to check on the safety of the key. "If you don't succeed, you die."

Crispus reached out and caught his leg. "But if I find her and am successful in killing Lucan . . . do I get to keep her?"

"Aye. She's yours."

CHAPTER TWENTY-SEVEN

LUCAN LED NIA AND BRANNA BACK THROUGH THE SE-
cret passageway that he remembered linked the prison to the
palace. They had a better chance of escaping if they made their way
through the palace, to the courtyard door in the eastern wing.

Passing through the palace was very disorienting. Memories
caught him at every corner. The dry, sweet scent of hapsinflower
assaulted him from a vase in a corridor. His mother had always
kept the palace filled to brimming with the bloom. A whiff of pol-
ishing oil drifting from the darkened armory suddenly had him
back in the palace lists with his father, blade to blade in training.
These things rose up, reminding him of the past, of his lost family.
And yet, he was such a different person now . . . melted down in the
fire of rebellion and remolded. It was as if he was passing through
scenes of another lifetime.

They had to make it out of the palace before Magnus discovered Nia's treachery and raised the alarm. Already there were signs the palace stirred, and Lucan wondered if it was too late. Gripping Branna's hand and with Nia not far behind, Lucan ran up a turret stairway and pushed open the door to the courtyard. All three of them stopped short.

Ah . . . *Sweet Solan!*

He inhaled and held his breath, then after a moment remembered to exhale. It looked just as it had the day he'd escaped so many years ago. Shadows fell deep and dark over the ground and cloaked the Valorian archers that lined the ramparts on guard duty. He heard Branna draw a sharp breath beside him. Aye, she now shared his memory of that day. She understood the familiarity of the scene that lay before them.

"Move slowly," he whispered. "Keep to the shadows." They had to make their way around the perimeter of the courtyard to a side door where Nia said the sorceresses waited.

Branna and Nia nodded, then slipped into the shadows near the rampart wall. Moving silently and with caution, they made it to the door and pushed it open. Naught but Tirian women stood on the other side. Lucan breathed a deep sigh of relief. They'd gotten out before Magnus could rouse the palace against them.

One of them carried *Draiochta Cothrom*. Lucan didn't want to think about that book. The key to it still hung around his neck and was growing heavier and more burdensome with every passing moment. They had everything now—the book, the key, the sorceresses, the priest . . . and the priestess.

Solan.

Lucan caught a glimpse of the surprised look on Branna's face as the sorceresses each greeted her quickly in turn. Each murmured, "Lady Raven," to her, curtsying and inclining their heads. As soon as the last sorceress paid her gentle homage, Lucan hurried them around the back part of the palace, staying very close to the rampart wall and moving slowly so the archers above did not see them.

A grassy plain stretched in back of the palace, lined by the edge of the Arbonne Forest. Where the distance to the forest was shortest, he bade them run as fast as they could to the tree cover. Lucan went last, making sure the women all made it to the tree line. Behind them he heard the archers cry alarm and begin to let arrows fly.

Quickly, they moved through the trees, skirting bramble and dodging fallen logs. Branches broke and leaves crunched under their feet. They moved like the wind, not catching themselves on the tree limbs or stumbling over fallen logs. He didn't know if it was magic or sheer fear that caused such fleetness of foot.

He glanced back. They were leaving a trail a babe could follow, but there was no help for it. Lucan wished fervently for a sword. Armillon had taken the Dragon Blade and long knife from him.

Long ago, Lucan had discussed with Morgan the best place for the Opposition to attack Ta'Ror from the Arbonne Forest. Lucan couldn't know if his second-in-command had escaped the Valorian, but if he had, he should've raised the Opposition and encamped there. Lucan could only fantasize that Ileria had sent troops their way. He'd been expecting a messenger with Ileria's answer to his proposal of an alliance.

A horse stepped out in front of them, and Lucan and the sorceresses stopped short. The horse reared and whinnied in surprise. Lucan's arm shot out in reflex, and he pulled the rider to the ground and restrained him.

"Lucan!"

A voice Lucan recognized came from the jumble he'd pinned to the forest floor. "Morgan." Lucan rolled off of him. "I thought you were gone forever," he rasped in sudden pain, doubling over on the forest floor. His side still hurt, and he was weak despite the healing.

"And I, you," Morgan replied. Lucan could hear affection in his voice.

Morgan stood and held a hand out. Lucan took it and stood.

"Arturo said you'd come this way and to bring many horses," said Morgan.

Lucan held his aching side and glanced around. There were Opposition there, all holding the reins of horses. His eyes closed briefly in relief. Thank Solan for Arturo and his skills.

"Come," said Morgan. "We don't have much time. The scouts say Ta'Ror is stirring . . . and readying themselves for war."

"The Ilerians?" Lucan asked with trepidation.

Morgan's mouth widened into a grin. "They're here, my lord, forces of them."

Lucan let out a breath of relief. Without the Ilerians, he feared they were lost.

"But . . . there is bad news," continued Morgan. "Magnus sent troops to Ileria earlier than he'd originally planned. The Ilerian troops coming to join with us fair passed the Valorian troops going there. Ileria's borders are badly weakened because of the absence of their men. Ileria will fall."

"Ileria would fall no matter if they sent their troops here or not," replied Lucan.

"That is why the Ritual of the Balance has to be performed . . . and performed soon," Branna broke in. "Ileria will fall regardless, but if the ritual is performed it will strengthen their magic tenfold, and they may be able to throw off the conquering force, even if many of their troops are here. If we cannot defeat Magnus on the battlefield, working the ritual will prevent him from controlling all the magic. It will undo Magnus completely."

Lucan could not find fault with her logic, except it meant Branna would have to sacrifice herself. That could not be allowed. Cold dread washed over him as he remembered his vision of Branna lying lifeless against him.

"Do you still have the key, Lucan?" she asked.

His hand found the key beneath his shirt, and he fingered it in silence for a moment. Finally, he made a low, angry sound and ripped it from his throat. He rounded on her with it in his hand. "Aye, the ritual will be done, but you'll not be a part of it," he said with finality.

She hesitated for a moment, taken aback by his anger. "I have to be a part of it, Lucan," she shot back. "You can't do it alone. There would be no equalization in the center of the circle. The imbalance of power would rip you to shreds and the ritual would not be successful."

"Better me ripped to shreds than to have the Balance take your life."

Moonlight limned her face and tipped her eyelashes in silver. She raised her damned stubborn chin to him. "Funnily enough, I feel exactly the opposite."

He hadn't wanted to tell her about the vision he'd had. It was as though speaking it aloud would make it all the truer, but now he felt he had no choice. "It will be you that the Balance takes. I have seen it."

She went silent for several long moments. He could not read her expression in the darkness. "What will be, must be," she said finally. "It is *cinnunt* . . . the *Parcae*. This is where the skein of my life comes unraveled, Lucan."

Lucan fisted his hands in helpless rage. He wouldn't let it happen. He just didn't know how he'd prevent it yet. "We'll see about that. You're not standing in that circle, Branna. I'll stand there myself and hold it for the both of us. I've strength enough to do that."

269

She shook her head, and there was sadness in her voice when she spoke. "You know not how magic works. Physical strength has naught to do with it."

"Then what about love, Branna? I've love strong enough to hold your place in the circle as well as my own and let the Balance take me instead."

"Oh, Lucan . . . you know not what you say. Don't you know we were doomed from the first time we met in Strobia?"

He didn't respond. He turned his back on her and found a horse. "Mount up, we've got to get to the encampment before daylight."

W HAT AN OBSTINATE MAN TO THINK HE COULD RE-strain the hands of *cinnunt*. Branna watched Lucan as he bent his head in a serious discussion with Morgan. He'd changed his clothes and now wore a pair of fresh leather trews and a clean shirt and jerkin, all unstained by his blood. Branna shivered, remembering just how much blood he'd lost from his injuries.

Branna had also changed her clothes and now wore a chestnut-colored woolen gown. Morgan had even brought her athame with him. When he'd given it to her, traces of Fiall's blood had still stained it.

Fiall.

She closed her eyes and pushed his name to the farthest reaches of her mind. It was far too painful for her to think of him. She could still sense him mentally. He was far away now, headed in the direction of Bah'ra.

She opened her eyes and found Lucan again. Her gaze had barely left him since they'd been reunited. Goddess, the man was galling, but it didn't change the fact that she loved him. She wished she didn't. It would make what was to come much easier.

They'd camped in a large clearing quite a distance to the south of Ta'Ror. She could hear the ocean not far away and knew it lay on the other side of the trees that flanked the camp. Opposition and Ilerian soldiers swarmed the area. A queer tingling flavored the air, caused by all the Ilerian and Tirian far-bloods.

Shadows and magic. The place was rife with them both.

The morning skies were overcast and heavy with the threat of snow. Branna wore a heavy black cloak, and her breath showed against the late autumn air.

She spotted Nia and the other sorceresses on the opposite side of the encampment, all standing with Arturo. The old mage hadn't left them since they'd rode in yesterday. Branna walked over to them.

When she reached them, they all curtsied, and Arturo bowed, causing her to take a step back in confusion. In Tir na Ban, no such formalities had ever been followed, simply because there weren't enough free Tirians or Tirian culture left to engage in them, but these sorceresses had been captured at the beginning of the Terror. They remembered the Tir na Ban of old.

Arturo took her hand. "When the time comes, he will have no choice but to let you participate," he said softly in Tirian. "Though I hate to see you do it." He patted her hand.

Branna couldn't help wondering what would happen after the ritual was performed and if the Opposition defeated Magnus. Would Lucan regain the Dragon Throne? Would he order the Valorian home from Tir na Ban and other provinces? Would he finally bring some peace and well-being to the land? Would he ever find peace and contentment for himself? If the answers to these questions were yes, she'd be able to go to the ritual with tranquility.

"How much else can you see, Arturo? Your powers of far-seeing are more developed than mine."

"All I see is the circle. That's how I know the ritual will come to pass," he answered.

Branna took her hand from Arturo's, then turned and walked toward the woods.

"My Raven?" Arturo called after her.

She turned to face him.

"The Goddess has allowed us to place a regio around this camp. It is the Goddess's will that only those with thoughts in line with the Opposition be able to find it. Beyond the regio are Valorian, my Raven, and therefore danger. Please be careful."

She tried to smile and failed. "I will."

She turned and silently walked into the shadowed forest, needing to be alone. Picking her way past bramble and fallen logs, she searched for the thrum of the earth under the dead leaves, for the heartbeat of Terrestra. Magic brushed over her skin when she passed the border of the regio. She didn't intend to stray far, just enough to be away from it all for a few moments—to seek solace and guidance from the trees and the earth below her feet. Anyway, she would not come to harm. *Cinnunt* would make sure she'd be safe enough to perform the ritual. The thoughts came with an edge of hard cynicism, and she drew a deep breath.

Maiden . . . Mother . . . Death Crone . . .

They were all the faces of the Goddess. She was all that was good, all that was evil, and every shade in between. She was the earth and the sky, the sun and the Sister moons, everything and nothing at the same time. Branna knew soon she'd see the Goddess wear the face of the Death Crone.

The sound of footfalls on the dead leaves came up fast behind her. A branch broke under someone's tread, and she whirled but saw nothing. The hairs along the nape of her neck rose. She backed up, keeping her eyes on the area where she'd heard the sounds, and ran into something hard, soft, and warm.

A hand grabbed her shoulder and spun her around. A scream bubbled up from her throat, but it died when she saw Lucan in front of her. He caught her up in his arms, pressing her against him. His eyes heated with intense need laid bare. He bent his head to hers and kissed her, parting her lips and possessing her mouth.

She relaxed against him, closing her eyes and molding her body to his. This was the only place she wanted to be . . . in his arms. All the tension left her body.

She knew with a certainty that made her heart beat faster that he wanted to be inside her every bit as much as she wanted him within her. Her hands instantly went to the lacings on his trews. She fumbled with the cord for a moment in her urgency and finally freed him to her touch.

His hands went under her cloak, pulling up her skirts. He found her undergarment and pushed it down to her ankles. She kicked it away. Then insistent fingers were on her, stroking her, pushing her to the place where she'd be ready to take him.

He must know she was already there.

His hips pushed against her, and Branna knew without a doubt that he was more than ready for her. Lucan slid his hands around her buttocks and lifted her from the ground, positioning her against him. He carried her a few steps to a tree and pressed her against it. Then in one long, powerful thrust, he pushed himself inside her to the hilt. A sound of animalistic pleasure tore from her throat, and her breath came in short little pants.

He held her there, pinned to the tree, and kissed her deeply. Then he began to move inside her. The pure and utter possession he claimed over her body, coupled with the deep pleasure she felt, drove all other thought from her. Gone were thoughts of the Ritual of the Balance, of losing Lucan, of death. For the time that he was inside her, it all blessedly disappeared.

After they'd pushed each other over their thresholds and were sated, Lucan held her against him in silence. Nary a word had been spoken by either of them since he'd come to her, and she knew if they spoke, the reality of their situation would again be asserted.

Branna searched his eyes and found both fear and love in them. Intense weariness etched lines around his eyes. He kissed her deeply again. Then, with clear reluctance, he released her.

He smoothed her hair back from her forehead in a domestic sort of way . . . the way a man who had a deep love bond with a woman and had been with her for years might touch his beloved. Branna's throat clogged with unshed tears. That one action brought all of reality crashing down upon her once more.

They only had this short time together. The Goddess would allow them no more. They held each other's gazes, both knowing the horrible truth of it.

"Come back into the regio with me," he said.

"Give me one moment," she choked out.

Lucan turned and walked away from her, back to the encampment, and she was left alone. She slid down the tree and curled up at the base of it, her face crumpling. Bitter tears rolled down her face.

CHAPTER TWENTY-EIGHT

CRISPUS FOUND THE CHIT AT TWILIGHT, CURLED against the base of a tree. Snow had fallen and had laid a light, white powdering over her.

She was sleeping, the silly little thing.

He reached down and gently bound her hands without awakening her. Then he slipped the blindfold over her eyes . . . just to be on the cautious side.

That woke her, and she started to pull at her bonds. He let her rise and stumble forward, catching her easily around the waist before she fell.

"Nay, girl," he said close to her ear. "I've a whole brace of archers with me. All their bows are taut and trained on your pretty little neck. I suggest you sheath those claws, my sleek black cat." As if in exclamation, the archers drew back their bows and the sound of arrows being notched filled the air.

She went still. "Crispus," she stated in a flat tone.

Interesting, he thought. She sounded tired. She sounded like the fight had left her. Oh, that was no fun at all.

"Aye. Did you miss me?"

He turned her in the direction he thought the Opposition's camp lay, and then pushed her forward. She tripped over the hem of her gown and fell to her hands and knees in the dead leaves. She stayed that way for a moment, her head bowed, then got to her feet.

"Walk," he ordered.

Crispus suspected a regio had been placed around the Opposition's camp. He'd lead the chit blindfolded to close to where he believed it was, then remove the blindfold and let her simply lead the way. Without a guide whose thoughts were aligned with that of the Opposition's, he'd never find it.

He took her by the upper arm and guided her blind march forward, letting her stumble and fall over the rocks and branches of the forest floor. The archers flanked them.

Straight into the camp, with only a brace of archers.

Some people said he was half-insane. Some said he was completely insane. Crispus smiled. Aye. Maybe he was, but he'd use the chit to draw Lucan out all the same. He was betting she meant a lot to him. It had been in his eyes in the prison. He and his uncle both pined for women. It was ridiculous. Crispus had never had such problems himself.

No love clouded his judgment. No passion blinded his eyes.

He'd use her to kill her lover, and then he'd take her back to Ta'Ror with him. She'd provide a few hours of enjoyment before she died from the strain of his attentions.

The girl stumbled over a log and went sprawling. Crispus helped her to her feet and realized belatedly the chit held a blade. Falling had only been a ploy. She'd used the opportunity to search out her dagger from the folds of her gown.

Clever chit.

She came up fast with her ladylike blade and tried to gut him with it. He dodged out of her way. She was blindfolded after all, and her wrists were bound. The advantage was all his.

She feinted blindly, out in front of her where she thought he stood.

"Oh, this is adorable!" said Crispus.

She made a low noise of rage and stabbed the air in front of him. He stepped out of her way and moved to her right. When she feinted right, he went left.

She made a sobbing sound.

This was fun. It was like that children's game, Baccaphan. He whispered low in her left ear and then moved to her right.

Left . . . then right . . . then left again. "Can't catch me," Crispus squealed with delight.

He dodged her dagger, went right . . . and made contact with her blade. Its silvered edge bit deep into his chest . . . right into his lung.

Interesting, he thought in a strangely removed way, the dagger seemed more serious now that it was embedded in him up to its hilt.

And the chit seemed far less adorable.

He grabbed her cloak as warm, metallic tasting blood flowed up from his insides and into his mouth. A gurgling sound escaped his lips, and he slumped to the forest floor, the blade sliding free of him as he fell.

BRANNA LET THE BLADE DROP FROM HER LIMP FINGERS. Warm blood coated her hands. She could hear the movement of the archers around her, and she braced herself for the stabbing of their arrows. Maybe the Ritual of the Balance wouldn't take her after all. Maybe it would be this.

For several long moments there was no sound, no movement. Then deadfall crunched under someone's tread. The person walked nearer and nearer.

"Rogan, stop, or I'll shoot you." The whine of an arrow string pulled taut filled the air as one of them notched their bow.

The footsteps ceased.

The whine of many arrow strings pulled taut sung through the forest. Branna's breath started to come in short, nervous gasps.

The footsteps resumed. "Karvyn, I'm pulling off her blindfold. If you want to shoot me . . . then shoot me, but seeing how many bows are trained on you, I don't think it would be a wise decision."

She felt hands on her face, pulling away her blindfold. Branna blinked and a young man's face came into focus. He took his long knife from his belt and used it to cut the bonds from her wrists.

Confused, she glanced around her. Lord Crispus lay on the ground at her feet. It was the first time she'd seen the man's face. His eyes were open, staring up blindly. Twilight had descended on the forest. The Sisters were rising. Around her stood a brace of Valorian archers. Most had their bows trained on one man. She suspected his name was Karvyn.

Branna wound her hands into her skirts so tightly her knuckles turned white. She stepped backward, making an agonized sound. It was all too much . . . too much.

"Shh . . . it's all right." Rogan reached a hand out to calm her as though she were a wild animal he was taming to take food from his hand. His face broke into a grin. "That was a pretty piece of blade work there, my lady."

"Rogan, this is sedition. The penalty for it is death—for you and for your family," Karvyn yelled.

"Aye," Rogan called back angrily. "But they can't kill us all, can they? They can't kill all our families. Anyway, it's not like they have any kind of a life under Magnus. All they have is hunger and fear," he finished fiercely. He whirled around and addressed the other Valorian archers. Some had their bows on Karvyn; others simply looked terrified. "It's time for us to take a chance! It's time to make a stand!"

There was a very tense moment when Branna thought Karvyn would let his arrow fly. Many bow strings tightened as the Valorian drew back and up, pointing their killing tips at Karvyn. Karvyn closed an eye and drew a line of sight trained on Rogan. The other archers did the same, trained on Karvyn. Then Karvyn's bow sagged and dropped to the ground. "Fine," he said wearily. "I'm with you."

Rogan smiled as he turned to Branna. "Take us to the man they call Gallus Navius Lucan."

W HEN BRANNA CAME THROUGH THE TREES WITH A brace of Valorian archers trotting alongside of her like dogs trained to heel, Lucan's jaw dropped. Many of his men drew their swords or long knives. Some notched arrows into their bows, but Lucan could see the truth written on the Valorians' faces.

They were joining with the Opposition. There was dissention in the Valorian. Magnus's hold was slipping.

He watched Branna walking toward him in the twilight, the men at her side. Her long black hair moved around her, displaced by the wind. Her face was tight, her mouth drawn. The tension of the situation weighed on her every bit as much as it weighed on him. He wanted to pull her close and kiss away the lines that framed her mouth. He wanted to tease her to laughter, drag her into his tent, and hold her all night long, safe and protected in his arms.

He wanted to keep her beside him for the rest of his life.

Lucan wildly entertained the notion that perhaps they'd be able to defeat Magnus without performing the Ritual of the Balance, and then he remembered Ileria. Even if they defeated Magnus there was still Ileria. The Valorian forces would ravage the country not knowing their emperor had been undone.

Curse Ileria.

Branna approached him, and he noticed right away that she wouldn't meet his gaze. "Lucan—"

He forced a smile. "These archers have come to join with us," he finished for her.

One young man stepped forward and went down on one knee. "My lord Navius Lucan, I swear my bow, my blade, and my fealty to you as the true and legitimate ruler of Numia." He placed a fist to his breast. "My liege." He inclined his head.

All of the men dropped to one knee and swore the same.

It took Lucan aback to see such formality. He bade them rise.

The one who'd sworn him allegiance first, spoke. "My lord, my name is Rogan. Our services are at your disposal." He smiled in a conspiratorial way. "And so is our information."

Lucan raised an eyebrow. "And what information would that be?"

"Magnus plans to attack at dawn the day after tomorrow. Still, he is making his forces ready for warfare. He will lead troops himself and strike from the north and west. Commander Armillon will lead from the south."

"Do you know when the Valorian forces that have been sent abroad will make landfall on Ileria?"

"Aye, my lord. They will be engaging by tomorrow morning at the latest."

Branna's gaze flicked up and caught Lucan's momentarily. He

had her until tomorrow morning. They had one more night to make up for a lifetime.

"My lord," said Rogan, jerking Lucan from his thoughts. "If you can kill Magnus, the Valorian resolution will disintegrate. When Magnus dies, so does the fear. With the fear gone, many will turn to the side of the Opposition. The lady here killed Lord Crispus, and it spurred us to turn."

Lucan had Branna by the arm before the man had even finished his sentence and led her away. He signaled for Morgan to go and deal with the archers.

Lucan guided her into his tent. Once inside, he sat her down on the bedroll. It was then he saw the blood on her hands and the fresh smears on the black of her cloak. "What did he mean you killed Crispus?" Fear made his tone rough. Just the thought of her anywhere near that twisted soul sent terror ripping through him.

Branna looked up at him, her eyes bright with unshed tears. "I've never killed anyone before, Lucan," she whispered.

His face softened. He acted as though he was angry with her when he wasn't. It was the situation they'd been put in that he was angry with. He was angry at Solan, the world at large, and most of all, he was angry with himself. He was failing yet again to keep someone he loved safe. "Aye . . . it's not a nice feeling, is it?"

She shook her head. A teardrop fell into her lap.

He knelt beside her and pressed her against him, smoothing her hair.

Branna struggled free of him, stood, and ran out of the tent. He got up and followed her just in time to see her running back into the woods. Lucan wanted to go after her, but knew she needed to be alone.

Aye, being near one another so close to the ritual was painful. She felt it too.

She felt safer in the woods, but he did not think it was a safe place for her. He would set sentries on her to make sure she stayed within the regio.

The pledging of the archers fealty had brought home the fact that if they were successful in their goals, by tomorrow night he would be a king.

A king without a queen.

B RANNA SAT IN THE LEAVES AND WATCHED FROM JUST inside the darkened tree line, fully aware that Lucan had sentries following her every move.

The rebels lighted fires for the night, and she watched as Lucan and Morgan worked to prepare for what would come in the morning. The Sisters were high in the sky before the camp calmed and soldiers began to drift to sleep.

The sorceresses slept in a tent at the heart of the camp, surrounded by Ilerian troops. Branna sighed. The archers had provided their paltry bit of information, not realizing that they would have an unlimited supply of it. The sorceresses had much to impart.

Lucan said good night to Morgan. They embraced briefly, clapping each other heartily on the back in the way of men, then parted. Morgan went to his tent. She expected Lucan to go to his own, but he walked past it and into the woods beyond.

Branna stood and followed him.

She found him the same way she'd seen him when they had been traveling to Kern the first time. His sword and long knife were to the side and he was on his knees, his face tipped to the night sky and bathed in silver starshine. His lips moved in a silent prayer.

She knew what he prayed for—the same thing she did.

Tirians did not pray the way Numians did. For a Tirian every moment was a prayer, every action in reverence to the Goddess. They communicated always with her, so there was never a reason to formally address her.

Branna thought perhaps it was time she spoke with Lucan's Gods.

She picked her way toward him, knelt, and tipped her head up. Silently, she paid homage to Solan of the Overworld and the four Gods of the Elements.

She felt something brush her lips, and she opened her eyes. Lucan's arms came around her as he pulled her to him, deepening the kiss. She reached up and twined her fingers in his hair. Hot tears stung her eyes, but she refused to allow them to fall.

She pulled away from him and rocked back on her heels. "If you'd been merely my consort, this would be difficult but not nearly as painful."

Lucan reached out and then let his arms fall to his sides. "I—I don't know what to do. I don't know how to avoid what will come tomorrow. I don't know how to protect you." A sharp breath escaped him. "I want to let Ileria fall. I want to let them fend for themselves and not conduct the Ritual of the Balance. I want to—"

"You want to sacrifice an entire nation of innocents to save one woman? We both know we can't do that, Lucan. I won't allow Ileria to go through what Tir na Ban went through. If I had the power to prevent it and didn't, I would never be able to live with myself. This is *cinnunt*. This is what I'm meant to do with my life, my magic."

Branna tried to read his expression in the darkness, but his features were shadowed.

"I want the Balance to take me," he said. "I don't want you to stand within the circle."

She shook her head. "I have the magic, Lucan. You have the

strength. We both must stand there. It won't work if one of us is missing."

"Branna." His voice broke on her name.

She reached out and touched his face. "I love you too, Lucan. More than anything, I love you." He helped her stand and then guided her back to his tent.

This was their last night together.

The Ritual of Balance would be performed the next morning, and they both knew it.

CHAPTER TWENTY-NINE

LUCAN AWOKE LYING ON HIS SIDE WITH BRANNA PRESSed against him. His arm was thrown over her waist and tucked up against her stomach, his fingers entwined with hers. Her head was pressed under his chin. Last night he'd prayed that morning would never come, but, of course, it had.

Someone pushed the tent flap in, and Arturo's wizened face appeared. Behind the mage, Lucan saw that the skies had broken clear with bright sunshine—in sharp contrast to the sorrow the day was destined to bring.

"My lord, the Ilerians are beginning to become agitated. They begin to sense what is happening in their homeland." His eyes flicked to Branna. "The time grows near."

Lucan tightened his arm around Branna. "Give us as long as possible."

"Of course." Arturo's head disappeared.

Branna stirred and shifted onto her back, parting her berry-colored lips. Her black lashes swept down on vanilla-silk skin, and her cheeks were tinged with the palest shade of healthy pink. Lucan knew her skin would not stay so. Soon it would be ashen . . . cold.

But not yet.

He lowered his mouth to taste her lips, and when he raised his gaze, her cat-green eyes were on him. Her lips moved under his, returning his kiss. He shifted over her, covering her body with his and catching her hands in his and pinning them to the bedroll. The full lengths of their bodies kissed.

A low keening of many male voices reached into the tent and surrounded them. The sound quavered, catching and rolling on the wind like some unearthly music. It chilled him to the center of his being.

Branna's eyes widened and she broke the kiss. Lucan held her under him for a long moment. Their gazes locked in silent understanding.

The time had come.

An agonized sound rose up from deep within him and ripped its way from his throat. He rolled away from her, releasing her. He lay on the ground beside her for a moment, willing himself to move.

It's time . . . it's time . . .

He shot up from the bedroll and out of the tent.

Outside, the Ilerian soldiers, normally a fierce and unforgiving breed, were on their knees, all of them experiencing some sort of mental connection to their homeland. If their reaction was any indication, Ileria was not faring well . . . not well at all.

Branna followed him out of the tent, her face drawn in surprise and fear. Arturo came up to them. He bowed low to them both in turn. They had to yell to make themselves heard over the keening. "It's time, my lord, my lady. The sorceresses have cast a circle outside the camp to the west."

All three of them stood still for several long moments. Lucan had half a mind to throw Branna over his shoulder and run for the forest.

Something black moved out of the corner of his eye. He turned his head and saw a single raven flying low over the tents of the camp, coming straight for them. He glanced at Branna and Arturo and saw they too saw it. It was no apparition caused by his tormented and feverish mind.

The raven perched a short distance from them and spread its wings. As the mournful sound of the Ilerians swirled around them, the raven cawed once. Then it took off and flew west . . . toward where Arturo said the sorceresses had cast their circle.

Branna's face transformed from a look of surprise and fear to one of determination. "Let's go. Let us put this suffering to an end." She swept past them both, leaving them to follow in her wake.

The sorceresses had cast the circle in a flat area far enough from camp that the sounds of the Ilerians could be heard only distantly. Nia was also in the circle, holding the *Draiochta Cothrom*.

Branna broke the circle and went within. Holding Lucan's gaze, she stood in the center.

This was going too fast . . . way too fast . . .

"Do you have the key?" Arturo asked him.

The question took a few moments to sink in. His eyes were on Branna. Her gaze held him motionless. A look of peace graced her face.

"Give him the key, Lucan," she said with a slight smile on her lips. "It's going to be all right, whatever happens."

Aye, she could say that when it was she who was doing the leaving. She would not have to spend the rest of her days alone, haunted by the memory of this day. She had the easy task of the Ritual of the Balance. Surviving it was the most difficult part.

Behind him, the far away sound of the Ilerians' keening reached a wavering crescendo. Lucan reached under his jerkin and shirt and ripped the key from the chain around his neck.

"Here," he growled, pushing it at Arturo. Then he parted the circle angrily and entered it. He walked up to Branna and put his arms around her.

Lucan watched as Arturo gave the key to Nia and then took his place in the circle beside her.

"Gallus Navius Lucan and Branna ta Cattia ta Sorcha, you are the Balance," said Nia. "You are the male and female, the priest and priestess. You represent the night and day, the sun and moons. You are the God and Goddess. By using your Balance and the gifts of your power and your life force, we'll permanently alter the Universal Fabric, freeing magic throughout this land." Nia smiled sadly. "We thank you for your sacrifice," she finished softly.

Nia placed the key into its place on the cover of the book. For a brief moment Lucan thought perhaps the key would not work. It was a copy, after all. There was a true *Draiochta Cothrom* and a false *Draiochta Cothrom*, according to Nia. The false one would not work, so perhaps a false key would not work either.

His hopes were dashed when the key slid in. A single, powerful tone resonated out from the book, going straight through him, thrumming to the soles of his feet. The Book of Magical Balance was awakened.

Nia opened the book and began to chant in Tirian. It took him a moment to realize he could understand what she said. He knew then that magic already worked within the circle.

The circle calls the wind to blow.
Come swift, come low.
The circle bids the magic rise.

Ride in on the lover's sighs.
Here stands the strength of one to hold, and the magic of another to
    mold.
Spread her soul over plain and field,
And magic for all it will yield.

The other sorceresses took up the chant. Their voices were whis-
pers at first, growing louder and louder until they all made one
single voice, drowning out the sound of the Ilerians' keening completely. As their voices rose, so did the wind. Dark clouds rolled in
from the north, growing blacker and blacker. The cold wind buffeted his hair and caused Branna's to swirl around her.

Branna caught and held Lucan's gaze. She smiled in acceptance
and peace. "I will see you in the next life, my love," she said over the
rising wind.

Lucan tried to answer her, to tell her that she wasn't going to
leave him. He was going to hold on to her so tightly the Balance
could not take her. The wind increased and caught the voices of
the sorceresses around them. The sounds pitched and whined and
flowed through and around them. The wind picked up his words as
soon as they were uttered and cast them into an abyss.

Lucan didn't need to have magic to feel the energy grow around
them. The air was pregnant with it. He pulled Branna against him.
She had her eyes squeezed shut and was mouthing the chant from
the *Draiochta Cothrom.*

The wind grew in force with every passing moment. It ripped
leaves from the trees, and they whirled around them madly. The
sorceresses of the circle seemed to be the only ones unaffected.
Nary a tendril of their hair stirred, nor were their skirts disturbed
by the cold northern wind.

Something built in the air, some sort of tension all around

them, ready to explode. Lucan pressed Branna against him, holding on to her as tightly as he could. Whatever it was, he swore, it would not take her with it.

Then light splintered in front of his eyes—the light of a million crystals breaking apart and swirling around them. The sound of a brittle shattering near deafened him. The force of it pushed him back, and in the process his grip on Branna faltered. He released her and fell backward into darkness.

CHAPTER THIRTY

MAGNUS FISTED NIA'S FINELY WOVEN SLEEPING CHE-mise in a shaking hand and turned from her bed. He stalked to the double doors leading to the terrace and hit them hard with the flat of his hand. The doors flew open, and he went to the railing, staring down into the courtyard.

Armillon stood with the commander of the Southern Valorian. Soldiers lined the courtyard and spilled out beyond the gates to the plains on the eastern side of the palace.

He suspected he knew the area in which the Opposition was en-camped, though a regio had thus far foiled all attempts at deter-mining their position for certain. Now he bided his time until the Valorian had strength enough to attack the area from every direc-tion, overwhelming them and preventing their escape. Their regio wouldn't matter if they were encircled and choked. He'd sent many troops to Ileria and that had weakened them. During the last day and night, he had gathered up every man from every village as far away as Pannonia. He'd gathered up every boy old enough to hold a long knife as well. Nay, he would not underestimate his nephew any longer.

Crispus was gone, the miserable cur. He'd left yesterday and hadn't come back. It made him nervous. He knew not what went on in Crispus's twisted mind.

The key to the *Draiochta Cothrom* was still in the politician's wing of the palace. That was the best thing he had discovered since Nia and the other sorceresses had left. At least there was that. They'd gotten the Book of Magical Balance, but they didn't have the key to open it.

A sharp gust of wind buffeted his hair, blowing the scent of Nia's chamber to him. She'd always insisted on having skyflower in her sleeping room. Magnus lifted her chemise to his nose, closed his eyes, and inhaled. He'd get her back, and she'd never leave him again. Nay, he'd never even allow her to see the light of day. He'd lock her in his chamber and make her work to win his favor, to wait upon his every whim, no matter how wretched or carnal. If he couldn't woo her, he'd simply subdue her.

Another gust of wind blew, and thunder boomed in the distance. That was odd, Magnus thought. The day was so fine. He opened his eyes and lowered Nia's chemise. He looked toward the west where the clouds were darkening and rolling over the land on the wings of a fast-moving and wicked wind. Lightning split the clouds, and thunder shattered the otherwise quiet air. The eastern sky was bright and cloud free, and the west roiled with chaos.

Magnus looked down at the courtyard and saw his men all looking to the west as though mesmerized.

That's when he heard the screaming. The wind made a low keening sound that grew louder as the clouds approached. The horses whinnied and bolted for the gateway. Where there had been neat rows of Valorian soldiers, there was now utter disorder as they also fled.

The wind grew incredibly strong. It ripped his hair from the queue at his nape and whipped it around his face. Magnus knew he should go back inside where it was safe, but he couldn't seem to move his feet. The wind tore Nia's chemise from his hand. It hovered in the air in front of him for a moment, taunting him. Magnus bellowed and made a grab for it, but the wind whipped it out of his reach and lofted it high into the sky. Magnus watched as the wind bore it away. It looked like a dove set free from its cage.

As he watched the chemise blow away, he saw that not only did the sun hang in the east, but the Sister moons had also risen. The three celestial orbs now hung in the sky together. It was unnatural. It was . . . the Ritual of the Balance.

His eyes widened in comprehension. Somehow, they had opened the book.

The wind pushed him forward, and he gripped the stone wall. He could hear nothing but the screaming of the wind around him. The courtyard below was now empty, save for a few confused horses who couldn't find the gateway and some men who'd been trampled.

A flash, almost like reflected sunlight, winked from the Arbonne Forest. It flashed again and then exploded. Light rolled out from that point, enveloping everything in its path. When the light reached the palace at Ta'Ror, Magnus cried out and fell backward.

L UCAN CAME TO AWARENESS SLOWLY. THE FIRST THING he noticed were the many birds that sung in the trees. But that was impossible. It was autumn; all the songbirds had flown to the southern reaches of Pira and Bah'ra where it was warmer.

The second thing he noticed was that it smelled like spring. The scents of fresh green grass, flowers, and trees in full bloom were in the air . . . mixed with skyflower.

Lucan forced himself to open his eyes, his head pounding. Above him was bright blue sky. Was it bluer than it should be? It looked almost indigo.

He shook his head and rolled onto his side, his eyes searching out Branna. He noted that all the sorceresses, and Arturo too, were also coming back to awareness. The shattering of that invisible crystal . . . if that's what it had been . . . had knocked them all unconscious.

Then he saw her. She lay in an unnatural position on the grass, her face pallid and her hair fanned out around her.

His breath caught painfully. He pushed himself onto his hands and knees and crawled across the ground to her. He pulled her into his arms. She was so cold . . . too cold. He put his fingers to the pulse at her throat. It fluttered like a dying bird. She was still alive . . . but her life force was rapidly slipping away. Lucan bent his head over her, a low sound of anguish tearing from his throat.

"I'm truly sorry, my lord," said Arturo, kneeling on the grass beside him. "It will be of no consolation, I know, but her sacrifice has wrought all of this." He threw an arm wide.

Lucan looked around. Spring had come to darkest autumn. Flowers bloomed at the edge of a full and lush forest. A warm breeze blew, buffeting bees that were heavy with nectar. Pollen floated through the air alongside innumerable dragonflies. Songbirds had perched in the trees, and their voices filled the air. Sunlight dappled the ground and limned the leaves of the trees in golden light.

The colors looked brighter . . . almost unreal. There was a new definition to the world that had been absent before. It was crisper, clearer.

"Within the circle, you were the strength and she was the magic," whispered Arturo. "You kept your strength to get through her loss. Aye, she's gone, Lucan, but she's left her magic behind."

Lucan had realized when they'd chanted the spell why the Balance had needed to take Branna and not himself. It was her magic the spell required. It was her beautiful, strong, magically imbued soul the Balance had spread over the world, making the colors brighter and the magic more powerful. He realized that every time he touched a flower or a tree, he'd be touching Branna. Every time he smelled rain in the air, it would be she.

Lucan dipped his head to hers and kissed her cold lips.

It was not enough by far.

He noted that the keening of the Ilerians had ceased. He dropped his lips to Branna's throat and felt that her pulse had also ceased.

Arturo said he'd kept his strength to get through her loss. Lucan realized that he didn't have enough strength for that. It felt as though a part of him had been ripped away. No amount of strength would ever bring it back. He would never be whole again.

Lucan said nothing to Arturo and eventually he left. Unwilling to let Branna go into the hands of the sorceresses to be prepared for burial, Lucan simply held on to her.

The sound of rapid hoofbeats approaching from the west met his ears. Lucan did not bother to raise his head until the gasps of the sorceresses around him had him looking up. A horse pranced in front of him, soaked with sweat. It gave a great whuffling snort, obviously content to have been brought to a halt.

He looked past the horse's lathered head and neck and saw the one face he didn't want to see. Fiall.

Lucan had no weapons with him other than his own rage. He laid Branna onto the grass and stood. Stalking up to Fiall's horse, he pulled him from it. Fiall made no move to resist and let Lucan slam him hard to the ground. He straddled him, keeping both hands fisted in Fiall's tunic. "What are you doing here, betrayer?"

Fiall's haunted eyes stared up at him from a face yet black-and-blue from their last confrontation. "I'm here to pay for my betrayal."

"Too late. She's gone."

"I . . . I had thought to save her."

Lucan's grip faltered. Was that why he'd given her into Magnus's hands? Had it been some misplaced attempt to protect her from the Ritual of the Balance, driven by rage and jealousy?

"I should have know that *cinnunt* is never denied, but . . . I can still save her," he whispered fiercely.

On Fiall's face and in his eyes, Lucan saw self-hatred of the highest level. He pushed off of him and rolled to the side, raking both hands through his hair. "You cannot, Fiall. She is in the hands of the Deities of the One. She's in Vallon now."

Branna's words came back to him. *I will see you in the next life, my love . . .*

Fiall stood, walked to Branna, and knelt beside her. "I can trade myself for her. I can bring her back from Vallon."

Lucan raised himself from the ground and went to him. Angrily, he pushed Fiall back away from her. "You've gone crazy, Tirian. There is no bringing anyone back from Vallon."

Arturo approached them. "There are certain rules in the universe, Fiall. She is gone. You must accept that."

"No!" The word issued from a throat constricted with pain. He drew a deep breath and shook his head. "The Ritual of the Balance has been performed, and it has changed all the rules. This is not the same reality you knew this morning. I will have the opportunity to make amends." He locked gazes with Lucan. "And if I am successful, I will save not one life . . . but two."

Lucan stared at Fiall in agonized surprise.

"She did not know it yet, but I sensed a child seeded within her the morning I turned her over to Magnus's hands." Fiall looked away from Lucan. "It makes what I did even worse," he said softly.

Still in shock, Lucan watched as Fiall gathered Branna against him. The birds sang in the trees around them, and the spring breeze blew loose petals and pollen over the two Tirian forms. Sorrow welled up from the depths of him, almost choking him with its intensity. She'd been carrying his child.

Fiall tipped his head to Branna's and closed his eyes. "I won't let harm come to you today," he said.

The guilt Fiall was experiencing must have driven him mad. But there was a part of Lucan that harbored a hope that he'd succeed in his efforts . . . and then he knew he'd also been driven mad.

For a long while, nothing happened. Fiall simply held Branna's limp body against him. The sorceresses reformed their circle and began quietly keening the Tirian death song. Their voices rose and fell and echoed mournfully around them. Lucan guessed they sang for the sacrifice their Raven had made, and for their loss of her presence.

Lucan stared down at Fiall and almost . . . almost . . . forgave him his actions. The lines of the Tirian warrior's body laid bare his feelings all too well. Fiall had thrust himself into an underworld of his own making.

Then something flickered between Fiall and Branna. Some tiny thing came to life and flashed between their bodies. He caught his breath, daring himself the smallest bit of hope.

If autumn could turn to spring, if the birds could return from the south, if all this could happen within the space of a heartbeat, then why not . . .

Fiall slumped backward onto the grass as though he were merely a child's rag doll. Lucan caught his breath when he saw Branna stir. The sorceresses broke off their keening, and Arturo gasped in surprise.

Lucan knelt beside her as she opened her eyes. Confusion clouded her face, and she gasped as though remembering something. "Lucan—" she rasped.

"Shush. Don't try to speak. Relax now." He stroked the hair framing her face.

She shook her head. "Fiall came and found me in Vallon," she whispered. "He bartered his magic for mine."

Lucan gathered her against him. "Aye . . . then he truly was your protector in the end." He placed his hand on her lower abdomen and could feel heat rising under his fingertips. He fancied he could also feel the flicker of life deep within her.

The sorceresses began their keening again, but this time it was for Fiall.

B RANNA PACED BACK AND FORTH OUTSIDE THE TENT she and Lucan had shared the night before. When she'd awakened, he'd been gone, and so had Morgan and most of the Opposition. The sorceresses remained, along with a force of rebel and Ilerian soldiers led by Varro.

Lucan had not used the sorceresses at all, she thought wildly. He'd simply left them behind, despite the advantage they would give him.

She opened her hand and looked down at Fiall's shield necklace that lay against her palm. She'd taken it from around his neck before he'd been buried. Her feelings for Fiall were yet jumbled and painful. She did not forgive Fiall for nearly killing Lucan. Never would she be able to forgive him for that. But he had tried to be her protector in all his actions, be they confused or nay. He'd given up his own magical soul in place of hers and had saved her and her child.

They'd buried Fiall in the woods, in a beautiful clearing dotted with bunches of skyflower, chambersweet, and freeleaf.

Skyflower was only found at very high altitudes. That it should be growing here, in the Numian lowlands next to the ocean, was strange indeed.

But all reality had changed now.

Bringing home that fact, a tiny female being with iridescent wings now skirted the edge of the tent. Branna watched it in awe. Aye, there were no more rules at all now.

Varro came up on her right side and swiped at the being with his sword scabbard. Thankfully, the being dodged it. The tiny thing made a faint, enraged noise, and Varro hefted his scabbard to take another swing.

"Varro, stop," cried Branna. She put a hand to his upper arm. "Stay your hand. That is no insect."

He lowered the scabbard, looking at the thing quizzically. *"Solan's blood,"* he breathed. "It's a tiny woman ... with ... wings," he exclaimed. With that, he collapsed at Branna's feet.

She sighed. So much for the protection Lucan had thought to leave behind. The mighty Varro had just been felled by a pixie.

Two Ilerian soldiers who'd seen what had happened came to gather up Varro and lay him comfortably on his back until he regained consciousness. They exchanged knowing looks with Branna. In Ileria and Tir na Ban, places of far-blooded magic, there was the occasional pixie, but in Numia, it was an unheard-of thing.

When she'd returned to the camp with Lucan the previous night, the Ilerians had been at peace, their mournful keening replaced by smiles and murmurings of gratitude. They'd bowed to her and paid her homage as the Tirian Raven. Branna was simply satisfied that Ileria had been spared what Tir na Ban had endured.

She and Lucan had made love last night. For every bit as possessive as their lovemaking had been in the forest the day before the ritual, their coupling last night had been tender. Passionately and slowly they'd given each other physical gifts of themselves and had known themselves to be truly one.

But that had been last night.

This morning she'd awoken to a cold tent and the colder knowledge that Lucan had already left to attack Magnus.

Goddess . . . His misplaced chivalry would allow Magnus to triumph and get Lucan killed.

Branna tried to access Lucan mentally, but all she perceived were blinding flashes of blade work, the sounds of steel meeting steel, all awash in blood . . . lots and lots of it.

She cast a desperate glance around the camp for Arturo and the sorceresses. The old mage's vision was more valuable than ever now. When she spotted them, she picked up her skirts and ran. They bowed and curtsied again, making her stop short. *Morrenna's stars!* She did not feel like the Goddess incarnate today. She felt far more like a woman afraid for her lover and not at all worthy of their esteem.

"I . . . I can see nothing," Branna stammered.

Arturo stepped forward and touched her shoulder gently. "None of us can. The threads of *cinnunt* are weaving wildly now. The Ritual of the Balance has broken all the rules. Fate changes with every passing moment."

It was chaos, he meant.

CHAPTER THIRTY-ONE

WHEN MAGNUS HAD AWOKEN, THE WORLD HE'D known before was simply . . . gone. In its place was springtime and rebirth. But, *Solan's blood*, it was a rebirth of the oddest proportions. It made his blood run cold.

The Ritual of the Balance had spread some strange enchantment over the land. He knew not how to rule in this new world. Deep down, he knew he was done for. Many of the Valorian had revolted after the Ritual of the Balance. Many had turned tail and fled from fear. Many, he knew, had joined the Opposition.

The magic his sorceresses had lent him had been fading rapidly since they'd left. Magnus felt years older than he had the day before. His campaign in Ileria had surely failed. There would be no new infusion of magic for him to draw from, since now magic was everywhere. It was impossible for him to control it all.

No. He now felt old and was a man without magic, but he was

not yet ready to admit defeat. That was why he had gathered his troops . . . what was left of them . . . and had planned his attack.

There was one positive thing. The Valorian that were left fought for him. They did not fight out of fear of reprisal against themselves and their families. They fought only for their emperor and the glory of the Numian Empire.

The day had dawned clear and bright, ready to be colored crimson by the blood that would be spilled. Magnus looked down into the valley below him, where his forces were now engaged with Lucan's.

He had not expected his nephew to be so well versed in the ways of war, of strategy and psychological manipulation. Lucan had directed the Opposition to attack the Valorian before dawn had even broken on the horizon. As a result, Magnus's troops had entered the battle on the defensive. They'd still been wiping the sleep from their eyes when the Opposition had begun to cut them down in the still of the early morning.

The Valorian had regained their lost ground, however. Now they fought on equal footing.

The sun reflected off his nephew's blade as he thrust and parried through the melee. When Magnus had known him, Lucan had been a young man who'd pledged himself to the Gods and had renounced violence as a way of life. But with every passing minute, Magnus saw that his nephew had changed much over the years. He did not know how much Lucan had retained of his pious ways, but one thing was certain, his nephew now worshipped his silvered, misery-giving blade.

Magnus tightened his grip on his weapon. Aye, Lucan's sword might have a bite that stung, but Magnus had the Dragon Blade, and Lucan would have to wrest it from his fingers himself.

There was not a sorceress in sight, so Lucan had no shield to protect him. Probably, Lucan had bid the sorceresses to stay in the Opposition's camp out of some silly notion of protection.

He'd soon show his nephew what a mistake that had been. He'd let his nephew fight and become tired. Only then would he seek him out and have an advantage over him. The Valorian and the Opposition were fairly well matched, but Magnus had extra troops he would be sending in soon. According to his scouts, the Opposition was rapidly depleting theirs.

The Valorian in the south were not faring as well. The damned Ilerians had been sent to block Commander Armillon's attack. They'd seemed to know just where to go to head him off. The Ilerians fought like the Tirian warriors had, hard-edged and unforgiving, with all their hearts thrown into the task. It was surprising they were so fierce, considering they came from a country where women ruled.

And they wouldn't fight normally!

Some of them fought on the ground in organized troop movements, but many hid in the trees. They would fall upon the Valorian from above at the most unexpected of times. It made Armillon's troops nervous and on edge. The Ilerians fought with vicious, serrated blades, as did the Tirians, but the Ilerians dipped their swords, long knives, and arrow tips in socausia, a debilitating poison.

Really, it was quite tiring.

As a result, the Ilerians had the Valorian in the south on a hasty retreat, and Magnus had ordered Armillon's troops to join his forces. That meant the Ilerians would also relocate, but here in the north there were no trees for them to hide in, only long, open plains. Magnus hoped it would be enough to take the edge off them.

He found his nephew in the crush once again. He'd sent his best to finish him off, but the man simply would not die. Besides the fact that his nephew had a tight circle of protective Opposition around him, Lucan seemed to have a charmed blade. It never missed its mark.

His mouth twisted in a smile at the irony. He'd taught his nephew everything he knew about swordplay. Apparently, the only one able to take him down was his teacher. It had been like warring with himself when he'd fought Lucan in Kastum. Magnus had taken his measure of him then, weighing out his weakness.

He turned and motioned for his brace of personal Valorian to flank him. It was time they finally put this to an end. He spurred his mount down the hill, heading straight for his nephew.

B RANNA OPENED HER MOUTH TO SAY SOMETHING TO AR-turo, but the pounding hooves of approaching horses drowned out her words. She whirled and saw the trees shaking so hard their leaves were falling. Then horses came through the trees. She squinted against the bright sunlight and saw they were retreating Valorian soldiers with Opposition and Ilerian forces following steadily behind. The battle had spilled back and was now in their camp.

Branna saw Varro, now fully conscious after his encounter with the pixie, order the rebel and Ilerian soldiers in the camp to battle.

The sorceresses scattered, but she remained rooted in place, her eyes searching out Lucan. A Valorian soldier rode past her, his blade angling for her head, and it was only then that she moved, dodging the silver edge and finding shelter behind a tent.

Lucan came after the man, his sword cleaving through the air like some deadly bird of prey. The soldier dropped to the ground near Branna, and Lucan whirled around, his eyes catching hers briefly and then searching out another opponent.

Branna ran out and took up the Valorian's sword. Her hand molded itself to its grip and she hefted it. It was heavy, but not so heavy she couldn't use it.

Nia and Arturo ran toward her and together they found shelter within the tree line. When Nia tried to take the sword, Branna let her. With wild eyes, Nia held it close and searched the melee anxiously.

LUCAN SAW BRANNA TAKE THE FALLEN VALORIAN'S sword and run into the woods with Nia and Arturo before he whirled and headed back into the fray. The Valorian had retreated toward the camp, and the rebels had no choice but to follow them. The safety of the sorceresses, the old mage, and Branna weighed heavily on him. Since he'd met Branna, he had learned quickly the price of love and fettering of emotion that came with it, but he could not allow himself to be distracted now.

Magnus was here.

He could see his uncle at the opposite end of the camp, working his way through the Opposition to him, even as Lucan worked through the Valorian to get to Magnus. He could see the Dragon Blade flashing in his uncle's hand.

He would have it back.

Lucan's blade bit into the side of a Valorian soldier who'd tried to behead him, and he reined around to find Commander Armillon in front of him. This was the man who'd killed Ren. The thought blazed through Lucan's mind, leaving intense anger in its wake.

"You won't escape this time, rebel," Armillon bellowed. They raised swords and engaged. Their blades arched through the air, meeting then parting, then meeting again in a deadly dance. The air around them fairly sung with the slicing and clashing of steel.

Lucan caught Armillon in the face with a shallow cut and then a deeper one on his upper arm. The man yelled in outrage and pain. Lucan wanted to make fast work of Armillon. He could feel Magnus at his back growing nearer with every passing moment.

Fueled by anger, Armillon lashed out with renewed energy, putting Lucan on the defensive. From the side, Morgan launched himself at Armillon, taking him unawares, and pulled the commander off his horse to the ground.

Armillon and Morgan engaged on the ground. Lucan watched with dismay as Armillon quickly asserted himself as a formable foe against his second-in-command. Morgan was a warrior tried and true, and his swordsmanship was excellent, but Armillon had not reached such a high position in the Valorian without also proving himself in battle.

Lucan would not lose Morgan. As Armillon pushed his second-in-command to his knees, Lucan swung down from his horse. He separated Armillon from Morgan with one well-placed swing of his blade, cutting the commander in the shoulder.

Armillon turned enraged eyes upon Lucan. Before he had a chance to react, Lucan swung his blade down and up, catching the commander deep in his midsection, cutting clear through his hardened leather vest.

Lucan had no time to watch Armillon fall. Malevolence was palpable at his back. He turned from Armillon just in time to block the Dragon Blade, which was arching fast toward his head.

MAGNUS HAD SEEN HIS NEPHEW CUT DOWN ARMILLON as though the commander were no more than an annoyance to him. Magnus swore Lucan would not find battle with him so easy.

His blade met Lucan's with a satisfying clash. He'd taken his nephew by surprise. He could see it on his face and was able to instantly push him into the defensive. Determination replaced surprise and settled on Lucan's features as his swordplay grew bolder. Magnus pushed back with a vengeance.

"How did it feel when you ordered your own brother's death?" yelled Lucan over the din of battle.

Magnus's blade faltered, and Lucan drew blood from his forearm. "It felt necessary," he rasped in answer.

"Necessary," echoed Lucan.

He watched his nephew closely, looking for an opening in his tight offensive strategy. Then he found it. Lashing out quickly, risking the bite of Lucan's blade, he aimed for his throat. He laid a stroke high on his chest instead.

It was enough.

That action turned the tide in Magnus's favor, and he pushed Lucan back. His nephew stumbled over the body of a Valorian and dropped his sword. Magnus thought for a moment he had him, but quick as a flash Lucan grabbed up his blade and slashed at Magnus's middle, causing him to jump back. Lucan sprang to his feet.

"Our father did not make the right choice when he selected Gallus to inherit the Dragon Throne. Gallus was weak," yelled Magnus.

Lucan made an enraged sound and forced Magnus back against a tent. Magnus tripped over a pole and stumbled, narrowly missing Lucan's blade as it came arching toward his head.

"My father was not weak. He was honorable and fair. You . . . you're the weak one. You're the one who must use fear to rule. How did it feel to order Valentina's death, Uncle?"

Magnus's parry failed, and he moved quickly to block. It had not felt good . . . not good at all. Valentina had been a beautiful child, full laughter and innocence. These were things he did not want to remember.

Lucan took the opportunity to lay a deep gash though the muscle of his sword arm. Magnus cried out in pain, his free hand covering the wound. He fell to his knees and waited for his nephew's blade to meet the back of his neck.

Everything suddenly moved in slow motion. Out of the corner of his eye, something caught Magnus's attention. It had skirts that rustled when it ran and long, thick hair colored like the sky at dawn, all jumbled reds and golds. It held a blade, its steel reflecting the sun. He turned and looked.

Nia.

Remotely, he wondered why Lucan didn't go ahead and finish him off, but his nephew also watched Nia run toward them. She held her sword high, an enraged battle cry coming from deep within her. Was he bewitched to stay so still and transfixed? He did not know. All he knew was that the hatred he saw on her face wounded him to the quick, far worse than a blade ever could.

Gods. What if he'd been a caring man? What if he'd been a man full of honor like his brother, father, and grandfather had been? Would she have loved him then?

Magnus got to his feet and let his arms swing open, allowing the Dragon Blade to fall from his hand. He'd take Nia into his arms any way she wanted to come, with a sword meant for his heart or nay.

When Nia plunged the blade through him he felt numb to the physical pain; he felt only intense sorrow and regret. Those emotions licked fire through him, stinging him worse than the edge of the sword. It was fitting that he be slain by her hand, he thought with a strange detachment. She'd always held ultimate power over him, even if she hadn't known it.

As Magnus fell upon the blade she wielded, pushing it deeper inside, he held her gaze.

She simply looked sad.

Then the entire world went dark, and Magnus felt himself slip to Vallon.

W HEN MAGNUS HAD OPENED HIS ARMS AND SIMPLY allowed her to plunge the blade through his chest, they'd stood and stared in shock.

Branna had run out from the tree line, with Arturo close behind, when Nia had taken flight with the sword.

Magnus had loved Nia.

It was impossible, but it was true.

Magnus fell to the ground, and Branna saw, even at a distance, that he wore a tormented expression on his face. When Nia swayed unsteadily on her feet and would've collapsed, Morgan caught her up in his strong arms and held her against him.

The camp went eerily quiet as the Valorian realized their emperor and Armillon had both been killed. The fighting stopped. Some of the Valorian now headed into the forest. Others simply threw their weapons to the ground.

Branna ran to Lucan, and he caught her around the waist. "It's over," he said, smiling.

"Aye, it's over." She returned his smile. "You will have your peace now."

A Valorian soldier came toward them and dropped to one knee. He swore his fealty to Lucan. One by one, many of the remaining Valorian did the same.

And Lucan made every last one of them swear allegiance to Branna as their queen.

EPILOGUE

Numia 1108

B RANNA PLUCKED A BLOOM AND HELD IT TO HER SON'S nose. He inhaled the flower's perfume and then twisted a chubby hand around a loosened hank of her hair.

The palace at Ta'Ror was much changed after the Ritual of the Balance. Lucan and Branna had returned to find the place awash in golds and silvers, instead of weathered gray granite.

It was an enchanted place now.

Ivy clung to the ramparts, sprouting sweet-smelling amberdine, lavender, and skyflower. Never mind that lavender and skyflower didn't grow on vines. Aye, the world on the other side of the Balance was definitely a strange and wonderful one.

Lucan, having taken his rightful place as king of Numia and its provinces, had long since ordered the Valorian forces home from Tir na Ban and Ileria. Lucan had much work to do in setting Numia, and the Valorian, to rights again. He meant to make the Valorian valorous once more.

Nia and the Tirian sorceresses had returned to their homeland. They also had much work ahead of them in setting Tir na Ban back to rights. It would take many, many years for the country to recover, but Branna knew that under Lucan's nurturing rule, the country would be a thriving place again one day.

After all, the Tirian Raven was the queen of Numia. Tir na Ban could not hope for a better alliance . . . and it would be an alliance, rather than a dictatorship. The days of iron-fisted and fearful rule were over. That was true not only for Tir na Ban, but for Pira, Angelyn, and Bah'ra as well.

Branna turned and walked into the lush palace gardens. The breeze blew golden petals and sweet pollen through the air. The seasons had not changed yet, and Branna wondered if they ever would.

Arturo had also left for Tir na Ban. He'd known he'd been close to traveling on to Vallon, and he wished to see his homeland again before it happened. Indeed, not long ago, Branna had received word that the old mage had passed on, but she knew she'd see him again one day.

Morgan had revealed incredible information to Lucan not long after the final battle. He'd kept the knowledge from Lucan in fear he'd be treated differently. And rightly so, for Morgan was not simply an Angelese soldier who'd come to Numia to fight—nothing as menial as that. Morgan was the prince of Angelyn, son of King Owain and Queen Anisa. The wife he loved and missed so very much was none other than Bria, the princess of Angelyn. He'd left soon after he'd made his admission, promising to return to Ta'Ro soon with her.

There were fears that along with the wonder and beauty of enchantment unleashed, there would also be danger. No light existed without the dark, after all, no good without evil. Always, there was a Balance. Always, there were costs.

But they would deal with those when the time came. Until then, they would enjoy the newfound world to which they'd given birth. For certain, after the defeat of Magnus and his Valorian, they felt as though they could take on anything that came their way, even the running of an empire.

But perhaps not the raising of a child.

Lucan entered the garden from the opposite side, and Branna knelt, letting their son, Killian, toddle into his smiling father's arms. Killian was just learning to walk and already there were signs he'd be a headstrong youth, full of fire.

Killian did not have black hair like his parents; his was a jumble of rich copper and reddish hues. The color of his hair put Branna much in the mind of the shade Ren's had been. Killian also shared the same lopsided smile Ren had sported.

Branna often wondered about that smile and how many more similarities the years would reveal. She knew well the endless circle of life, death, and rebirth. Never was the circle broken. Always, there were meetings, partings, and then meetings again.

And the wheel continues to turn.